Enjoy th—
Jeffrey!

Whit E S[signature]

My Island Beach: A Summer Read
By R. E. Salter

Book One
of the
My Island Beach Trilogy

Coyote Moon Books

Arizona

Copyright © 2011 Robert E. Schwartz

This book is a work of fiction. Names, characters, places, and incidents are used fictitiously, and any resemblance to actual persons, living or dead, and actual events is entirely coincidental.

All rights reserved. No part of this book may be used or reproduced by any means, graphic, electronic, or mechanical, including photocopying, recording, taping or by any information storage retrieval system without the written permission of the publisher except in the case of brief quotations embodied in articles and reviews.

Reviewers may quote passages for use in periodicals, newspapers, or broadcasts provided credit is given to *My Island Beach* by Robert Schwartz and Coyote Moon Books, LLC.

Coyote Moon Books, LLC
www.CoyoteMoonBooks.com

ISBN: 978-0-9844319-5-3

Printed in the United States of America
First Edition

Dedication

This book is dedicated to Connie Lee, my editor, who deserves all the credit where the narrative flows, but none of the blame where I was too stubborn to take her advice!

Contents

Preface	
Prologue	*The Story and the Teller*
Chapter 1	*Precious Interlude*
Chapter 2	*Reunions*
Chapter 3	*The Restaurateur*
Chapter 4	*Destiny's Child*
Chapter 5	*Trial by Fire*
Chapter 6	*Marshmallows*
Chapter 7	*Daniel*
Chapter 8	*The Sedge*
Chapter 9	*Beach Blanket Bingo*
Chapter 10	*The Plot Thickens*
Chapter 11	*Samantha*
Chapter 12	*Jersey Girls*
Chapter 13	*Opposites Attract*
Chapter 14	*Close Encounters*
Chapter 15	*Perspective*
Chapter 16	*Indiscretions of Youth*
Chapter 17	*Del*
Chapter 18	*The Story of Island Beach*
Chapter 19	*X Does Not Mark the Spot*
Chapter 20	*The Conundrum*
Chapter 21	*My Island Beach*
Chapter 22	*Sea Glass*
Chapter 23	*Undercurrents*
Chapter 24	*Simpler Times*
Chapter 25	*Look Who's Coming?*
Chapter 26	*Seeds of Discontent*
Chapter 27	*When You Wish Upon a Star*
Chapter 28	*Losing Focus*
Chapter 29	*Smoke and Mirrors*

Chapter 30	*Putting it on the Line!*
Chapter 31	*Let's Make a Deal*
Chapter 32	*Acid Test*
Chapter 33	*Oil and Water*
Chapter 34	*Truth*
Chapter 35	*The Devil You Say!*
Chapter 36	*Grandma Katy*
Chapter 37	*The Whole Truth*
Chapter 38	*Parting*
Epilogue	*The Teller and the Story*

Preface

This note is included as an explanation for the provenance of the three manuscripts donated to the Friends of Island Beach Historical Society. I purchased the beach cottage in question as a tear down. In the process of removing the existing fireplace, a metal box containing the three manuscripts hermetically sealed in plastic was discovered along with a fourth document, similarly stored, which did not survive.

While the new house was being built I took the opportunity to read the manuscripts. The first, A Summer Read, was apparently written by an individual named R. E. Salter. It describes the relationship of Dr. Philip Brace with his 17 year old granddaughter Kathleen, both previous owners of the cottage. It also describes a number of historical claims having to do with Island Beach, some of which were facts that I was able to verify, while others have no records that I can find to support them, but still seem reasonable. Lastly, though, many of the assertions presented in this manuscript are clearly fabrication in some cases, and sheer fantasy in others. I can only conclude that this is some sort of unpublished novel or fiction.

The second manuscript, Winter Journals, was written by a D. Hawkins. It describes the experiences of the same Kathleen Brace from the first manuscript, now in her first year of college. It also refers to an ancient diary, which I now believe to be the fourth,

R. E. Salter

decomposed document found in the metal box with the other three. Again, the content of this second manuscript is part historical fact, and part invention, some of which is, frankly, quite disturbing. In fact, as I was reading Winter Journals I came to realize that one of the characters in this manuscript, a Dr. Robert E. Salter was presumably the author, R. E. Salter, of the first manuscript!

The third manuscript was written by a J. Dufrense. J. Dufrense turns out to be Jasmine Dufresne a Quebecois co-ed who translated the old French diary mentioned in the second manuscript. The author of the second manuscript, D. Hawkins is a child from the third manuscript (these strange attributions are confusing but are partially clarified in the third manuscript). This third manuscript is a continuation of the experiences of Kathleen Brace, who has returned to the cottage 22 years later. The bizarre assertions mentioned in the first manuscript and amplified in the second go beyond the pale in the third manuscript. These fantastic claims are especially unnerving in that there is a strangely persuasive ring of truth to them!

Being an amateur historian, I felt compelled to make these documents available as a primary historical source and to provide what provenance I possessed for them. I have chosen, for reasons that I will not explain, to remain anonymous in my donation. If one carefully reads the descriptions in the first journal, the location of the original cottage and my identity can be determined from perusal of the public record. I sold the house upon completion of construction and never actually resided there. Be assured, I know nothing more than has been written in the three manuscripts and this note. Please do not contact me; I have no interest in further discussing, considering or speculating on the nature of these artifacts!

Prologue

The Story and the Teller

"Okay children settle down."

A group of 15 or 20 small children and their parents surrounded the fire that was just starting to evolve as the day was dimming. While the children romped, the adults huddled, whispering amongst themselves. It was officially summer, but it was early in the season and cool enough at night for a sweatshirt and jeans—and perfect for moving a little closer to someone you cared for in front of a roaring fire on a deserted ocean beach.

This scene could be unfolding anywhere on the eastern seaboard of the United States, the beaches of the East Coast of North America being distinct and easily distinguishable from West Coast beaches. But more importantly, and with little imagination, it could be taking place *anytime* in the last 500 years.

"As you know, Park Service regulations don't allow fires on the beach, *except* for the park-sponsored storytelling and sea shanty singing every Sunday night during the summer—tonight, in fact!" explained the chubby ranger named Sally.

"And this particular Sunday night we have a special treat for you," she continued. "Dr. Philip Brace, a scientist and local resident, renowned for his knowledge of the history of Island

Beach State Park and his ability to spin a yarn. Dr. Brace."

The anonymous gentleman—previously indistinguishable from the generic parents and grandparents around the fire—stood and, out of sheer body language, was transformed into a wizened old storyteller. He confronted his audience and began the introductions.

"First of all, people who know me call me Dr. Phil. And now you know me so that, as they say, is that. Now then, children, what's my name?" he asked.

"Dr. Phil," came the timid response from a minority of the children.

"Hmm…it seems we have a problem," he ruminated, rubbing his chin and looking upwards. "How can you tell your friends who the best storyteller in the world is if you can't even remember my name? So what's say we try again?"

"So, what's my name?" he repeated after a pause.

"Dr. Phil!" they responded.

"I don't hear you?" he insisted.

"DR. PHIL!" they screamed.

"Right! Good. I can see we're going to get along. Now, before I tell my story I need to explain a few things about Island Beach. First of all, does anyone know why it's called 'Island Beach'?"

Silence.

"Well. Is it an island?" he asked.

"No, it's a peninsula," answered an anonymous voice from the crowd.

"That's right," he replied. "So why call it 'Island Beach' when it's not an island?"

Silence again.

"Because in olden times it was an island," he explained. "At the point where you came through the gate at the entrance to the park there used to be an inlet, making this an island called Lord Stirling's Beach, Nine Mile Island, or the name that stuck—Island Beach."

"But the inlet's not there anymore, is it?"

When no one responded he stopped.

"Is it?" he repeated.

"No," the children answered uncertainly.

"No, a storm that occurred around 1720 closed the inlet, known at the time as New Inlet, but which became Old Inlet after it closed. But even then, it was still an island because another inlet opened. Does anyone know the name of *that* inlet?" he asked.

"Cranberry Inlet," supplied the same anonymous voice.

"Hmm...children, either your parents are very smart, or someone here has heard my tale before," he said, puzzled. "Looking at this group, I suspect they've heard my story before," he offered, drolly.

"Cranberry Inlet is correct," he confirmed, "And that's going to be important for our story later on, so don't forget it." He inspected the crowd as he inquired, "But since this isn't an island now, what must've happened?"

"That inlet must've have closed, too," answered a tow-headed little boy in the front row. He looked to be eight or ten, with a shock of blond hair and a square jaw that gave him an air of seriousness not usually found in a boy his age.

"That's right. And I'll have more to say about that, too. But, enough history lesson, now for the story." He scanned the audience for the right child and spotted her easily.

"Young lady, can you tell me what your name is?" he asked the one most innocent-looking youngster in every group of children. She was freckled-faced with a strawberry-and-cream complexion that would make her look 10 years younger than here real age for the rest of her life.

"Cecilia," she chirped.

"Amazing—incredible in fact!" he exclaimed to her delight.

"And how old are you, Cecilia?" he continued.

"Eleven," she giggled.

"Outstanding!" he said, and let the silence hang for a moment, waiting for the inevitable query.

"Why is that so amazing?" she finally asked.

He sauntered towards her, with his left arm folded to support his right arm. He stopped to consider the group and then continued towards Cecilia, rubbing his chin and mumbling to himself.

"The story I'll be telling you tonight is about another little girl, from a different time. Her name was Cecilia too, and she was also eleven. Do you believe in ghosts, Cecilia?" he asked, directing his question solely to the little girl and ignoring the rest of his audience.

"I don't think so, do I, Mommy?" she replied looking around for her mother whom she couldn't locate due to the fire blindness. "Why?" she asked suspiciously, turning her attention back to the storyteller.

"Because the other times I've told this story, she's showed up. The ghost, that is. Always looking different, but always as a little girl named Cecilia, who is eleven. Can anyone vouch for this little girl? Does anyone claim her?" he cried, suddenly turning his attention away from Cecilia and engaging the entire crowd.

The ranger Sally had taken the parents aside and let them in on the joke so that they, along with everyone else, denied knowledge of the child.

Dr. Brace turned his attention back to his involuntary ward. "So, Cecilia, have you come again to hear your story told? Don't you ever tire of hearing about yourself?" he asked the little muffin who was now just about ready to cry. Finally her parents showed themselves and gave her a wink, as did the storyteller. Aware of the joke, and feigning exasperation but enjoying the attention, she slugged her Dad on the shoulder and giggled along with the rest of the crowd.

"And," he whispered directly to Cecilia, but in a stage voice loud enough for others to eavesdrop, "even though the story didn't start here, it ended right here on Island Beach!"

At which point he began telling "The Story".

"Cecilia was a little rich girl, living on a tobacco plantation on an island in the Caribbean," he began.

"What was the name of the island?" interrupted the boy seated next to Cecilia.

"Well, what a lively bunch! Good. Now I'll bet you're

Cecilia's brother?" The boy sighed, indicating that yes, brotherhood was his burden in life. He had flaming red hair and a face full of freckles that hinted at his natural exuberance.

"Well, the Cecilia in our story didn't have a brother, but her best friend was a native boy, whom her parents did not approve of. In fact…"

"But *what* was the name of the island?" the boy interrupted again.

"I'm getting to that. But first you need to know that Cecilia loved her life on the plantation. She even had her own pony. Would anyone here like to have their own pony?" As the children's hands shot up their parents frowned indulgently.

"On the island, she had the run of the plantation, the beach, and the jungle. She loved her life, the animals, and most especially that native boy," he continued wistfully. The storyteller stopped for an instant to stare down Cecilia's brother before he could ask about the name of the island for a third time. Everyone laughed at the mock conflict; the boy got the message and was silenced—at least for the moment.

"The only problem," he cautioned, "was that her parents had always planned on returning to England after they made their fortune, so that Cecilia could be in brought up in English society. Her mother was French, but her father was a very proper English gentleman. But already at the age of eleven, though well-mannered with adults and well educated, Cecilia was growing up to be a wild child. And, although her parents had already turned a tidy profit, they were still a long way from meeting their ultimate financial goal. After much soul-searching her parents decided that they would temporarily separate; Cecilia and her mother would return to England on the next outgoing ship." He paused momentarily, inadvertently leaving an opening for the comments from the audience.

"Return to England from *where*?" inserted the persistent lad, smirking.

"From where do you think?" he asked the young heckler, pretending to be exasperated.

"From Treasure Island!" Cecilia's brother responded enthusiastically, surprised that someone would actually ask his opinion.

"No, but you're not far off," encouraged the storyteller. "The name of the island," he paused for effect, "was *Serendiph*, as in serendipity or good luck!" Cecilia's brother accepted the designation, delighted to finally having a name assigned to the island at his insistence.

"So they sailed on the next barque from *Serendiph*," he continued, emphasizing their port of embarkation for the boy's sake.

"But they didn't go straight to England. Who knows why?" he asked the crowd.

No response at first.

"They usually stopped off on the East Coast of the United States," offered one of the parents.

"The Colonies, not the United States yet. But that's right. Children, perhaps your parents are smarter than they look." That got a laugh.

"They typically rode the Gulf Stream up the coast of the Americas and across the Atlantic Ocean to England. But they usually stopped to trade with the Colonists before making the long ocean crossing to England."

"This barque was indeed headed north to trade molasses from the islands in exchange for pelts to sell to English furriers and tall pines logs to be used for the ships masts. But besides her mundane cargo of molasses, this particular ship carried all the revenues from the plantations on that Caribbean colony, to pay off English investors and taxes owed to England. So while it looked like a run-of-the mill cargo ship, it was really a…" he paused expectantly.

No response.

"What kind of ship?" he prompted.

Still no response.

"Come on! Doesn't anybody know? Guess!" he pleaded, looking directly at Cecilia.

"A treasure ship!" screeched Cecilia.

"No fair, you were there!" he accused.

"I am *not* a ghost" she said. "Just smart!"

"Smart indeed," he agreed, grinning. "It was, in fact, a treasure ship disguised as a common barque in hopes of fooling privateers lurking in the Atlantic. Who knows another name for privateers?"

"Pirates!" whispered the tow-headed boy sitting cross-legged in the front row. His wide eyes seemed ready to burst free of his head.

"Exactly right!" Dr. Brace said. "Did everyone hear? Pirates, cutthroats, scoundrels, and murderers!"

"But the privateers attacked the vessel in spite of her disguise as a common barque, as we had very thrifty pirates here on Island Beach," he continued, generating a laugh. "Does anyone know where the privateers hung out around here?" he asked.

"Cranberry Inlet," was offered, again anonymously, from the crowd. Now he was intrigued. People, with their busy lifestyles, are usually blissfully ignorant of the history of where they live, much less where they vacation.

"Bingo! I am truly impressed!" he said. "It was, in fact, the perfect place. Sheltered from the weather, these pirates skulked in this deepwater inlet, and then pounced on the unsuspecting and defenseless ships. They transported the ships and the booty, usually Caribbean molasses, into Cranberry Inlet and up Toms River for auction to the tavern owners who used it to make rum."

"But this little barque had the King's soldiers, disguised as common seaman, and a few cannon to protect the treasure they were carrying," he continued. "And what do you think happened?" he asked. No one answered this time.

"The King's soldiers were enough to thwart the pirates but not enough to save the treasure ship. Both the barque and pirate ships were incapacitated and both crews were killed in the battle!" He paused to let the children absorb the gravity of these latest revelations.

"Cecilia, however, had hidden in the bowels of the ship and somehow survived the onslaught," he continued. "But her mother, whom she loved dearly, mercifully died."

"And what do think happened next to these crippled ships?"

"A sea monster ate them!" howled Cecilia's hyperactive brother, which providing a bit of comic relief to the melancholy atmosphere.

"No...a storm," said the tow-headed young lad with an inexplicable certainty; he was obviously fascinated by the idea of pirates. This reestablished the tension.

"Quite right," the storyteller said. "A storm, the likes of which this coast had never seen!"

"History informs us that David Mapes, a colored Quaker man from Tuckerton was tending cattle near Cranberry Inlet when that tempest struck! So violent was it that it closed Cranberry Inlet, like New Inlet before it; where, what is now known as Ortley Beach is, making this the peninsula it is today. And, in spite of several attempts to open the inlet, it has remained closed ever since."

"What color was he?" asked a little girl.

"What?" asked the storyteller, perplexed by the inquiry.

"What color was he?" repeated the curious little girl without further explanation.

"Oh, honey, 'colored' is what they called African Americans back in those days," he explained, which seemed to disappoint her; she had probably been hoping for a more unusual hue.

"At the height of the storm, it took those two ships," he said, leaping to his feet, "and drove them onto this Island Beach with the dead bodies of the pirates, the King's soldiers, the crew, Cecilia's mother, and..." he swept his arms with a grand flourish, indicating the exact spot on which he and his audience were perched "...the treasure!" he revealed in an exaggerated whisper.

Not one person spoke or moved. Everyone was completely engrossed in the tale, wondering what was coming next.

"And what do you think happened to Cecilia?"

Silence.

"Anyone?"

Still no answer.

"Somehow she survived the barque's destruction. She dragged a sword that was almost as big as her and hefted it so she could slit

My Island Beach

open the bodies of the two dead pirates who had killed her mother. She let the birds and the bugs feed on their innards—and peck out their eyes." He paused to let the gruesome image set in. "Then she buried her mother in a deep, deep grave to protect her body from animals, saying a few Christian words she remembered from her Bible lessons."

"And then?" asked Cecilia's brother, sedate now, totally absorbed by the tale.

"And then," he continued, "she went totally wild, living off the berries, clams, bird's eggs, and anything else she could lay her hands on. Cecilia was an ingenious young lady. She even learned to eat bugs and other things that are edible if you're hungry enough!"

This drew the expected "Yuck!" from all.

"Tragic as the circumstances were that placed her on this island, that courageous girl not only survived—she thrived. Her pony Lilly, which had also survived the pirate's onslaught, made the island a virtual Eden for our free-spirited young Cecilia."

"Folks around here say that, to this day, you can still spot this wild little rich girl playing in the surf or riding Lilly in the dunes," he said.

"But she'd have to be over..." the tow-headed boy hesitated, doing the math in his head, "three hundred years old!"

"That's right! Good lad. Say, what is your name anyway?" Dr. Phil asked.

"Jimmy," he replied.

"And Jimmy—or anyone, why do you think that she's still lurking around?"

He waited. "No one?" he asked finally.

"She's a ghost?" hazarded Cecilia's brother.

"No, that's not why," he said and lingered until he realized that no further suggestions were forthcoming.

"No one knows for sure, but it's said that she's having so much fun that she never grew up..."

"Like Peter Pan!" a previously unheard-from child said.

"Like Peter Pan," Dr. Phil agreed enthusiastically, as not every group noted the analogy. "And until she tires of playing, she'll never grow up—and she'll never die."

"Will she ever die?"

"Well, legend has it that someday when she's done playing, for whatever reason, she'll grow up and die like anyone else. But before she passes on, she'll reveal her secret to the last person she sees," he teased, setting the bait.

"Does anyone know what that secret might be? Anyone? C'mon, Jimmy, what could it be?" he asked.

Jimmy considered the question with a perplexed look, but then enlightenment spread over his face like a spotlight moving across the sky. "The treasure!" he blurted out.

"The treasure," Dr. Phil confirmed. "Jimmy, what's your family name?"

Jimmy looked up, confused.

"Your last name?" the storyteller said.

"Hawkins," Jimmy said.

"Jim 'awkins then? Aye and a right smart lad, you'd be. Smarter than paint, I'll wager?" he said in his best Long John Silver impersonation—which actually sounded more like Popeye.

Jimmy stared at him impatiently, suggesting that he was, unfortunately, aware of this reference to his namesake in Robert Louis Stevenson's *Treasure Island*.

"Now I'm going to ask you all a question and I want you to think about it for 30 seconds. No one is allowed to answer until then. Who thinks they can do that?"

They all shook their heads. "OK. Here's the question: 'Would you rather 1) have the little girl stay young forever here on Island Beach, or 2) have the treasure found and have her grow old and die?'"

As usual, a few children were bursting at the seams, but he hushed them pointing at his head, then his watch, pantomiming that they should take the additional time to think.

After 30 seconds (he had tried 60 seconds once, but discovered that a full minute was practically an eternity for children this age) he indicated that they could answer.

"The treasure!" was the enthusiastic answer of the first few children, mostly boys. The majority of girls voted for Cecilia staying young and keeping her secret, some of them simply rejecting anything the boys said, but most were swept up by the romance of the tale.

Having finished his tale, the storyteller closed with a bow, said, "Thank you for your kind attention and good night," and moved away from the firelight while Ranger Sally launched into an old sailor shanty.

He gathered up his things and moved away from center stage. There was a time when he would have stayed until the end of the evenings activities. His favorite tale was about Captain Kidd and the treasure buried beneath the three-trunked dogwood tree on Money Island in Toms River. But, by now, he knew all the songs and all the stories so well that he could practically recite them by heart. Tired and with a long trek ahead of him, he set out down the beach towards home.

Chapter 1

Precious Interlude

"That tale's gotten taller than I have," I remarked, when we were out of earshot of the tourists. He turned, startled, unaware that anyone was following him.

"Don't you recognize me?" I teased as he turned around.

"How can I recognize you when I can't even see you?" he stalled. "You've heard my story before? You were the one that was answering my questions!" he concluded, asking the first and stating the second.

"I have...I was," I said. "But the last time I heard it the little girl was named Angela and the time before that, Beatrice, I think." I waited to see if he would make the connection. When he didn't, I added, "And there were other names before that. But the first time I ever heard it, at my very first bonfire, that plucky little girl was named Katy," I giggled.

"Katy!" he exclaimed and rushed to embrace me. We stood hugging on that moonless beach for what seemed like an eternity, without exchanging a word.

"No fair, it's so dark that I can't even see you—can't see how you've changed!" he said, ending the physical portion of the reunion.

"Then for tonight, think of me as being eleven again—still! I never grew up, Grandpa, I'm eleven and on a beach walk with my favorite grandfather," I suggested.

"Would that it was true. But I detect a note of cynicism not found in any eleven-year-olds that I've ever known," he said.

"But Grandpa, I was cynical even at eleven. I just knew how to hide it better," I said.

"That's true," he allowed, "but you're not supposed to be here for another two days," he said, realizing why my presence had taken him so completely off guard.

"Busted," I admitted. Responding to his silence, I explained, "Things got a little uncomfortable at home, so I decided to come a few days early."

"Besides," I said, not giving him a chance to pursue the subject of domestic problems with my father, "I wanted to hear your famous pirate tale *incognito*. Grandpa, you are really quite shameless!" I said. "The storm that closed Cranberry Inlet was in 1812, about a hundred years after your tale was supposed to have taken place. And Serendiph is in the Indian Ocean not the Caribbean? Really Grandpa, I thought your story was a way of force-feeding a little history to the tourist masses?"

"I have great respect for our summer visitors—I used to be one myself," he protested. Instead of responding to my charges he changed tacks. "Katy, I'm amazed you remember all that. I was never sure you were listening. But even then you saw right through my bluster and were just humoring me, weren't you?"

"Sometimes," I said chuckling. "But I was afraid if I called you on anything you'd start acting like all the other adults—all serious and stuff, always trying to teach us a lesson."

"And, well, Serendiph!" he grimaced, "You know that feckless little freckled-faced bugger wanted a name and that was all I could come up with. Can you believe that in all these years no one's ever asked me the name of that island?"

"It's OK Grandpa, it's still as enchanting as ever. Let's go home. I'm hungry and tired and I need a drink!" I said.

"A drink?" he asked. I couldn't see his expression, but I could sense raised eyebrows.

It was a tramp back to the house along the beach—over two miles in loose sand. But the exercise and ocean breeze kept us awake and gave us an opportunity to get reacquainted without distractions. We discussed my school, some of his projects, and family. We touched upon our divergent philosophies, tinted by the chronologically disparate parts of our lives that we were passing through. And simply enjoyed each other and took up where we left off as if it was last week, instead of a pair of years since we were last together.

In retrospect, I'm heartened we had that short but sweet time together before events starting unfolding.

Chapter 2

Reunions!

As we approached the house I was flooded with memories. This was the old beach house I remembered so well from my childhood with white cedar shakes weathered gray by the sea, sun, and wind. Mother and Grandmother complained about the lack of amenities, while the kids whined about the absence of TV. Looking back, it had been a joy to be here because there were no distractions from physical activities and family interactions. We swam, read, and played board games together as a family instead of branching off into individual pursuits, as was our natural inclination at home.

Grandpa liked it primitive here; he lived by the motto KISS (<u>k</u>eep <u>i</u>t <u>s</u>imple <u>s</u>tupid). In fact, after he sold the family house and moved permanently to the beach house, Father was disappointed that he never made any significant improvements. Grandpa told him that he was "simplifying his life and shedding the accoutrements and complexities that modern society demanded". Grandpa's latest theory, Father informed me derisively, was that "things own you and not the other way around."

The yard was sand, with road gravel in the front to support

parked cars. A deck was positioned on the eastern side of the porch so that it was sunny in the morning when the temperature was still cool, and shaded from the afternoon sun setting in the west. A shed and plenty of rope and other maritime trappings completed the minimalist ensemble. The house was a small, one-story, three-bedroom cabin, fourth house from the beach.

The kitchen was equipped with an ancient gas stove that looked to be from the fifties, no dishwasher, a newer, but cheap refrigerator and a microwave. It was more of a galley than a kitchen, sufficient for a family for a week or two of vacation, but inadequate for more than a single person for any extended period of time.

The layout of the bedrooms was inefficient; they were too small and had too many windows and doors to handle a bed any larger than a double. The closets were built for tourists limited to a beach wardrobe of swimsuits, flip-flops and a change of underwear. The walls were made of old-fashioned, knotty pine, and there was a small fireplace fabricated from hand-hewn beams that Grandpa's father had recovered from an 1800's barn.

The screened-in porch at the front of the house was the natural meeting place for the family. Outfitted with a picnic table and benches, it was the place we retired to when the sun was too hot, the bugs too voracious, or the rain too heavy. It converted into a dormitory where the kids slept *en masse* on makeshift beds, couches, and sleeping bags, not to mention the creation of complex constructs of blankets, picnic tables, benches, and beds known generically as "forts". Punishment for any bad behavior was banishment from the porch to sleep in one of the regular bedrooms with the adults. The porch was not just the coolest place on a hot summer night—it was the most fun.

There was only one bathroom inside the house fitted with those old-fashioned canary yellow tiles and a yellow porcelain tub that prevented modification of the color scheme without a makeover of the entire facility. It was so small that you had to keep the toilet seat down so you didn't accidentally drop your toothbrush or some other article of personal hygiene into it.

Outside was an incredibly ugly but *amazing* shower, which was heaven to use in the summer under the stars. Of course, if someone stood on the back step on their tiptoes, they could get a pretty good peek at whoever was in the shower. Eventually, when I hit puberty and my brother's friends got curious, I had to give up showering without my bathing suit on, except after dark. Both the indoor and outdoor showers were equipped with showerheads that delivered a virtual cloudburst of fresh, hot water. Wasteful, but heavenly!

Grandpa's one concession to making this his year round residence was the installation of central air-conditioning and heat. Since there was no ductwork in the house this upgrade was installed in the attic and vented through the ceiling into the rooms. Unfortunately, this retrofit wasn't terribly efficient—hot and cold spots coexisted in the house since it was designed to let the ocean breeze in—not to keep it out as it was now required to do. Ceiling fans helped to homogenize the interior environment.

As we entered the house, I had a moment to observe my Grandpa standing under the porch light searching for the right key on a key chain that, by the look of it, held every key he had ever accumulated in his entire seventy-five years.

He had aged well—still vigorous and full of himself, like always, but he definitely looked older, especially after a long day and a longer walk. His hair, while still the thick mop it had always been, was grayer. He was thicker in the waist but still fitter than many men half his age. His skin was wrinkled from years of exposure to the sun, but the result was a craggy look, rather than an aged one. He was a handsome man who was, in all likelihood, the object of many a merry widow's designs.

"Now let's have a look at you," he said as he switched on the light in the living room and turned to face me. I removed the band from my makeshift ponytail and was shaking out my long, unruly hair as I turned to face him. He smiled curiously when he first glimpsed the long tresses framing my otherwise unremarkable face, but then abruptly staggered backwards and plopped, ungraciously, into an old rocker. The color rapidly drained from his face, and his formerly ruddy complexion turned ashen. He seemed locked in a fugue-like state.

"What are you looking at?" she asked. I shook my head, realizing that I'd been staring.
"Sorry" I mumbled and turned a bright shade of red.
"Don't be sorry" she said. "What's your name?"
"Philip," I replied sheepishly. "Phil," I corrected, unable to come up with anything more intelligent to say.
"From around here?" she continued.
"We're from up north, but my parents have a summer house in South Seaside Park. My mother, sister, and I spend the summers here and my Dad comes down on the weekends," I said finally finding my tongue. "What about you?" I asked.
"My father's an ornithologist," she said.
"He studies birds," she explained, in response to my look of complete ignorance. "We live here year-round."
This girl—this budding young woman—was not what you would call a classic beauty. While she had a pretty figure and stunning, wild hair, her face was more interesting than beautiful. But she was interesting in a way that was compelling to me—piercing eyes and a way of holding herself with her shoulders thrown back that expressed self-confidence, intelligence, and ambition.
"It must get sort of boring in the winter?" I said finally.
"That's what all you summer people say!" she blurted, anger flashing in her eyes.
I can't imagine the look of shock and regret on my face for making that unintended slight—but its result was to soften her demeanor immediately.
"You know what," she said, "You're right. It is kind of boring. But it's beautiful, too, in a different way than in summer," she said diplomatically.
"You never told me your name," I pointed out.
"Kathleen—but my friends call me Katy," she said with an engaging smile that I'll never forget.

"Grandpa—Grandpa—are you OK!" I demanded.

He was back in the present but still speechless apparently at the sight of *me*. By the time I'd convinced myself that he'd was having some sort of a stroke, he managed to regain the power of speech.

"Kathleen…Katy. I'm so sorry. It's just that you've changed so much since I last saw you." He hesitated and then continued. "You look *so* much like your grandmother, the one you were named after…when she was your age I mean…" he stammered, "that…well…I wasn't prepared is all." Finally he surrendered, knowing he wasn't making any sense.

He continued staring at my face; it was unsettling, to say the least. After several minutes of the stony silence, I decided to change the subject. "You know Grandpa; you're the only one who calls me Katy. Dad encourages people to call me Kathleen."

That was my way of letting Grandpa know that I was uncomfortable with the subject of my dead grandmother and my resemblance to her. Apparently he was also uncomfortable, and let it drop. We moved on to other, safer topics, punctuated occasionally by his furtive glances in my direction when he thought I wasn't looking.

The next day things were a little better, although our conversations weren't as open and carefree like they were during our beach walk that first night. It was obvious to both of us that it was going to take some time to reestablish the relationship we'd had in the past. But we sincerely loved each other's company so I wasn't too concerned about our relationship getting back on track.

After breakfast we decided to walk over to Evelyn's, the restaurant where Grandpa had arranged a summer job for me. Evelyn had been a close friend of Grandpa's for years and years. As we entered the restaurant, Evelyn was delivering someone's lunch, directing the waitresses, and kibitzing with the patrons all at the same time. She was all business and in total control; somehow making it look completely effortless. When she spotted Grandpa her face lit up until someone interrupted her with what *must* have been a foolish question; my first impression of Evelyn that she doesn't suffer fools well. After dispensing an appropriate dose of her wrath upon the unfortunate individual, she once again turned to greet Grandpa with a light in her eyes.

"Well look who's deemed to grace us with his…" At that instant she spotted me and her expression evolved rapidly from curiosity, to confusion, and finally to fear, as Grandpa's had last night. The color drained from her face and, for a moment, I thought she was going pass out. She dropped the plate she was carrying, pasta, sauce, and all! It shattered on the floor making a horrible mess, and called the attention of the patrons to her distress.

But *still* she stared wordlessly at me, anguished by my presence.

"Evelyn," Grandpa said trying to rouse her from her catatonia. "This is Katy…" at which point Evelyn unceremoniously fell back into a chair next to an unsuspecting patron, clasped both hands to her face, and gasped out loud!

"Oh God—Philip!"

"Evelyn—Evey" he pleaded. "This is my *granddaughter*, Katy!"

"Kathleen," I said.

"Kathleen's here for the waitress job, Evey. Remember we discussed…" but Evelyn rushed into the kitchen before he could finish.

"Grandpa, I think we'd better go," I said. And, despite his concern for Evelyn, he reluctantly agreed.

The usual group was relaxing at the beach, horsing around, riding waves, and kicking up sand. I looked up from the merriment, and there she was. Recognition registered on her face and a quick wave was followed by daggers emanating from Evelyn's eyes piercing the back of my head. In spite of the fact that we were just friends, Evelyn acted possessively where I was concerned.

"Who's she?" she asked, trying to sound casual.

"Just one of the locals," I replied trying to sound equally

nonchalant.

"Who's that she's with?" Evelyn said.

"I don't really know." And I really didn't, but I definitely did not like him. "I think his father owns the fishery. Del, I think," I said as if Evelyn wasn't even there.

"What's her name?" she said to me while I was obviously distracted by the person in question.

"Katy," I replied. "Her father's an ornithologist."

"An ornithologist?" she asked sarcastically. "Been doing the Times crossword puzzle again?" she said, openly hostile now as I continued to ignore her.

"Study of birds," I replied, finally aware of her "fowl" mood. "I didn't know what it was either," I offered in my defense.

Having regained my attention, her attitude lightened.

"I'll bet he smells like fish," she said, and we shared a good laugh.

Outside the restaurant, we walked home in silence. I was confused and emotionally drained.

"Grandpa," I said as I stopped, turned, and confronted him. "What the hell is going on?"

Grandpa's reaction last night and Evelyn's reaction today were really aggravating me. And when I get upset, I don't get weepy, I get pissed. Just, I imagine, like my grandmother Katy.

"First you and now Evelyn! What the hell is going on?" I demanded, waiting for Grandpa to explain. "Evelyn knows me—why did she react that way?" I insisted, still angry but now actually starting to cry.

"Kathleen, you haven't been here in over two years, and I'll bet Evelyn hasn't met you ten times in your whole life." He paused letting it sink in. "And you've changed a lot. A real lot! You just caught her off-guard. She probably doesn't even remember you," he said, but I wasn't buying his feeble rationalization.

"Grandpa, I could've been Marilyn Monroe in Times Square and I wouldn't have gotten a response like that! Please tell me what's going on?" I pleaded.

"Kathleen, I don't remember you having the slightest resemblance to your grandmother the last time I saw you," he said, finally acknowledging the issue that must have been nagging at him all night. "And it wasn't that long ago."

I was starting to understand. "What can I say, Grandpa, people grow up. From what people tell me, I've changed a lot. I guess it happened so gradually that, I just didn't see it."

"Let's talk back at the house," he said and walked away, expecting that I would follow.

I really didn't have a choice.

Back at the house Grandpa sat me down, put his fingers his lips to signal silence and exited to another room.

After a long while he returned, gently placing a well-worn photo album on my lap. I leafed through one or two pages until I found "The Picture", a female figure clothed in blue jeans and a tee shirt—exactly what I was wearing at that very moment—her hair wild and unruly in a fashion strikingly similar to my own locks.

"Whoa, I see what you mean," I said, staring almost reverently at the photo. It was black and white, of course, but this two-dimensional chemical representation captured the very essence of Grandma Katy. God, it was like looking in the mirror!

I glanced at other pictures of her but eventually returned to *The Picture*. At last I turned to Grandpa and stated, "The resemblance is bizarre, I'll grant you, but that still doesn't explain the way you and Evelyn reacted. You guys almost had a stroke!" I said.

"What do you know about your grandmother?" Grandpa asked after a short silence.

"I don't know. Not much. Father never talked about her," I replied.

"Well, did you wonder why you never met her?" he asked.

"Not really," I replied defensively. "She was never there, so it never occurred to me, I guess."

"So?" he asked.

"So, I don't know, I guess I figured she was dead," I replied, sitting back to reflect about my namesake.

Grandpa waited.

"So?" I parroted, realizing that I would be forced to take the initiative if I wanted any answers out of him.

"Your grandmother disappeared when she wasn't much older than you are right now," he said.

"You're kidding, right?" I asked.

He nodded his head.

"No shit!" I responded.

"Your father didn't tell you!" he said, beginning as a question but ending as a conclusion.

"No," I replied, knitting my brow, pondering the implications.

"And you never bothered to ask!" which began as a question but this time ended as an accusation.

"Actually, I seem to think that I *did* ask when I was little. He avoided it, as he does with all really difficult questions, and I let it drop. It never occurred to me again," I said, unapologetically. "Damn—disappeared?" I asked again.

"Without a trace," he confirmed.

Chapter 3

The Restaurateur

At that moment, the telephone rang.

"Hello," Grandpa said as he picked it up. I was only privy to his portion of the conversation.

"Yes," he replied.

"I know Evey. I'm sorry," he said, after listening for several moments

His apology was followed by a contrite silence. "You have every right to be angry," he said, before being interrupted. "For as long as you like—mea culpa, mea culpa!" he shouted in exasperation.

"I am sincerely sorry, Evelyn, and I am also sorry about my tone of voice just now. But believe me, I was bushwhacked just like you were; I wasn't thinking straight," he said.

From his increasingly relaxed demeanor, I inferred that both his explanation and apology had been accepted.

"I'll tell her…," he said but was interrupted again. "I think I can handle it," he said after a long silence. "Goodbye Evelyn."

Turning to me he said, "I'm to 'Please tell you….' That is, 'Please *request* that you to come around to the restaurant.' It's not a request though, but I'm to make it clear that it is a request. Is that clear?" he asked.

"I think so," I replied. "She's being as polite as she can."

"Something like that," Grandpa replied, still irate, but calming down.

I stared at Grandpa, hoping for some additional explanation. "She's stunned!" he said, responding to my demanding silence, as if that explained everything. "Will you go?" he asked, concerned, obviously hoping that I would—and quickly. She must be quite a lady to have my Grandpa hopping.

"Oh, I don't mind, but maybe you'd better have the paramedics meet me there?" I said, irreverently.

"I think you'll find that she's recovered," he responded dryly to my well-intentioned sarcasm and sent me on my way.

As I approached the restaurant for the second time that day I was, once again, singularly *unimpressed* by the outward façade of the establishment. It was a single story building, with several unintended and unplanned additions. Covered with forgettable white clapboard and gray shutters, it was marked with an inconspicuous neon sign that read ***Evelyn's*** in script. The landscaping, likewise, was the washed-out beachfront style seemingly designed to deflect, rather than attract, attention to the establishment.

Entering the building this time around was an altogether different experience from earlier this morning. I was immediately confronted with an ambience that can only be described as "Robber Baron/Summer Cottage Class." While a little old-fashioned, it clearly established that a premium price would be paid for service here, but the experience would be worth every penny.

The walls were adorned with rich, dark woods, and covered with paintings of typical shore scenes. In addition, an eclectic mixture of oils depicting English castles, fox hunts, native Caribbean islanders, and figures from early American history were at hand. The chairs were of the Windsor, spindle-backed variety and were most likely very good reproductions. Real Windsor chairs were rarely used by the original settlers for dining, but were considered a special chair for sitting. They were made of a variety of woods that were especially well-suited for the particular part of the chair where they were employed. Therefore, these types of chairs were rare to start with and very few survived due to their delicate, if surprisingly strong, and elegant construction.

The bar was constructed of a single unjointed piece of chestnut, the likes of which a spoiled e-millionaire couldn't find, even if they could afford the price. The bar fixtures were wooden or neon promotional devices from brewers and vintners 50 to 100 years before, that would bring tears to the eyes of an assessor on "Antiques Road Show".

The kitchen was reasonably modern, equipped with stainless steel grills and ovens of a vintage from 10 to 30 years ago when professional equipment was over-engineered to last a lifetime or more. More importantly, it exuded an incredibly rich aroma despite the fact that nothing was currently cooking, since the lunchtime business was finished and dinner had not yet begun.

As I entered the restaurant I once again took note of the stern, business-like woman after whom the establishment was named. Evelyn must have been in her early to mid 60s, but looked easily a decade younger. She was reasonably athletic, with only the slightest hint of sag in her face and the back of her upper arms— the place to best ascertain the true age of a woman. Her hair was dark and rich looking without a touch of gray, accomplished I'm sure, through chemistry rather than genetics. Her makeup, like her clothing, was understated and impeccable. I couldn't help but think that Evelyn was the kind of woman that it would be difficult to be stuck in an elevator with for an extended period, but who you'd want for your advocate in a murder trial.

When she noticed me, confusion momentarily flashed across her face, but this time she regained control of her demeanor almost immediately.

"Kathleen, thank you for coming. Come with me. There are some things we need to take care of," she said, ushering me to an inconspicuous little table near the kitchen. Moving through the restaurant, it became painfully obvious that we were the main attraction in the place.

My Island Beach

As we sat down, I said, "Are they staring because I look like my…?"

"No child, that's not the reason," interrupted Evelyn. "Most of them never met your grandmother."

"Then what?" I asked with sincere curiosity.

She sighed. "Well, two reasons. First of all, they're waiting to see if I…well…lose my composure a second time," she said, pausing for me to comment. I remained silent.

"I will not," she answered the unasked question.

"Secondly, I rarely allow anyone to join me at my exclusive little table—this unimpressive little platform. Only your grandfather and a few selected others—on rare occasions—and never, ever the help."

"I see" I replied. "Like Rick."

"Rick?" she asked.

"In *Casablanca*. Humphrey Bogart never mixed with the patrons until Ilsa came along," I explained.

"Uh huh," she said, politely dismissing the analogy. "Anyway, young lady, the reason I wanted to see you again so urgently was that I owe you an apology," she said smiling in the warmest, most endearing way you could imagine. She was transformed. "I don't like owing anything to anybody and especially not apologies."

"Apology accepted," I responded to her unmistakable sincerity.

"Not so fast," she said, unwilling to accept my unconditional absolution. "These things need to be done properly, or why bother?"

I nodded and waited.

"I can only tell you that sometime after my first meeting with your grandmother, Kathleen, we became the best of friends. However, at first I hated her for being so many things that I'll never be, but *especially* for being so beautiful and free and stealing your grandfather away from me. When you showed up here this morning, out of the blue and after so many years—well you know she disappeared when she wasn't much older than you are now?"

I nodded and she pressed on. "Well, unlike your grandfather and me, she hasn't aged, at least in our minds. Seeing you earlier was like seeing a ghost." She paused, momentarily considering past events. Returning to the present, she continued, "Which is not your fault, of course, and is why I am apologizing to you from the bottom of my heart. Can you forgive me?" she implored.

"You're finished?" I asked this time, to which she nodded.

"Of course," I said.

"I would, however, appreciate it if we never mention this again!" she said with an intensity that startled me. I agreed, and we never did.

"Now, back to business," she said. "You'll be working Thursdays, Fridays, Saturdays, and Sundays. Every other week you'll have a Friday or Saturday off, because even waitresses need a life. Four o'clock till midnight, usually. Is that a problem?" she asked. I said that it was not.

"We have a liquor license, so the bills tend to be a higher here than in other restaurants in the area. But the food is a lot better, too, and still reasonably priced. What that means for you is that, even though I pay slave wages, the tips are large, especially for attractive young girls." She stopped to gauge my response

"This is my table, as I said before," she said. "Never, ever seat anyone here unless they are so intractable that you absolutely cannot handle them. No more than once a season—handle all the others yourself. Understand?" she asked.

I nodded and she continued, "But if you get a good one, don't hesitate," she said, smiling wickedly.

"I wanted to see you today to dispose of that item about which we will no longer be speaking…and also to inquire if you could work tonight? Janie has a cold and we're short."

"Four o'clock?" I asked.

"That would be fine. And Kathleen, your grandfather will want to know if I'm still upset with him for not warning me…about you, that is. I'm not, and you can communicate that to him." She smiled mischievously and continued, "But you might want to wait three or four days to tell him," she finished, standing up and taking off to attend to business.

I had been summarily dismissed and left to find my own way out.

Chapter 4

Destiny's Child

"You're destined to have a momentous life, child," my mother announced as she peeled the potatoes for dinner that night. In spite of the calm manner in which she stated this, the content of what she said was so out of character with her pragmatic, and mostly colorless outlook on life, that I cringed.

"What?" I said.

"You're destined to have a momentous life," she repeated.

"Oh, I heard you," I responded. "What the heck's that supposed mean?"

"What it means is that you'll be present at times and places when great events occur," she said, even more cryptically.

"What the heck are you talking about?" I asked sarcastically.

"Watch your tone!" she responded in her normally brittle voice.

"Mother, I'm sorry, but I've never heard you talk like this before!" I was only 15 but smart for my age and college-bound—well, I hoped I was anyway. I was becoming an adult and was ready for an adult approach to discussions, which probably made me sound like a smart-mouthed little kid to real adults. "What I meant to say is, 'What in the world are you talking about?'" This time my tone of voice was one of sincere wonderment instead of a cocky smart aleck.

    I took a good long look at her. My mother was in her early fifties but looked ten years older. It wasn't that she was out of shape. Her hair was still mostly dark, and she was as lean and fit as a thirty-year-old woman. But she wore her hair in a tight bun and always one of two or three clean but frumpy housedresses. But her clothing and hairstyle just made her look unattractive; it was really the way she held herself that made her seem old.

    She was hunched over like a giant had stepped on her; she seemed to carry the weight of the world on her shoulders. She lacked enthusiasm for living. In fact, her approach to most tasks, whether she enjoyed them or not, was "OK, let's get it over with". And her breathing, her very existence, was punctuated with so many sighs of frustration that I found that I had adopted this mannerism myself.

    "I have to tell you some things," she said, after a particularly deep sigh. "You need to listen carefully, because we'll never speak of this again."

    I nodded.

    "Does the date May 6th, 1937, mean anything to you?" she asked.

    I thought about it for a minute and then replied, "No..."

    "Think about it again," she encouraged, looking up from those potatoes for the first time since the conversation began. She looked at me hopefully—she'd never done that before.

    Ever!

    I thought about it again.

    "No," I repeated, disappointed that I couldn't impress her by gleaning the significance of that date. I should have known or she wouldn't have asked with that piercing, expectant look that I'd never seen from her before.

    "No," I said feeling annoyance with her for her cryptic question. "Not a clue," I continued, feeling more and more dejected.

    She returned to her potatoes and sighed—as deeply as a person can sigh; still disappointed in life—and now in me.

"Except your anniversary," I said, grasping for straws. "That's close—the day before, wasn't it? May 5th?"

Still not looking up but quietly triumphant, she continued, "Remember what year your father and I were married?"

"1937," I said after a moment. "So it was the day after you were married," I concluded.

Back to the potatoes.

"That's it?" I asked when she didn't say anything.

"You remember your own birthday?"

"Yes," I replied as sarcastically as I dared. It was January 8th of the next year, 1938, as we both very well knew.

I still didn't get it.

Then I did.

I was conceived on my parent's wedding night.

I refrained from saying, "So that's the news flash," or something equally sarcastic, since I suspected it wasn't her only point. There had to be more.

This was new territory for Mother and me. We had never admitted to each other that sex even existed, much less that she and Father had ever engaged in it. My curiosity was piqued but with a deepening sense of doom, not unlike the anticipation of impending slaughter one experiences at a horror movie.

"Now listen," she said putting down the potatoes and looking directly at me. This was really getting serious. "I have to tell you some things that that will make both of us uncomfortable, but they have to be said. OK?"

I nodded unenthusiastically.

"On May 5th, 1937, your father and I were wed in the Union Hall," she started, staring off into the distance. "One of his friends had a band: a guitarist, an accordion player and a drummer. We had a wonderful time. Your father is quite a good dancer, by the way." I couldn't recall her ever saying anything nice about Father before.

Ever!

"The reception went on well into the night. It was a wonderful time and a very special night," she said wistfully. My mother was definitely not the wistful type.

"It was after midnight when we got up to the room—the bridal suite." She looked at me to see if I had anything smart to say, but I didn't want to say anything or hear another word on this topic.

"Mother!" I interjected desperately.

"Do you think I feel comfortable telling you about this?" she asked, before I could respond. *"Now be quiet and listen!"* she commanded.

"When you're father and I had relations, it was shortly after midnight. That would make it May 6th, 1937," she said. *"That's the day I want to tell you about."*

Why she insisted on describing the details of her relationship with my father was so outside of my experience with her—with both my parents —that I couldn't and didn't want to comprehend what she was saying.

"MOTHER!" I protested.

"PHILIP, JUST LISTEN!" she ordered, *"Don't you think there's a reason I'm telling you all this?"*

I didn't respond. This was one of those things in life, like gallstones or hemorrhoids (as I would later discover), you just had to survive until they passed. There was just no way out. The pain would diminish but not before it got more painful.

"Afterwards," she said in a dreamy way which I knew meant that it had been wonderful. *"Right afterwards,"* she emphasized, *"I knew I was pregnant with you!"*

Whew!

"How did you know that?" I asked, unable to prevent the unanswerable question from being voiced.

"I don't know," she said. *"I just knew. It was different."* Different from what, I pondered momentarily and then blocked that thought process out completely. The thought of parental sex was disgusting; the thought of premarital sex was inconceivable. This was a side of my mother and father's relationship of which I was completely ignorant—and happily so.

When I didn't respond, she continued reminiscing. *"I found out for sure in the morning. Starting at around 9:00, I became violently ill. I threw up until there was nothing left to throw up. Then I continued with the dry heaves into the early afternoon. And*

My Island Beach

it wasn't a hangover!" she said. "But it didn't matter. I was happy because I knew I was pregnant."

"We'd borrowed your grandfather's car and were going to drive to Florida for our honeymoon. But there was no way I was traveling that day, the way I was feeling," she continued.

"Finally, at around 6:00 p. m., I was feeling better and guilty enough to suggest that we start out on our honeymoon that night. Your father protested that it was too late, but I finally convinced him that I was all right. I knew he was dying to get on the road, but he was being so considerate. He really was sweet back then," she said, implying that he wasn't sweet like that any longer.

"We'd been driving for about an hour when we spotted a dirigible on the horizon, headed our way. God it was impressive!" she gushed. "I'd always been fascintated by those grandiose airships. I'd fantasized about flying in one, and this was the most majestic one I'd ever seen. It was just starting to get dark and when the lights on the airship came on it looked so festive. I asked your father if we could follow it, since I knew they landed somewhere around there."

Grandiose? Was this my mother speaking?

"We were coming up on Lakehurst," she continued, "And, in spite of the fact that we were way behind schedule, he agreed. He really was sweet back then."

"I turned on the radio and flipped around the stations until I happened on one that was describing the arrival of that very dirigible," she continued. "I can still remember some of what the radio announcer said: 'Well, here it comes, ladies and gentlemen. And what a great sight it is, a thrilling one, just a marvelous sight. It's coming down out of the sky, pointed directly towards us and toward the mooring mast.' The announcer called it a 'great floating palace,' I think. It did look like a floating palace, too!" she said.

"At that point, we arrived at the landing field and stopped to watch it grow larger and larger. It was grand! It filled the sky!" I was still surprised to think that anything could impress my mother that way.

"But then, when it was nearly on the ground, flames

appeared," she continued. "And the announcer on the radio screamed, 'It burst into flames! Get out of the way! Get out of the way. This is the worst of the worst catastrophes in the world! Oh, the humanity, and all the passengers screaming around here!'"

And then I realized what she was talking about. "The Hindenburg!" I whispered.

She just nodded and even cried a little. "She was so majestic and elegant as she lit up the sky. And even more beautiful in the throes of death!" she said with the intense fascination of an unrepentant arsonist. "God, it was magnificent!"

"Momentous?" I whispered.

She nodded her head, weeping and began peeling potatoes again, with a long excruciating groan. It was then that I realized then that she hadn't expelled a single sigh as she was describing her—our—brush with history.

Chapter 5

Trial by Fire

Figuring that I didn't know how flexible Evelyn was about the 4:00 start time, I returned to the restaurant at 3:45 sharp, especially since I was the new kid on her first day. I'd noticed that the waitresses didn't have a formal uniform; I'm certain Evelyn would have said something if they did. The others wore a short black skirt, probably because it was cool and the customers liked it. White socks, running shoes, and crisp, ironed white blouses completed the ensemble. I conformed exactly to that unofficial uniform, since I had already called enough attention to myself earlier that day.

Grandfather told me that there were four waitresses, Janie who I was replacing tonight, Rose who was the oldest, Samantha, and Flo. It seemed to me that if your parents named you Florence, you were pretty much *doomed* to be the crusty but good-hearted head waitress in an earthy eatery.

Flo, Janie and Rose were lifers; Samantha was like me, here for the summer crowd. Flo was the head waitress.

"Good," Evelyn said, "You're here early. Samantha, this is Kathleen. Kathleen, Samantha can show you the ropes and introduce you to the other girls." Girls? Humph, sometimes it seems like women are the worst chauvinists, but maybe, in this case, it was a class thing more than a gender thing.

"Although, tonight it looks like you might have to hit the ground running. They're already lining up outside. Good luck Kathleen!" With those words, Evelyn was off.

I turned my attention to my mentor. Samantha was definitely a beautiful girl, and just as definitely a party girl. You could tell just by looking at her. "Oh I like to *play* when I play, but I can work when I need to—or I wouldn't be working here," she said, reacting to my all too obvious assessment.

"So is it 'Kathleen' or something else for the rest of us?" she asked referring to Evelyn's formality.

"Kathleen. That's just what everyone calls me," I responded trying not to sound too particular about using my formal first name.

"Not a problem," she said. "It fits you better than Kathy."

"I, on the other hand am to everyone but Evelyn, Sam. Sam, I am. Unless we get to be drinking buddies; then it's Sammy, OK?" she said. I was confident it would be Sammy pretty soon. It was hard not to like this one.

"No problema," I said.

"You can take tables 7, 8, and 9, over by the kitchen, OK?"

"Fine"

"We don't split tips with each other, but if you don't give Julio 10% of your take, your tables won't get bussed the next night and you'll lose more than the 10% you would have given him," she continued. "OK?" The now expected but dreaded question.

"Got it," I said, determined to meet the constancy of her "OK's" with an infinite variety of affirmatives, instead of the mundane "OK". I often find myself playing these word games with others who are rarely aware of it—unless they're extremely perceptive or similarly warped.

"The bartender is Bruno. Do not split tips with him! Do not agree to go out, be transported or meet with him for any reason outside of work. Encourage him just enough that he'll provide you with free alcoholic beverages after the doors close at midnight. No matter how much you reject him, he'll "buy" you a drink since he doesn't actually pay for it, and there is any possibility that you'll change your mind and agree to be his sex slave. Like believing in God, just in case." She paused to take a breath and to give me the *tiniest* hope she wouldn't pose *the* relentless query.

"OK?" She came through in the clutch.

"Understood," I said. Besides, at only 17, I don't think anyone would be serving me drinks in this establishment.

"Well hike up your panties and let's let the proletariat in. OK?"

"Consider them hiked," I said, which drew a smile. I was beginning to think she was getting it. I only hoped she realized it was meant to be friendly wordplay rather than mocking.

"You just might fit in to this loony asylum," she mumbled as she walked over to open the door. "OK?" she said, winking.

The first hour wasn't bad—busy, but *OK*. Oh God, now I was starting to *think* like Sam talks.

Sam didn't introduce me to the cook, which was fine, since he didn't speak English, but thankfully, he reads it. Around 6:30 the line started to back up out the door and, by 7:00, there was almost an hour's wait for a table.

Flo blew off an older couple who didn't have reservations and who were obviously drunk and upset. But Flo, like Evelyn, wasn't a person to be messed with.

A few minutes later the same couple approached me when the other three waitresses were occupied. As competent as I knew I was, my young age and lack of experience in this particular establishment must have been conspicuous.

"Miss, we have a reservation but the other waitress would not seat us," the gentleman said.

"Your name?" I queried, figuring I would simply confirm their lack of a reservation as Flo had.

"Hanson," he said.

"Sorry, don't see your reservation," I said after carefully examining the list.

"Really, miss, it must be there," the husband insisted as I moved away.

"Darling," he said, speaking to his wife, "I was there when you made the reservation."

"To Jillian's?" Sam suggested as she passed by.

"That's right!" exclaimed his inebriated wife.

"This is Evelyn's, not Jillian's," I explained. "Jillian's is in Bayhead." Now the matter was settled.

"I hardly think we can be held responsible for your restaurant having a similar name to the one that we have a reservation for!" stated Mr. Hanson in florid, if irrational seriousness.

"Please miss, just find us a table and no mention will be made of this little difficulty." With that bit of convoluted reasoning he tried to slip me a $20 bill.

"Sir, with all due respect, you made the reservation at the wrong restaurant. Your mistake, not ours," I said. "I don't even know if I'm allowed to accept a tip for special consideration, but I'm betting I'm not. And there are about 50 people who have been waiting patiently, who'll lynch me if I seat *you* ahead of *them*!" I explained.

"Your name, miss?" he asked, switching from a conspiratorial tone-of-voice to a confrontational one and producing a pad of paper as if to write my name down.

"Kathleen," I said, becoming irritated. This wasn't getting us anywhere, so I decided to change tacks. "Wait here a moment and I'll speak to my manager to see if we can accommodate you," I stated as if capitulating to his implied threat.

I retired to the kitchen to find Evelyn—but no luck. Sam was there, though, so I consulted her.

"Ignore them," she advised when I explained the situation.

"They're really giving me a hard time. They took down my name."

She peered out the door. "The guy with the toupee and the woman with the makeup troweled on her face?" she asked.

"Yeah," I said, hoping that someone else, like Sam, would deal with this.

Rose overheard our conversation and said, "Do them!"

"That's easy for you to say," Samantha said. Rose shrugged and left with her order.

"Do them?" I asked, perplexed.

My Island Beach

"*Evelyn* them," Samantha said, as if 'to Evelyn' was a verb.

"No one's Evelyned a customer on their first night. Hell, Rose has never Evelyned anyone," said Flo. "Who's bothering you?" she asked, only having caught the tail end of our conversation.

"The older couple without a reservation. The ones who talked to you first," I replied.

"Oh, the guy with the bad toupee," pronouncing it toop, like poop. "Evelyning is definitely an option. He's picking on you because he can tell you're new. No offense."

"None taken. What's Evelyning?" I asked.

"Did Evelyn mention to you about seating difficult customers at her table?" Samantha said answering my question with another question. I nodded.

"Well, if you do that, Evelyn will deal with the problem. That's *Evelyning*," she said, as if that explained everything. Didn't seem like much of an explanation to me.

"But Flo said that no one's…" I started.

"Evelyned someone on their first night. That's right. I haven't done it yet, but I was here for one once. Gets your juices going. It's up to you. Gotta go," Sam said and sprinted off with her order.

"Sir, I'm sorry but I haven't located my manager yet, so you'll have to wait like the rest…" I said having decided to give them one last chance when he interrupted my offer.

"Miss, I don't seem to be getting through to you. Either find us a table now or suffer the consequences!" he threatened quietly but emphatically.

"All right, sir, why don't you follow me then? We have a reserved table for our special customers."

Our *especially difficult* customers, I thought to myself.

I escorted them to Evelyn's table, hoping that this wasn't some kind of initiation goof being played on the new girl, or that these weren't international dignitaries or something.

"Someone will be with you momentarily," I said and returned to the kitchen.

Back in the kitchen the other waitresses were peering out, and they pulled me aside as I walked in the door.

"Oh shit, you did it!" exclaimed Sam, obviously impressed. "I can't believe it!" she said looking alternately at me and outside at Evelyn's table.

"You got a set. I'll give you that," said Flo. "You wouldn't know it from looking at you—oh shit, they're smoking!"

"Evelyn's gonna have a cow!" contributed Rose. "You did the right thing kid. I can't wait to see this!"

"There's Evelyn," I said as I started out the door to explain the situation to her. Flo grabbed my arm and stopped me.

"Honey, wait!" she whispered and looked outside. "Let Evelyn handle it now. If...when she calls you, just *gooooo* along with the program."

Evelyn was returning from wherever she'd been when she spotted the interlopers at her table. She then glanced towards the kitchen, smiled mischievously at us, and headed toward her unsuspecting prey.

"Good evening," she said politely.

The couple continued their conversation, aware of Evelyn's presence, but arrogantly making her wait until they finished their discussion. "Good evening," said the gentleman, at last.

"My name is Evelyn. I'm the owner of the restaurant. I assume that there's been some sort of difficulty?" she asked, all peaches and cream.

"You could say that!" began the gentleman loudly. "In all my years I have never been treated as cavalierly as I have been in your restaurant tonight!"

"Well, we'll just have to rectify that right away," said Evelyn with a diffidence that was just plain frightening, it seemed to me, and I've only really known Evelyn for a few hours. "With whom did you have this difficulty?" she asked.

"A young woman with unruly hair," he complained. "She refused to give us her name!" he accused, even though I *had* given them my name. He was probably too drunk to remember, or just plain mean.

"That would be Kathleen. Kathleen, could you come out here please?" she called out, signaling to me.

"Go go go!" said Flo, shoving me out the door with unconcealed enthusiasm.

"Yes?" I said as I arrived, not knowing what to expect.

"Did I not explain to you that the customer is always right?" she said in a patronizing manner, but accompanied with a wink that the pompous couple could not see.

"Yes," I said, looking down and acting chastised.

"I won't even ask for an explanation," she said with a smile that only I could see. "Sir," she said sternly, "This girl is new and obviously did not understand my instructions. I believe she understands them now. I usually give my girls a second chance, but say the word and I'll sack her now," she said, waiting for his response.

"I believe that your establishment would be better off without this particular young *lady* as an employee," he responded, uttering *lady* with particular disdain.

Turning to me, she barked for all to hear, "Kathleen, please clean out your locker at the end of the shift."

"Dismissed!" she said impatiently, when I didn't leave right away.

"Sir, I'll be back in a moment to take your order," Evelyn said and headed towards the kitchen.

As she entered the kitchen she grabbed an apron, put it on over her formal hostess dress, placed a pencil behind her ear, and grabbed a pad and a pair of menus. I tried to talk to her as she turned to leave, but she just held my wrists, looked me in the eye and said, "I was serious out there when I said no explanation was necessary. Don't worry, I haven't had this much fun in years," she reassured, then returned to the couple-from-hell.

"Bogus wine," she instructed Flo as she returned to her *special* table. "Put it in a really good bottle!"

"First of all, let me mention that we have a restaurant-wide no smoking policy here."

No response from the couple!

"However, in view of the rudeness with which you have been

treated, we'll be making a special example...that is, exception for you tonight," she said to the couple who continued to smoke in spite of the plethora of No Smoking signs.

"Does anyone have a problem with that?" she polled the adjacent patrons.

My previous experience with customers in restaurants suggested that there should have been a militant protest to letting these pschyos continue to smoke. Instead, the other patrons were all smiles, murmuring, "No problem," and waving it off as if it were a minor distraction not worth mentioning.

Except for one couple.

"Sorry to bother you, Evelyn, but I'm extremely allergic to cigarette smoke," said an older woman, smiling.

"Jennifer, of course. How could I forget that? Well, we'll just to have to move you. Would that be all right?" she asked Jennifer, but glanced towards the offending couple to see if they would relent.

No response. They just blinked at her insolently!

"Steve, would you and your wife be willing to change tables with Jennifer and Frank?"

"No problem," he said, and the deal was done.

Everyone was acting like this was completely normal, which was totally weirding me out. There was some underlying dynamic going on here that was way beyond my comprehension.

"Now please accept a complimentary bottle of our best wine," she said, returning her attention to the pair of misanthropes, as she opened the bottle of adulterated wine.

The man sniffed the cork, swirled his glass, held it up to the light, swished and swallowed. The whole nine yards. "Quite satisfactory," he remarked. "Excellent, in fact!"

"Fine, now here are your menus," she said handing them the opened folders. "I'll be back in a moment," she concluded and returned to the kitchen.

Well, it was between thirty and forty five minutes when she returned, but instead of her elegant hostess outfit underneath an apron, she had completed the metamorphosis. She was wearing a plain, and I might add dingy, pink polyester uniform. It was a dress-like affair with huge pockets for order pads and other paraphernalia, like crayons for kids. She had mutated into a waitress you'd find in a greasy spoon at a truck stop. She was equipped with an order pad in hand, chewing gum in mouth, and her hair pulled back into a bun. And, I swear to God, she had pencils sticking out of the bun. The transformation was mind-boggling!

She went through the "Hi, I'm Evelyn, and I'll be your waitress for the evening" bit, followed by a list of 10 or 12 specials described in glowing detail, with just a hint of a Brooklyn accent—including several specials I knew we didn't have.

"Is the orange roughy fresh?" inquired our difficult gourmet a bit ruffled at first at her tardiness but impressed by the deference she was showing him. Talk about thick! And the other diners, so agreeable. I don't get it! It was like being in the *Twilight Zone*.

"Of course," she said, as if she wouldn't have it any other way. "Flown in daily!" she reassured. Even *I* knew that orange roughy, while a delicious fish, came from New Zealand and that Evelyn's only served fresh, locally caught seafood?

I turned to Samantha who was totally engrossed with the vignette that was unfolding, covering her mouth to stop from bursting out laughing. She turned towards me, giggled and said, "Katy, I've only seen this once before, but it was nothing like this. Nothing like this!"

Samantha was not the type that giggled, but, then again, Evelyn didn't seem like the type that tolerated fools or played practical jokes.

"Samantha," I said breaking her fascination with the ongoing sport on the floor, "Why are the other customers putting up with those people? They forced their way in, ignored the No Smoking signs, and, in general, are acting like total assholes. That usually pisses people off, but these people seem—I don't know—entertained!" I said.

"They know what's going on," she said dismissively.

"They're tourists. How would they know about *Evelyning*?" I asked.

"They're not tourists," she said, still focused on Evelyn and the whackos.

"But Evelyn told me that in the summer, 90% of the trade was tourists!" I insisted.

"They're locals," she said, again without explanation. "They know about *Evelyning*."

"What are you talking about?" I demanded, giving her a shove to get her attention and, hopefully, some kind of meaningful response.

"Look," she said impatiently, finally turning to face me for the first time. "They're locals. They came to see you—and Evelyn. They heard about how you unhinged her earlier. You asked—now you know. What's going on now is just an added entertainment."

"Great!" I replied. "Now I'm a side show!"

"Get over it. But to answer your question, they're in on the joke. They've either seen it or heard about it before. But, I swear, it's never been anything like this before! Katy, these freaks are doomed!" she said, turning her attention back to the show.

"Excellent choice!" Evelyn confirmed and returned to the kitchen after taking the couple's menu and practically genuflecting.

"Samantha, get the Polaroid and make sure there's film in it," Evelyn ordered. "I have an errand to run."

She returned in a few moments from Hawkins's Fish Market next door, holding a skate up to Samantha. "Give this to Alejandro and tell him to punch 'scallops' out of it for our illustrious gourmets. Make sure he understands to makes 'scallops' out of it!" she said whirling around to speak to me.

"Kathleen," she addressed me smiling. "I've got a feeling we're in for an interesting summer! What do you think?"

I was relieved that she wasn't angry with me, but still apprehensive. "A little *too* interesting so far," I said, thinking about the apoplectic response my appearance had caused earlier—and now this.

"I suppose it is a little much on your first day. Don't worry, it should quiet down after this," she said.

She brought their "scallops" appetizer after about 30 minutes and provided another bottle of bogus wine. They raved about both, genuinely enjoying Evelyn's deferential manner. Not to mention that they were totally in the bag about three drinks ago.

After that they waited…and waited…and waited. Half an hour…an hour…ninety minutes. Finally they started to grouse.

"Ma'am, where are our dinners?" asked the little bully politely, confused by the two faces of Evelyn.

"I'm sorry," replied Evelyn, back in her hostess outfit—and attitude. "I don't wait tables. Let me get you a waitress."

Before she could leave he shouted angrily, "But you're our waitress! You took our order! Orange roughy, remember?"

She turned around and walked deliberately—and ominously—back to the table. "Oh, that's right," she said, as if recalling a distant memory. "I'm sorry, we're out of that item," she explained. "And now the kitchen is closed."

"What do you mean you're out of that item!" he demanded, turning an interesting shade of red.

"Yes, well, all the people that had reservations and waited their turn ate it all," she said, innocently. When they didn't comprehend her meaning she added calmly, but loudly enough for everyone to hear, "You insufferable little prick."

Low-level snickering broke out everywhere in the restaurant.

"How dare you!" he bellowed, totally infuriated when he finally realized, in his befuddled state, exactly what Evelyn had said.

"Do you know who I am?" he asked.

"I think we already covered that," she replied, mugging to her audience—the other diners. "Insufferable," counting off her thumb, "Little," she continued indicating her index finger and pausing to let everyone absorb what she was saying. "Prick!" she finished with a flourish, refolding her thumb and index finger, followed by the prominent display of her solitary middle "finger", and triumphantly looked to her audience for support. They roared with laughter!

"You old bitch!" he screamed. "I'll destroy you!"

Instead of being cowed by his attack, Evelyn was infuriated. "You little fuck!" she said, showing the first real indication of the intensity of her anger. "You'd have had me fire a girl who gave in to your relentless bullying, and made everyone suffer from your filthy habit, including complete disregard for a person's health. And you're going to destroy me?" she said, enraged. With that she whipped out the Polaroid and snapped their pictures while they were screaming at her. The effect of the flash was as if she'd pulled out a gun and shot them. They were utterly stunned.

"You know what *these* are for?" she continuing shouting, making no pretense at concealing her rage. "These are for the 'asshole' board, so that the waitresses who aren't here tonight will know to kick you're asses out of here if you ever show your ugly faces here again! And considering that most of the town is here tonight, if I were you, I wouldn't be caught dead in any of the other businesses in this burg!"

"Capiche?" she said with a flourish.

I figured they were finished. I would have been finished if I was in their position. I'd have slinked out with my tail between my legs—hell, I'd have wet my pants and run out as fast as I could.

"You bitch," he repeated, demonstrating not courage, but a limited vocabulary and a complete lack of comprehension for the precariousness of his situation. "I'll bury you and your little restaurant!" he said quietly, taken aback by Evelyn's unanticipated fury, but still kicking.

"Yeah, you said that, already. Now get out!" she said firmly, with undisguised disdain.

"I'm the food critic for the *Daily Record*, bitch, and you're done here!" he informed her, then waited expectantly for her to buckle.

"*Oh—my—God*!" she exclaimed, leaving everyone wondering if she was finally being flustered by this imbecile. "This just keeps getting better and better!" she said laughing.

"Oh, Harry," Evelyn sang out towards a corner of the restaurant. "You're not going to believe this! He's one of yours."

Harry McVickers, I later learned, had a summerhouse in Mantoloking and his favorite restaurant in the area was Evelyn's.

My Island Beach

Oh—and he also *owns* the *Daily Record*!

Our *prima donna*, to his credit, immediately assessed the situation, and shifted gears in such a calculated and practiced manner that you immediately knew that he was experienced at weaseling his way out of this type of jam.

"Mr. McVickers, I'm sorry, no excuses, I messed up. They moved me from 'Advertising', after twenty years, to 'Food'. I don't know what the hell I'm doing. My apologies to the owner and the other patrons and to you and you're wife," he said with a sincerity that was almost believable. But it was a little too fast and a little too smooth.

Harry McVickers was enjoying this immensely. "Ignorance, sir, is no excuse for rude behavior. In fact, rude behavior might even be tolerable, but you—you have put on a display of abusive behavior the likes of which I have never seen before. Do not say another word to me or the people in this restaurant. It's difficult for me to believe that anyone could be so offensive—as despicable as you have been this evening," he said, then waited, hoping for a response from our misanthropic gourmet that would reenergize his ire.

Again, Mr. Hanson had the good sense to remain silent. He had survived worse, but not much worse. All was not yet lost.

"Your office will be cleaned out and your personal items returned to your house. Do not, I repeat, do not return to the *Record* or I will have you arrested for criminal trespass. And, believe me; I will press charges to the full extent of the law!"

Well, that was too much even for our little weasel to absorb without reacting. With that, our ersatz gourmet and his escort stood up to exit the restaurant seething. As he passed Evelyn he allowed his temper to finally overwhelm his cowardly survival instincts and sputtered, "Stupid whore!" loud enough for her to hear.

Her response was a swift kick in the pants that put him flat on his face!

"I'll sue you, you bitch! I'll own your restaurant for that!" he spat.

"Sir," said Steve (remember Steve, one-half of the couple that traded to sit next to the smoker). "Do you know what the punishment is for breaking the fire code in this town?"

Fear flickered over Mr. Hanson's face, but he remained silent.

"I don't either," said Steve, admitting his ignorance. "You see, I'm only the sheriff and the fire chief in this little hamlet," he said, smiling and holding the troublemaker by the collar. "It's up to the judge and he won't be here until Monday. And seeing as it's only Friday night, you'll have to spend the whole weekend in jail."

"Unless I hear that you're going to forget about any threats, say to sue or something?" Steve said making his case.

"Just let me out of here!" he replied. Steve's response to his request was to slam him up against the wall—ever so gently.

"No lawsuit!" Steve insisted quietly.

"No lawsuit," Mr. Hanson conceded. "Just get me out of this psycho bin."

"Just remember us psychos if you ever decide to change your mind," said Steve in a sinister tone-of-voice that scared the hell out of me.

Off he slinked. And I swear there was a stain on the front of his pants, just as I'd predicted.

The patrons' response was roaring applause and a standing ovation. Evelyn took a bow, gave way to Harry McVickers, who likewise took a bow, followed by Steve who, to the cooing of "My Hero" from Evelyn, stood flexing his biceps and strutting like the head rooster. Engrossed as I was in watching this burlesque from the kitchen, Evelyn managed to sneak around and, with the aid of the other waitresses, pushed me out into center stage.

"This is who you all came to see," she said over the noise, indicating me. "I hope you weren't disappointed! I know I wasn't."

The crowd went nuts. Truthfully, I was undone by the turn of events on this, my first full day on the island. Grandpa and Evelyn's distraught responses, "The Picture" of my grandmother, and now a grand *Evelyning*!

At that moment I don't know if I felt more like Sally Fields at the Academy Awards having a "You like me—you like me" moment, or Dorothy after she landed her house on the Wicked Witch.

Dorothy, I think.

Chapter 6

Marshmallows and Other Delights

"Wake up honey. Time to get going," Grandpa said nudging me.

"Huh," I grunted, turning away.

"Wake up. Rise and shine," he said, shaking me now.

This time I turned over, sat up on my elbows and stared at him dumbfounded.

"Are you OK, Katy?" he asked, not sure what my perplexed look was all about.

I made a last ditch attempt to dive under the sheets.

"Katy!" he scolded.

"*What*!" I whined, pulling my pillow over my head.

"Time to get up," he repeated, laughing.

"Grandpa, what time is it?"

"6:30," he said sheepishly.

"In the morning?" I asked, uncovering my head and staring at him in disbelief. "6:30!" I protested. "Grandpa, I didn't get to bed until after midnight."

"I know, honey, but there's something I want to show you," he insisted. "I've been waiting the better part of two years to show you this and I decided I can't wait another day."

That perked me up. I sat upright and stared at him, intrigued. Sitting up woke me up a little more. "Can't you show it to me at 10:00?" I complained, but I knew I had already lost the battle. I had shown weakness.

"C'mon sleepy-puss. Go grab a quick shower and we'll be off," he said.

"What about breakfast?" I grumbled.

"All packed and ready to go," he said. Damn, he had all the answers.

"And do something with your hair!" he said as I headed for the shower.

"You've got to admit it's beautiful," he said when I eventually appeared outside.

"My hair?" I considered saying. But the sunrise stopped me in my tracks. It was that dramatic. The glow was just beginning to peek over the dunes, a "special effect" they'd never be able to duplicate in Hollywood. In the distance was the sound of waves gently lapping against sand, the whisper of a sea breeze, and that beachy smell. And underneath it all, if you listened closely, was the soothing silence of the inactivity of a day at the beach that hadn't yet begun.

It was truly a delightful time of day in a truly glorious place in the world—but I didn't have to admit anything of the kind. I was just plain too tired.

"Here, put this on," he said, handing me a helmet.

"Somehow demolition derby doesn't appeal to me first thing in the morning," I said sarcastically.

"Maybe this will?" he said, ignoring my surliness. He rolled out what I can only describe as a truly magnificent bicycle!

"I had Harry, down at the cycle shop put it together special for you. Ultra-light frame, shock absorbers, special handlebars for low or high profile riding, which is critical when you're riding against the wind. What do you think?" he asked. "You can change the tires if you like, for off-road riding," he added solicitously, mistaking my silence for disappointment.

"Grandpa, it's beautiful," was all I could say.

"Let's go."

Without waiting for my reaction he grabbed his helmet, mounted his bike and took off.

I followed.

"Katy?" he said, ending the mutual silence we enjoyed during the first leg of our journey.

"Grandpa, I thought we decided that you would call me..." I began as we pedaled along into the park.

"You decided, I never agreed," he protested. "Katy, you are one of the two people in the world I've loved the most, and I've called both of you Katy. In spite of the uncanny resemblance, I won't get you mixed up! I'm not a doddering old fool. Please don't make me call you something else?"

"All right, Grandpa, 'Special Dispensation'".

"Katy?" he said a second time.

"Yes," I responded, acknowledging the familiarity of the diminutive with a smile.

"Do you recognize that?" he asked, indicating the area on our left. At first glance it looked like an expanse of nondescript beach greenery growing in a depression in the dunes. On closer inspection, however, I realized that beneath the dense foliage resided a swamp of some sort. The slight, but distinct odor of sulfur, suggesting decomposition, confirmed my hypothesis.

"No," I said not trying to be difficult, but not really making an effort, either. "A swamp I guess?"

"No?" he prodded. "Think about it."

So I did. "That's the mallow marsh, isn't it?" I said, suddenly remembering, but not comprehending, the meaning of the words I recalled. What a strange thing to say. Mallow marsh? "But where are the flowers?" I asked without understanding why.

Then it finally registered. "That's where the marshmallows grow!" I declared, awake now and recalling bygone days.

"That's right!" he said. We were stopped now. "The flowers show up at the end of July, or the beginning of August."

I remembered witnessing the flowers in bloom. It was impressive, a field of enormous pink and white flowers swaying in the sea breeze.

"And the marshmallows?" I giggled.

"Oh, could be along any day now," he said. "Gotta get 'em while they're fresh!"

"Grandpa—I remember now. You showed up at a barbecue that day carrying a bush with marshmallows growing off the ends of the branches," I recounted the returning memory. "You broke off the branches with marshmallows and told us it was the only way to know if they were fresh. And we'd roast them right on those sticks."

"Do you know how long it takes to attach a bag of marshmallows to a bush?" he asked, laughing. "You were three years old the first time I pulled that stunt and you insisted I bring you fresh marshmallows from then on. No store-bought marshmallows in plastic bags for my granddaughter Katy!"

"Why'd you do it?" I asked.

"As a way of teaching you kids that the flavor of that particular confection originally came from a plant" he said. "But really it was just to be silly."

"By the time I was four I knew it was a joke," I confessed. "And I told all the other kids."

"You always were a sharp one," he said thoughtfully. But then it struck him. "But why'd you keep up the pretence if you all knew? It was a lot of work, decorating those bushes with marshmallows."

"To be silly," I said. "And because that kind of cute shit kept parents, and grandparents, happy."

"Sharp and cynical," he said. "Even then."

And we continued our ride into the ark.

Island Beach State Park is part of a thin barrier peninsula—and sometime island—off the coast of central New Jersey, adjacent to the Town of Toms River. From the Garden State Parkway it's a short hop down Route 37 and over the Thomas Mathis Bridge to Pelican Island, a true island in the bay between the mainland and Island Beach. Both the Parkway and Route 37 vary from six to eight lanes. After the bridge off of Pelican Island, drivers must choose between 35 North and 35 South. Choose 35 South and the road now alternates between four and six lanes instead of the six to eight, a subtle indication that fewer people are required here. After D Street the highway narrows to a definitive four lanes—two in each direction—again acting as a subliminal filter to the onslaught of humanity. Between 13th and 14th street another lane is stripped off in either direction, leaving only two lanes in the four or so blocks that comprise the frontage for the cottages of Midway Beach. This is an unmistakable admonition that fewer people can be tolerated by the island as you move further south towards the point.

An attempt by the local government to widen this section of road to four lanes defied logic in that it required the destruction of 60 houses, thereby reducing the upper limit of potential occupancy while granting greater access to the area! The good people of that town soundly trounced the proposal.

After Midway Beach the highway momentarily swells, like an incipient aneurysm, to an inexplicable three lanes, two in and one out, through the four blocks of South Seaside Park. This provides access to local eateries such as the Atlantic Bar and Grill, Bum Rogers, and, of course, Evelyn's. Entering the park, the road is again reduced to two lanes down its midsection with the token concession of two bike lanes, the paths we were riding on now.

There are two adjacent bathing pavilions with lifeguards near the beginning of the ark. Continuing down the road are the Northern and Southern Wildlife Areas with sections set aside for fishing, beach buggies on the ocean side, and kayaking on the bayside in the sedge islands. The southernmost point of the peninsula is ultimately only accessible to the hardiest of individuals, for the road is now gone completely; only four-wheel-drive equipped fishermen with deflated tires dare proceed through the treacherous sand.

After we had covered three-quarters of the nine-mile-long park, Grandfather veered into one of the small parking areas and pulled up to a white, cinder block outhouse.

"We'll leave the bikes locked up here and walk the rest of the way," he said pulling a cable-lock out of his knapsack. "Better use the facilities if you need to. Not elegant but it's a long walk back."

I took his suggestion, and, boy was he was right! "Not elegant" was at least two or three steps above this. First of all there were flies, and, second of all there were more flies and—ooh the smell! Not to mention the *flies*! Grandpa told me once that that's the way it should be. Keeps the masses out.

We followed the path to the ocean then walked south, parallel to the beach. No one else was around at this ungodly hour, and it was just as gorgeous as I remembered. More than that, really—it was breathtaking! The sun was resting on the edge of the water, looking as if it were balanced on the horizon. The winsome cry of a gull was the only sound complementing the pulsing of the surf. I was fully awake now and moving without thinking, savoring the intersection of my life with this place at this moment. Then Grandpa abruptly turned away from the ocean and invaded the dunes!

"Grandpa, you're not supposed to walk on the dunes," I protested. "You were always telling us that!"

"Don't worry honey, it's OK," he reassured me.

"But Grandpa, we'll damage the ecosystem. You pounded that into our heads," I persisted.

"Honey…Katy, it's OK. We can't have everybody trampling the dunes. But I'm not everybody. This is My Island Beach."

"But Grandpa…" I said renewing my protest.

"Katy, its fine. Trust me please?"

"But Grandpa, won't we get in trouble? There's signs posted all over!" I asked still fretting.

"Don't let the tourists see you or they get upset."

"What about the Rangers?" I asked.

"I have a 'Special Dispensation'," he said. "Like I do for calling you Katy." With that, he straddled the partially submerged hurricane fence and proceeded into the dunes. Reluctantly I followed. I felt like I was walking into the Men's Room, a taboo so strong that you don't even have to think about it.

"Do you know what this is?" he asked. "Or what it was?"

My Island Beach

Before I could answer an orange streak sprinted past me! It was so close that it brushed my leg. "Whoa! What the heck was that?" All I could tell was that it was a small, furry animal.

"You don't remember the foxes on the island?" he asked.

"I guess I remember something about them, but I don't think I ever saw one," I said catching me breath. "They're so small!"

"Tiny really, ten to twelve pounds. Like a really big housecat. If you come into the park at the right time of day you'll see one or two," he said. "That was Q."

"Q?" I asked.

"Q," he said. "They're my Special Dispensation. I keep a census of the fox population in the park. I'm a volunteer."

"What did you do, alphabetize them?" I asked.

"No, I assign names, but I don't make the names up," he said cryptically. "To help me remember *and* for my own amusement."

"Right now there're around 11 breeding pairs in the park. More than 50 kits this spring, to the best of my knowledge, and I am the expert. Twenty seven kits are still alive," said Grandpa.

"That's pretty brutal," I said.

"The first months are the toughest: disease, predation, but mostly cars! We don't really know what happens to them. We lose most of the rest during their first winter. A few of the kits will endure and a few of the adults will perish. If they make it past the first season, they average 3-5 years, and the wily ones can live a lot longer. Overall, there will be no real change in the population; there's been between 9 and 16 breeding pairs since I started the census 10 years ago."

With the explanation complete, we sat on an old piece of timber and Grandpa started unpacking his knapsack. He had packed freshly baked bread, jelly (beach plum from last fall), strawberries, and hard-boiled eggs. This was followed by juice, coffee, and wonderfully seasoned cold crab legs. A veritable feast all laid out on a blanket.

"We're lucky the west wind stopped," he commented making conversation. "No flies." They were apparently all attending the convention in the outhouse.

"So?" he asked after we had devoured the better part of the meal.

"Good," I said with my mouth full.

"No?" he said impatiently.

"What?" I asked.

"So, do you know what this was?"

I looked around. We were sitting on the remains of an old wooden beam surrounded by sand situated in an immense depression. Unlike the adjacent areas, there was a dearth of vegetation. Just sand, like the beach or a desert.

"Hmmmm. Driftwood. Some kind of structure. An old beach house?" I ventured.

"Things made by man are of little consequence compared to the constructs of nature!" he replied cryptically.

"Darwin?" I asked.

"Grandpa," he responded. Sometimes he thought he was Confucius or something.

"Meaning?" I asked, to which he did not respond, so I continued. "This is a natural structure? Well, it's between the primary and secondary dune of a barrier beach," to which Grandpa raised his eyebrows, impressed. "But it seems to be a hollow of some sort. A break in the ecosystem."

"It's called a blowout," said Grandpa putting name to place. "It's caused by the concentration of wind on a section of dune. It occurs where the dunes have been weakened by damage to the primary or secondary dune."

"By what?" I asked.

"By a lot of things," Grandpa offered. "Storms, disease, but especially people trampling the dunes and killing the vegetation that hold things together."

I contemplated the dune, trying to imagine how it evolved.

"This is where we used to come as teenagers—for 'privacy'," he said sheepishly, an emotion I believed him incapable of.

"Sort of a 'Dune of Iniquity'?" I said. Pretty sharp, if I do say so myself, especially considering the hour.

"Don't be smart," he groaned then laughed. Then seriously, "Your grandmother and I used to come here."

My Island Beach

When he didn't go on, I said, "I never really thought about it but Dad doesn't talk about Grandma much. Why is that?"

"Well, first of all, your father didn't know his own mother; she died before he was two. But there are other reasons." He paused to emphasize what he was about to say next. "There are a lot of things I want to do with you this summer, but the most important thing is to tell you about your grandmother and what happened," he explained as I experienced perfect contentment, soaking in the morning and digesting that delicious breakfast.

The first time we came here it was really Katy's idea, but somehow I suggested it. We talked about everything and nothing. Not about important things...just things.

Katy told me what it was like to be here year round; I told her what it was like in the real world. She told me her hopes; I told her my dreams. We didn't make love that first night, but we knew we would soon. It was truly love at first sight. I was 17, she was 15. We were too young, but we really weren't. This was a once-in-a-lifetime thing, and only an idiot wouldn't have realized it.

Neither Katy nor I were idiots.

I took her home at three o'clock in the morning. Her father didn't know it was me that kept her out so late. I wasn't that brave or stupid. And we hadn't actually done anything wrong that first night—just fallen in love—so I didn't feel too guilty.

I never felt guilty about anything I did with Katy; never had a need.

"Time to go," Grandpa said, roused from his musings.

"But Grandpa, you hardly told me anything about Grandma," I protested, unprepared for our precipitous departure.

"We were young and in love, and she was the most extraordinary person I ever met and," he said. "We have all summer...and this is harder than I thought."

I was silent, so he changed the subject. "How was breakfast?" he asked.

"Delici...!" I started to answer, but two of our fox friends bound by and startled me again.

"Was that Q?" I asked, after I caught my breath for the second time that morning.

"Granddaughter, Q is a male. Those were vixens. Solitaire's the mother," he said as we retraced our steps out of the dune, "with one of her kits."

"Pretty," I said as we headed for home. "At least you didn't name her after another letter. What's the kit's name?"

"Pussy Galore," he said grinning impishly.

"Grandpa!" I objected. But then it struck me. "Her mate wouldn't be named Bond—James Bond, would it?" I asked.

"You always were the quick one. But no, her mate goes by the name Goldfinger!"

Chapter 7

Daniel

Grandpa was surprisingly busy for someone who didn't have a real job and, even though I only worked Thursday through Sunday, so was I. I was frequently a substitute for one of the Monday through Wednesday time slots, which were reserved for the full-time waitresses. These were considered choice shifts because they were less frantic with fewer tourists. But you also made less money in tips, so I usually got requests to sub at least once a week.

On one particular Tuesday night, Jim Hawkins (remember, the lad from the campfire) came in with his family. He was with what looked to be his father and an older boy. They were at one of my tables.

"Hello Jim Hawkins," I greeted as he sat down.

He looked up at me suspiciously, and then stated with perfect candor, "I don't know you." But after a minute, he said, "But you must have been at the campfire the other night."

"So I was," I said, distributing the menus. "Your son's very perceptive," I commented to the eldest of the three males who, based on the resemblance, was undoubtedly Jimmy's father.

"He is," the "apparent" parent agreed. "New here?" he asked, making conversation as he declined the menu.

"Sort of," I said. "I used to come to Island Beach as a child. My grandfather was the storyteller at the campfire where I first saw your son," I explained.

"So you're Katy Brace," he said. He shouldn't have known my name—but, ok, maybe he would. My first name was on my nametag and I think practically everyone knows Grandpa. I always feel vulnerable supplying strangers with my name—they don't have to tell me theirs. But then again, they were the customers.

And I had just pulled the same little name game on Jimmy. Nevertheless, I preempted the expected reaction. "I know, I know, I'm the spitting image of my grandmother. And the name is Kathleen, not Katy."

"I never knew your grandmother," he said. "Do I look old enough to have known her?" he asked, his ego apparently bruised by my comments.

He was, in fact, a handsome man, probably in his early fifties but could pass for a decade younger. He had a full head of blonde hair, sprinkled with gray if you looked closely. A stony face squared off and punctuated with a prominent, cleft chin. Strong but short and a stocky. In any case, he was certainly too young to have known my grandmother. "No," I said simply, after considering the chronology.

"Sorry," he apologized. "Talk about a loaded question. My name is Ken Hawkins. You know Jimmy, of course, and this is my other son, Daniel." At this point handshakes were offered all around.

"The reason I know your name is…well…it's just that everyone knows about you and Evelyn," he trailed off apologetically, "and that customer." So it wasn't just the nametag. "Small town," he explained.

Well if Ken Hawkins was a handsome man, and Jimmy a boy who would someday grow up to look just like his father, Daniel was totally unique and just plain delicious; dark complexion, big bedroom eyes, and a strong but lean build. He resembled neither his father nor his brother. Quiet though—troubled even. I think the term they used to use was "brooding". Anyway, gorgeous but not my type; too complicated. His mother must be a knockout.

My Island Beach

Anyway, they must be regulars as they ordered without opening their menus.

As advertised, it was a quiet night, and I was able to take a few minutes at an empty spot at the bar to tabulate the checks for my tables.

Evelyn materialized on the stool next to mine and said, "I see you've met the Hawkins."

"Actually, I met Jimmy at the beach bonfire the other night. He was giving Grandpa a run for his money."

"Yes, an unusually talented family. But who's that with them?" asked Evelyn, indicating the back of Daniel's head. She was trying not to show it but seemed unusually curious about this talented family.

"Daniel," I informed her.

"What!" she exclaimed, momentarily dropping any pretense of indifference. "It can't..." she started to protest but caught herself. She couldn't get a really good look at him from here.

"My God, he's changed. I wonder?" she murmured more to herself than to me.

Then the interrogation was over and it was back to business.

"You're waiting on them?" she asked.

"Yes."

"Well, then give them the bill like usual, but whatever money they leave is for your tip. The meal's gratis," she said. "They supply all the fish to the restaurant. We get a small discount, but more importantly, Ken guarantees that Evelyn's gets the best of the catch," she explained. "If it's not up to his standards, he won't sell it to us."

I handed him the bill, and he immediately handed it back to me with a very generous tip, and folded my hand over it in an overly familiar manner. As they were leaving he said, as if it had just occurred to him, "Ask your grandfather about my Uncle. He was good friends with him and your grandmother." Only I don't think it had *just* occurred to him. In fact, I'm beginning to think that he came to Evelyn's expressly to see me and to tell me what he just told me about his uncle.

Or maybe I was being paranoid.

Jimmy whispered to me, "Your grandfather's pretty cool. But I don't think my Dad likes him." I was beginning to think they all had hidden agendas when Daniel pulled me aside as his father spoke with Evelyn and Jimmy headed for the restroom. Now I knew they did.

"We're having a clambake in the park on Friday night. Ask Samantha, she usually comes if she's off. Mingle with the locals. It's usually a lot of fun."

At that moment Evelyn looked up from her discussion with Ken and got her first good look at Daniel. She caught herself very, very quickly, but there was no missing that look. The same look she had when she saw me for the first time.

I told Daniel that I'd think about it, since it was one of the rare Friday nights that I had off. Harmless enough, I suppose. He wasn't really even hitting on me, just being friendly.

Then why did I think that Daniel knew I was off on this particular Friday, the way his dad knew I was on tonight, a night I didn't usually work? The feeling was a bit disconcerting. No, it was more than a bit disconcerting.

"What's your uncle's name?" I asked as they were walking out.

"His name was Del," Ken Hawkins said, accompanying his answer with a very strange look. "Del Vechionne."

Later that night, as we were closing up, I approached Evelyn, who was installed at her little table. She didn't invite me to sit, and she didn't stand, which I suppose was her way of keeping conversations short and to the point.

"Evelyn," I said, without knowing what I wanted to say but knowing that I'd better figure it out fast. I took a breath which gave me time to figure out what I wanted to say. Evelyn looked up from her work when I didn't immediately say anything.

"Did you know Del Vechionne?" I asked.

I had her attention now. Without any real concrete evidence I knew I'd hit a hot button with both the topic and timing of my question. She looked at her paperwork, then at me, then folded it and stood up. "Come on," she said, propelling me gently by the elbow. "I'll buy you a drink," and steered me towards the bar.

Bruno brought her over some wine, without having to be asked, and a Coke for me as we sat at one of the few tables in the now-empty bar. After a few sips Evelyn asked, "So why do you want to know about Del?"

Not "What did I want to know?" or an acknowledgement that she knew him, which was the original question, but "*Why* do I want to know about Del?"

"I guess because Ken Hawkins told me that I should mention to Grandpa that I'd met some of Del's relatives. That is, Ken, and his kids," I said.

"This *is* going to be an interesting summer," Evelyn said, enigmatically.

I didn't know how to respond to that.

"If I were you, I wouldn't mention the Hawkins family to your grandfather," Evelyn cautioned without explanation.

What I really wanted to ask her was why I had the feeling that the Hawkins had hidden motives with regards to Grandpa and me. But Evelyn was being so cryptic that I was beginning to think that she had hidden motives regarding the Hawkins and Grandpa—and maybe me, too. She hadn't answered my original question but just asked questions of her own.

Too bad Sam was off that night. She's sure to know something about this. Or at the very least would concoct something interesting if she didn't.

All in all, it was a very unsettling evening.

Chapter 8

The Sedge

My next scheduled quality time with Grandpa was a trip to the sedge islands. Before embarking on our adventure I tried to talk him into taking out a double kayak, which I knew he could borrow if he wanted to, but he convinced me that two singles would be better. They were sit-on-top ocean kayaks; the type that floats even when filled with water.

As we unloaded our crafts I noticed the disembodied heads of people moving about in the open water. Next to each was an inner tube. I can't begin to explain how bizarre this appeared. Positively Medieval! I eventually realized that bodies were attached to the heads, underwater, and were walking across the sedge loading up their floats with clams. I later learned that these clammers go out at or near high tide, since at low tide the lack of flotation leaves them bogged down in the muck.

"This, my dear granddaughter, is courtesy of the inimitable Pete McLain," my grandfather pronounced as we began our outing.

"How did Mr. McLain get 'inimited'," I asked playfully.

"Do not take the name of McLain in vain," he said lyrically. "First of all, he not only recommended the purchase of the sedge but acquired the grants to buy it."

My Island Beach

"I thought Island Beach was purchased from the Phipp's heirs in the 50's," I said smugly.

"Katy, you've been reading up. Bravo! And they say there's no substance to our youth."

"So what did Mr. McLain have to do with it?" I repeated.

"A reasonable question," said Grandpa. "Wait! Quiet! See the heron in the small sedge to the left?" he whispered.

I did. We glided close to it for several moments. It was quite majestic. Blue and gray with black highlights, its body was topped with a white head at the end of a long gray neck. And a dashing black tassel sweeping backward off the top gave it a rakish appearance. Not to mention that it was an absolutely enormous bird. As the current brought us closer, it took flight, followed sequentially by six others that were hidden in the sedge!

"Magnificent!" I said, no longer preoccupied with silence.

"Katy, those were Great Blue Herons. *Ardea herodias*. I see isolated ones, usually; never seen a flock like that before! We were lucky today."

We drifted silently, again, toward a sand bar covered with seabirds.

"So tell me about Mr. McLain?" I said, as we landed on the bar. The spit of sand was covered with seabirds, mainly sand pipers, gulls and cormorants. They were unexpectantly tolerant of our presence.

"Well, the Sedge Islands are not actually part of Island Beach State Park," Grandpa replied. "The park is run under the auspices of The Division of Parks and Forestry under the Department of Environmental Protection."

"But I remember the Island Beach Interpretive Staff runs the kayak tours in the sedge," I pointed out. "Why is that?"

"Because the New Jersey Division of Fish and Wildlife, which is responsible for the sedge, chooses not to. The Parks Department's presence in the sedge is at the forbearance of the Division of Fish and Wildlife," Grandpa said.

"If you say so," I thought.

"Grandpa, I know the black birds there are cormorants, but why do they air out their wings that way—like Batman's signal?"

The look on his face intimated that he knew what I meant about the cormorant's wings, but he didn't understand the reference to Batman's signal.

"Most water birds have oil glands that they use to waterproof their wings: gulls, ducks, and the like. Cormorants lack oil glands and, therefore, need to air-dry their wings to keep them from getting waterlogged."

"Weird," I commented. Glancing around, I noticed a peculiar-looking bird perched on a piece of driftwood sticking out of the sand bar. "Ooh, what's that ugly one? Looks prehistoric."

"Katy, you know what that is," he said. He's right, I did, but I couldn't remember what it was called.

Finally it came to me, "A pelican! You always see them with huge, bucket-like beaks in the cartoons."

"That's only when they're full of fish," Grandpa said, which I'd already realized. "Wait till you see him fly."

So we waited, and when he didn't fly, Grandpa rousted him. Sometimes Grandpa really did think this is "His Island Beach" put here specifically for his pleasure. Anyway, when the pelican took off it was no longer ugly. It was impressive—but still prehistoric.

"It looks like a pterodactyl!" I said as it soared overhead.

"That's because it has such a small tail and such a large head," he explained.

"But I don't remember seeing them here when I was a kid," I said.

"That's because there weren't any. They only returned in the last year or two. Water's getting cleaner and the fish and birds are coming back."

"Want to see some other long-lost inhabitants?"

He took off in the kayak before I had the opportunity to voice an opinion. Guess it was a rhetorical question.

"Bay men harvested the eel grass to feed cattle, and hunted ducks and other waterfowl. Eventually the inhabitants and visitors started cutting down the trees for lumber. This resulted in the demise of one of the most majestic inhabitants of the sedge. Do you know what I'm talking about?" Grandpa asked.

"No idea."

"Not only is the sedge a resting place for migrating birds in the spring and the fall, but there is a special visitor who graces the sedge for the whole summer, breeding and raising their families here," said Grandpa. "That visitor is the osprey."

"The fish-hawk?" I asked.

"An accurate and descriptive, but totally inappropriate, name for this majestic bird," said Grandpa. "Their demise was due to DDT weakening their eggs and the destruction of the trees."

When I didn't say anything, he explained, "They nest in the upper branches of tall trees. When that niche disappeared, so did they."

"What do you see?" he asked as we paddled out into the heart of the sedge.

"Grass islands—sedge," I said uncertainly.

"Anything else?"

There was something else. Towers. Man-made wooden towers.

"Look closer. Squint," he said.

I did and what I saw were birds of prey, raptors, populating the towers.

"Tree surrogates for nesting. At last count there were 28 breeding pairs of osprey in the Island Beach sedge, the highest concentration in New Jersey. And all because of Pete McLain. He initiated the program to build the towers and seeded them with healthy eggs from osprey nests in Maryland," Grandpa finished.

As we silently glided towards a group of platforms we saw osprey chicks being fed with regurgitated food from their parents. The ultimate sushi, partially digested raw fish. Yuck!

"It's especially important, this time of year, that we don't disturb the families," Grandpa whispered. "If you scare off the adults, crows and gulls move in and kill the chicks."

I watched an adult osprey swoop down to the water, in a Kamikaze dive, and pull up with a sizeable fish in its talons. "You know, Grandpa, that's kind of disturbing. They're obviously good parents, but they tear the flesh off live fish. Seems kind of barbaric."

"That's because people romanticize primitive animals and

cultures. Chimps practice murder, in particular, infanticide. When a new male takes over a harem of females impregnated by the previous dominant male, he kills the offspring. And virtually any primitive human culture will opportunistically incorporate new technology that will give them advantage over their competitors. The way Native Americans become expert horseman and riflemen," he said. "King Kamehameha used cannons to become the first King of the Hawaiian Islands," he finished, winding down, or more likely, running short of breath.

We paddled on, peacefully observing the majestic flyer.

"One more thing you should see while we're here," he said pointing off into the distance.

As we drew close, we confronted an imposing, manmade platform. This construct was not only significantly larger than the osprey nests, but it was the only one of its kind within my line of vision.

"What is it?" I asked.

"It's called a *hacking tower*," Grandpa said.

"Like it sounds," he proceeded. "It's where they come to hack their prey apart."

"And who are they, and who are their prey," I said poetically.

"'They are peregrine falcons, and their prey is other birds. What better place to live than in a bird sanctuary," said Grandpa.

"Why only one 'hack box'?" I asked. "Seems like the perfect place to breed a lot of them."

"I don't know," replied Grandpa. "But if you want to see something impressive, it's the sight of a peregrine taking down another bird, as big as it is, in midair. Breathtaking! They've been clocked at 180 miles per hour in a dive. And they're as murderous as they are beautiful, once they've returned to the hack box. They eat their prey with their beaks, unlike the ospreys that use their talons."

"Here with the help of Pete McLain?" I asked, suspecting the answer.

"I have an article on it at home—National Geographic, you can see for yourself," he confirmed. "He lives out here in the sedge."

Having been introduced to the neighbors, we headed for home.

Chapter 9

Beach Blanket Bingo

"So he invited you to the beach party?" asked Samantha.

Sam had dragged me to the beach, and we were relaxing, soaking up rays. She was wearing a bikini that did little to cover her obvious assets, but was decent enough. Not a thong or anything. Not her working suit either, a one-piece Speedo that allowed her to indulge in her joy of the water without fear of being charged with indecent exposure. It was her "if you got it flaunt it suit," as she put it.

It was a little intimidating being at the beach with her, as numerous males stopped by to chat her up and check me out in the bargain. But I suppose there are worse fates to suffer.

"No, Sam, he really just kind of told me about it," I said.

"Well that's good. I was going to tell you about it; too, I just didn't get around to it yet."

"What do you mean 'That's good'?" I asked.

"Well, it's just that Mr. Daniel Hawkins is, well....what do you think of him?" she asked.

"What's this? The great Sammy, without an opinion, a sound-bite, a thumbnail biography of one of the inhabitants of Peyton Island." I said. Sam knew everyone and wasn't shy about sharing her opinions.

"Well, it's just that I haven't got this guy quite figured out yet. Doesn't fit into any of the easy categories. Sometimes I think I'd give him a tumble if he asked. Other times he gives me a little bit of the creeps. But, so far he hasn't asked, so I haven't had to decide. Nice butt though. Maybe he's gay!" I was mistaken. Apparently Sammy had a laundry list of opinions about Mr. Daniel Hawkins.

"You think he's gay because he has a nice butt?" I asked.

"No," she replied indignantly, "Because he hasn't come on to me. He must be gay. What about you?"

"I'm not gay," I said, purposely misunderstanding her question. She shot me an exasperated look.

"He hasn't come on to me either." Another exasperated look.

"I don't know. I guess I'm leaning towards the creepy side," I said, finally answering the intended question and, like Sam, uncertain how I felt about him.

"You're off this Friday, right?" she asked.

"Yeah."

"You should go then. It's fun. Something to do."

"Who am I supposed to go with? You're on Friday, right?" I asked.

"I always go after work. Night owl, you know. We'll go then," she said as if it was settled.

"Too late for me. I'm lucky if I'm still awake by midnight," I protested.

"Don't worry; I'll sneak out by 11:00. Rose will cover. She owes me and, besides, it's pretty quiet by then." And this time it was settled.

It was more like 11:30 by the time Sam showed up. She'd gotten "started" with a couple of drinks at Evelyn's. It was a quarter to twelve when we parked at the end of the park and started walking down the beach.

As we were walking, a 4WD pulled up alongside us in the sand. "Would you ladies like a ride to the party?" asked one of a pair of California-looking beach types.

"Billy!" shrieked Sam. "Where have you been? I've been looking for you all summer!"

"You work nights. I work days. It's a vicious cycle," he shrugged. "Come on, get in."

"So Billy, who's your friend?" asked Sam as we motored towards the bonfire.

"Sammy, Jason. Jason, Sammy. I'm Billy, and you must be…?" Billy paused, eyeing me.

"Kathleen," I answered. "I must be Kathleen since all of your names are taken." That got a laugh. But at that point a good loud fart might have been funnier.

Billy had a football player body type, big and muscular; Jason was more like a swimmer. Leaner, huge shoulders and a tiny waist. He must be twenty pounds lighter than Billy and two or three inches taller. Very firm looking but not so clean-cut. A mullet, earring and one eyebrow piercing. Not an unattractive guy, lean and kind of edgy.

"So Katy, you're a waitress too?" asked Billy, his interest in me totally undisguised.

"Of course she is. Now Jason, don't tell me you're one of those slow-witted, sun-baked, lifeguard dullards like Billy here?" asked Sam. "You look far too intelligent for that."

"'Fraid so," answered Jason, aware likewise, of Sam's interest in him. As it turned out, Sam ended up matched up with Billy and me with Jason, which I didn't have a problem with.

After a few beers, we had marshmallows and I decided to explain that the park contained the key ingredient for this snack. This was met with interest, followed by derision, followed by more beer.

"You know, I thought you weren't allowed to drive on the beach except to fish. And I know alcohol isn't allowed in the park. I don't see any fishing poles!" I said.

"Sorry, this is my first party, too. Haven't got a clue," said Jason with a winning smile. This guy must be used to getting pretty much anything he wanted with the girls. And I could understand why.

We discussed colleges before that. Jason was going to UCLA to study Communications and Far Eastern Culture. Weird combination, but he was on a full scholarship. I was actually impressed by more than his scholastic talents.

"It's an arrangement between the lifeguards and the Parks and Recreation Rangers. All totally illegal," said an anonymous voice.

I looked to see who was interrupting my unofficial date with Jason. Unfortunately, his back was to the fire which shrouded his features.

"Daniel," he supplied. "From the restaurant, remember?"

Of course! Once more I sensed something disturbing about this individual. I don't know what. It was more instinctual than rational.

"You sound like you don't approve," I said. "And yet, here you are."

"Well, its harmless enough," he said, unprovoked by my tone of voice. "Only beer and wine. No hard liquor or drugs," he informed us and sauntered off into the camouflage of the firelight.

"Friend of yours?" asked Jason, unfazed by the encounter.

"Nooo," I responded. "Just one of the weird ducks from the restaurant."

"I remember now," he said. "I heard about you and Evelyn. I know Evelyn!" he exclaimed. "You must be way cool to rock her world the way you did."

Instead of playing it down, which was my natural inclination; I told Jason the whole story, embellishing it here and there to make me look better. Sam was having a decided effect on my outlook on life, for better or worse. He was impressed and I was tempted.

"Hey Katy, check this out!" yelled Sammy during a lull in the conversation.

Coming across the sand was an old, old jeep. "Beautiful," said Jason. "That's got to be a '56 or '57 Willy. Mint condition!"

I recognized the driver of the vehicle. It was one of the local characters who the kids called "Surfer Dude," but who Grandpa told me was named Ray. He had a full head of hair, but it was gray and cut in a flat-top, and skin like leather aged by decades of summers in the sun. He had a little middle-aged spread but was really in pretty good shape. He was pushing 60, but he was out there every day religiously, riding the waves on his big board. Seemed like a happy guy.

"Yo, Surfer Dude!" the kids yelled out as he drove up.

"What's that on the back of his Willy?" asked Jason.

"You'll see in a minute," said Sam.

I could see what he meant now. While I wasn't a connoisseur of classic SUVs, I could tell that there was some kind of contraption strapped to the back of his jeep that wasn't standard issue.

"Watch this," said Sammy.

After he stopped, "Surfer Dude" circled around to the back of his jeep, pulled a lever, and the contraption unfolded and started lowering down to the sand. It looked for all the world like a wheelchair lift, which I later learned that it was, recovered from a wrecked van. Sitting on the lift—and I'm amazed I recognized it—was a full-sized movie theatre popcorn popper! Not of recent vintage. It had to be from the 50s or 60s, all chrome and glass! Ray fired up a tiny Honda generator, plugged the beast in, added oil and a whole lot of popcorn and let it rip. He finished up with butter and salt when it was done. He whipped up the best batch of popcorn I have ever had. Way better than you get in the movies today. It tasted heavenly with the beer.

Which brings up the topic of gadgets. The wheel chair lift/popcorn popper was definitely the extreme case, but there was a high concentration of other one-of-a-kind gadgets down the shore. (FYI, nobody ever goes to the "beach" in New Jersey. They go "Down the Shore".) Anyway, there are lots of homemade carts to transport kayaks and surfboards behind bikes or to just to make them easier to drag across the sand. I once saw an old four-wheel-drive International Harvester, the precursor of the Hummer that looked like a tank from World War I. Out of the back they pulled a platform holding a full kitchen—range, fridge and sink with running water—all on heavy duty rollers, like a drawer, so that it just hung out over the sand counterbalanced by that huge monstrosity of a truck. Or a school bus/mobile home with a chopped down jeep angle-winched in the back so that it wasn't being towed but was housed inside when they traveled!

There was also every kind of nautical decoration imaginable, mailboxes standing on an anchor base, planters inside an old Dory. You name it. Definitely not the kind of stuff you'd find at Home Depot.

"Jason, can you take my SUV home? Sammy and I are going home on Jerry's boat," said Billy.

"I guess." Jason said.

"Hey, what about me?" I asked, feeling a little out of control of the situation.

"Well, duh! You take my car home," said Sam.

"Sam, I just got my license a couple of months ago," I told her. "I have no idea how to drive a stick."

"Jason can take you home," said Sammy. Wink, wink, nudge, nudge. She pulled me aside. "Listen, I really want to spend some time with Billy. He's kind of special," she said. "And it's really tough with our schedules. Help me out?"

"I guess," I said. "But I don't really know this guy and you don't either, do you?"

"Billy says he seems like an OK guy. He doesn't know him that well either, but he's talking to him now. If you want to go straight home, that's where he'll take you. If you want to do anything else, that's up to you and Jason. But Jason will do whatever you want, or he'll pay the price with Billy. He's making that clear to Jason right now. Please?" she begged.

"Don't worry, I'll get you home safe," Jason assured me, having heard the latter part of Sam's request. I guess I didn't fight it too hard.

"What about your car Sam?" I asked, at the behest of my better judgment.

"Don't worry, Billy can run me out here tomorrow before he goes to work," Sam said.

Having run out of arguments, I figured my karma was to go with Jason.

It was about two in the morning and, in spite of the setup by Sam and Billy, I was feeling exhilarated as we tooled out of the park with the top down.

"Look, I can either take you home or over to my place for awhile?" Jason asked hopefully. To tell the truth, I was really thinking about it. I mean, I didn't want to tease, but I also didn't want him to think I wasn't interested.

I was considering all the possibilities, when we hit something!

"What the fuck!" Jason exclaimed, stopping and backing up and running over whatever it was again, so we could see it with the headlights.

I rushed out of the car when I realized what it was. A fox!

"Oh no!" I screamed.

"Don't get too close," Jason warned, concerned.

"I won't," I said. "Oh shit, that's Solitaire."

"The fox?" asked Jason incredulously.

"My grandfather..." I stopped, not wanting to go into a lengthy explanation of my eccentric grandfather. "Do you have a cell phone?"

I called Grandpa, knowing full well that I'd wake him at this hour.

"Why don't we just go?" Jason said, impatiently, as I called.

"Hold on," I said. "Grandpa, I'm fine," I reassured him quickly, realizing he might be concerned by a late night call. "But Grandpa, I was coming out of the park and hit a fox!" I confessed hysterically.

"OK, Katy," he said reassuringly. "How bad is it?"

I walked around to have a closer look. "I think her hips are crushed!" I said finally. Jason was pacing.

"Her?" asked Grandpa.

"I think its Solitaire, Grandpa!"

Silence.

And more silence. It went on for several seconds.

"Grandpa?" I pleaded.

"Katy," he said. "She's going to die." He tried to sound clinical, but I could tell it was a blow for him.

"No!" I shrieked.

"Katy, listen to me," he said. "She's had two litters of three kits each. The latest litter is already weaned, so they'll be fine."

"Grandpa, I can take her to a vet or something?"

"Katy it's a part of the cycle of life in the park. Without predators, cars are part of the equation, the balance. With 40-50 kits born each year, we'd be overrun in short order and the bird populations would pay dearly if the foxes had no predators. The problem is that people stop and feed them, so they come out to beg and sometimes get run over."

"But Grandpa!" I screamed.

"Katy, even if you could save her, which you can't, she'd spend the rest of her life in a cage as a cripple. Katy, you know that's not right."

"Come on, let's get out of here!" Jason said irritably as I weighed what Grandfather had said.

"Hold on," I said, starting to wonder what it was that I saw in this guy.

"Grandpa, there has to be something I can do?" I persisted. I was going to do something to make this situation right, the only question was what.

"Nothing, Katy. Just leave her. I'll see to her in the morning," he said sharply.

"Grandpa!" I implored. I couldn't just leave her.

"Katy, no matter what you do she is going to die. That's the way it's supposed to be!" he said getting more aggravated by the minute.

"Grandpa!" I screamed. Jason looked shocked.

"Katy, she's going to die!" he shouted, losing patience with my moral conundrum.

This was followed by a very, very long silence.

"There's one thing. Normally I don't believe in interference, but if you've got the courage, you could save her some suffering."

"What?"

"In the trunk of the car. You should have a tire iron or some such bludgeon?" he said.

"Grandpa!" I said, realizing what he was getting at.

"Katy...darling...we all have to make tough decisions in life.

My Island Beach

This is one of those." When I didn't respond he said, "If it's not in your heart to do it, it doesn't matter. The outcome will be the same. Come home and forget about it."

I found the tire iron in the trunk. "Goodbye, Grandpa. I'll be home in a while."

I looked at her for a moment, and then realized that if I considered it instead of doing it instantly, I'd lose my resolve.

I finished her off with three savage blows!

Jason and I continued our drive. He seemed a little hesitant about me now, but that didn't stop him from asking, "So, would you still like to come over for a while?" after the minimum decent interval. Even after all that has happened, he was *still* hoping to get laid!

I never said that I would…come over that is. Finally, I said, "You know Jason, you're a sweet guy and if I didn't know you lacked one iota of sensitivity, we could probably have had some fun. But I do, so I guess I'll just have to pass. It's a shame though."

Like Grandpa said, we all have to make tough decisions in life. I don't think Jason appreciated mine.

Chapter 10

The Plot Thickens

"Katy, time to get up. You have to be at work in a few hours." Grandpa was shaking me gently.

I felt tired, deep down tired. Achy, like I was old. My muscles were fatigued and my eyes were crusty and oversensitive even to the meager light filtering into the room. Grandpa was being a royal pain, shaking me, pestering me. I wish he'd stop and let me sleep, damn it!

"Grandpa!" I snapped, taking a wholehearted swing at him!

"Whoa! Aren't you the feisty one!" he exclaimed, laughing and grabbing my wrists before I could take another swing, which I would have. His preventing me was just making me angrier. But I was finally waking up.

"What time is it?" I asked as I came back to my senses, figuring it was 6:30 a.m. like the last time he woke me.

"It's two in the afternoon," he said. I looked at him with frank disbelief. "Honey, you had a long hard night, but you've had plenty of sleep now and it's time to get up," he said, trying to sound stern, but only sounding concerned.

When I didn't answer, he gave up on sounding strict. "Katy, are you…?"

I interrupted his question by vaulting out of bed and dashing to the bathroom. "I gotta pee!" I said. A second later I peeked my head back into the room, "And shave the fuzz off the inside my mouth."

"Go, go," he said. "More than I wanted to know."

"Thanks, Grandpa, much better," I said smiling, as I crawled back into bed where he was still waiting. "Did I punch you?" I asked, pretty sure I knew the answer.

"You tried," he said smirking. "Do you wake up like that often?"

"It's happened once or twice before when I went to bed upset," I said. "I almost put Dad in the hospital when I was thirteen." Grandpa smiled at the thought of it. So did I.

"Are you OK?" he asked finishing the question he started before I headed to the john. I stopped grinning, suddenly recalling the events of the previous evening.

"I'll be alright," I said stoically. "It was Solitaire, wasn't it? You've already been out there?"

"It was," he confirmed. "Everything's taken care of." He didn't tell me then, but he didn't believe in burying the corpses of wild animals or putting them into the trash. He moved the body into the dunes, where the birds and bugs took care of everything. In retrospect, I'm OK with that, but I'm glad he didn't tell me at the time.

"Oh Grandpa, I should have done something!"

"You did do something, Katy. You stopped her suffering. That took a lot of courage, darling."

"But Grandpa, there must've been some way to save her," I said.

"You don't believe that," he said looking at me sternly, then fiercely. "If you did, then you murdered her. You didn't murder her. You made a tough choice."

"But did I make the right choice?"

"You may have to wait till Judgment Day for the answer to that one. And don't ask me what I would have done!" he said. "I won't tell you because I don't know and it doesn't matter anyway. You took the responsibility for what you did. Don't try to give it up now. Responsibility's not just a duty," he counseled, "it can also be a privilege, and one that shouldn't be denied."

I *was* about to ask what he would have done. I bit my upper lip and started to cry, but when Grandpa tried to comfort me with a hug, I pulled away. He understood, I think, and didn't take offense.

Grandpa went downstairs to make a late lunch for me. After I showered and dressed for work, I came down. Before he could speak, I put my hand up and said, "I'm OK Grandpa. Let's talk about something else."

We ate and didn't talk at all for a long time.

Finally I said, "You remember little Jimmy?"

"Jimmy who?" Grandpa asked.

"'Jimmy 'awkins—smart as paint!' Remember?"

"At the campfire!" He smiled. "Cute kid. Sharp too!"

"Well, I waited on him and his family at the restaurant last night," I said.

"I don't think I know his family," he replied. "Summer folks?"

"No, they know you," I said. "Jimmy's father said you knew his uncle, you and Grandma, both."

"Not that I recall."

"Grandpa, it seemed really important to them," I said. "It was kind of weird."

"Hawkins?" he said thinking out loud.

"His uncle's last name was Vecchione," I prompted.

The attraction between Del Vecchione and Katy was palpable, even after she chose me—even after we were married. I wasn't blind. I only questioned her about it twice, once when we first started dating and once right before we got married. She didn't deny it; she said she'd always been drawn to him. Her only explanation was that she chose me and, though she never said it, that was going to have to be enough. And it was, but it was still hard on the ego.

They were together before I arrived on the scene. Intimate too, I suspect, but probably not all the way. She was only 14, that year before I got there. Katy was definitely precocious, but not THAT precocious.

There were rumors, even after our marriage. I'd asked her before the wedding and she'd denied them. I didn't insult her by asking again. Besides, if she'd lied the first time, she'd lie again. I loved her with all my heart and, above all, I loved her free spirit. But it was that free spirit that I didn't trust, the one that I loved so much. The one that would do what it had to do to stay free.

When Katy disappeared, so did he. And eventually people stopped bothering to whisper when I was around. It was nothing compared to the loss of the love of my life, but on top of it, it was just too much to bear.

"Grandpa, you're going catatonic on me again," I said, rousing him from his musings.

"Stay away from the Hawkins! All of them!"

"But Grandpa, Jimmy's a dear and you…"

"Stay away from them!" he said again. Finally realizing how he must have sounded, he took a breath, pulled himself together and said calmly, "Katy, you did something really *courageous* last night with Solitaire and, right or wrong, I admire you for it. Now do something really *intelligent*. Stay away from the Hawkins!" he ordered, raising his voice once again.

After that he got up, agitated, and left me to my lunch, wondering if my beloved grandfather was bipolar or something.

Chapter 11

Samantha

Sam swooped in, just in time for our shift, dressed provocatively in a miniskirt, halter top and platform sandals. She always changed at the restaurant before and after her shift, refusing to be seen outside of work in her work uniform. Looking at her, I realized that the things about her that I admired were the same things I was jealous of.

First of all, she had a fantastic figure: slender, tall, firm and pointed heavenwards in all the right places. Though I was blessed with some of the same attributes, I would never, for example, be considered tall.

She also had a gorgeous face with high cheekbones, heavy eyebrows turned upward at the corners, petite but strong features and dark, stunning hair.

To top off the whole package, she dressed cheaply (slutty, really) emphasizing virtues that would have been more sensuous if they were understated rather than broadcasted. Though I didn't admire her wardrobe, I did having a grudging admiration that she could pull off that kind of outrageous look. I couldn't.

"Hey Katy, how'd it go last night?" asked Samantha curiously.

"Not too well," I said. "Guy turned out to be a well-disguised creep!" I went on to describe the events after she and I had parted last night.

"Bummer," she said. "But so he doesn't like animals. Nobody's perfect."

"It was more than that, Sam...just a feeling that he wouldn't be the guy you'd want to be stuck in a lifeboat with if you were short of food."

"Whew," she cringed. "When you put a take on people there's not a lot of room for slack?"

"Hey, I know what I know," I said, not backing off from my opinion, which got me a look. Maybe I deserved it.

"How about you and Troy Donahue?" I asked.

"Yeah, well, you know. He gets it done," a statement which, even to another teenager is pretty obtuse, but I got the gist.

"Well, look what the cat dragged in," I said indicating that the topics of our discussion had just arrived.

"Hey, Billy," said Sammy, winking and mugging.

"You know Sammy," Billy said, slurring his words. "Your friend wasn't very nice to my boy, Jason, here last night," he said in a voice just a little too loud for this establishment.

Sammy grabbed Billy's arm and shuffled him off to the bar whispering, "Well, maybe it wasn't a match made in heaven like us?" which got her a squeeze on the ass and a squeal of delight.

"Bruno, give this man a beer," Sammy said. She sure knew how to handle men. Later, when we were alone Sammy whispered to me, "He's a real sweetie when he's sober. But he can be a real mean drunk."

Billy quieted down after that. Jason didn't say a word, just glared at me from his seat at the bar. At one point he pulled me aside and asked if I'd like to get together when I got off. I mumbled something about "Cruising for more road kill?" which pissed him off but "got it done", as Sam would say.

Everything was quiet until Ray arrived in the bar at about 11:00. "Surfer Dude," was murmured as he moved through the clientele. Ray waved and smiled at everyone then went and chatted with a couple on the other side of the room.

The next time I was at the bar, I heard Billy saying, "You know, I don't know why everybody likes that fuckin' guy. He's just an old lech that likes the young girls. Some kind of pedophile, if you ask me," he said, pronouncing the single word "pedophile" loud enough for everyone to hear. Everyone looked away when they realized it was just some drunk blowing off steam. Of course, the worst thing you can do to a mean drunk is to dismiss him.

"I'm talking about that fucking Surfer Dude!" he said loud enough for *everyone* to hear *everything* this time. He stalked to the other side of the bar and said, "You know he's just hanging around hoping to get a little teenybopper ass!" to the couple Ray was sitting with.

"Leave Ray alone!" said Sammy with fire in her eyes and an ominously calm tone in her voice.

"And you!" he said, turning towards Sam. "Why are you standing up for him?" She stood her ground not saying a word.

"Did you do it with him?" he said, finally. "I'll kill him!" he screamed before Sam had a chance to confirm or deny it, and lunged across the bar.

A couple of guys intercepted him, when Evelyn suddenly appeared. "Get him out of here!" she ordered.

"They can throw me out, but I'll be waiting for you Surfer Dude!" he warned Ray who was shaken by this unprovoked attack. "I'm going to kick your fat old ass," Billy threatened.

"Out! Now!" yelled Evelyn.

"Evelyn," said Sammy, after pulling her aside. "Let me handle this?" Billy was starting to calm down; in his inebriated state he seemed to have the attention span of a two-year-old. Evelyn looked from Billy to Sam and finally consented. As much as she wouldn't tolerate brawling inside her establishment, she'd be happier if nobody got beaten up later on either.

After Evelyn left, Sammy walked up to Billy, gave him a big kiss and started whispering in his ear. He was smiling and then laughing. But as she continued whispering he started getting visibly irritated, at which point Sammy paused to catch her breath.

He was quieting down again when she started whispering again. He was grinning, engaged by her endearments, when he abruptly shouted, "You bitch!" and backhanded her with such force that her head snapped back and sprayed blood over several of the patrons! She was physically lifted off the ground by the force of the blow and shot backwards several feet before landing on her backside! And, despite all the pain and insult she must have been feeling, she had a look of wry amusement on her face as she sat on the floor wiping the blood off her mouth and staring at Billy.

Now Sammy's behavior usually evokes either militant criticism or militant support. In this case, framed as the underdog, her supporters were mobilized. I wouldn't say Billy was beaten within an inch of his life, but I was surprised he walked out under his own power. But before he left, Sammy crawled over to his prostrate form and whispered in his ear one last time. No smiles, no anger from Billy—not this time. Just fear!

"Samantha, you want me to call the cops?" asked Evelyn when she showed up to witness the ruckus.

"No cops!" said Sammy emphatically.

"I'll take her to a doctor," I said.

"No, we can't lose both of you in one night. Sorry. I'll call your grandfather," said Evelyn.

"I'm OK, OK?" said Sam.

"You're not OK!" said Evelyn.

"I'm not great, but I'll live."

"OK, no cops, and I think you can wait till tomorrow to see a doctor, but I'll get Phil to run you home," said Evelyn.

"Evelyn, let me stay?" Sam pleaded.

"Sammy, I can't have you waiting on people looking like that. I don't want to scare you…I'm sure you'll look better when the swelling goes down. But right now I'm not so sure the customers will keep their dinners down the way you look."

"I'll work the bar, Evelyn," Samantha said. "Don't send me home right now. Even dogs look good to these guys after a few drinks."

Evelyn considered Sam's proposition. Then she changed her mind. It was the only time I've ever seen Evelyn convinced to do something that I believe she really didn't want to do.

"Alright, Sam, against my better judgment. And Sam, I know

what you did and, as noble as it was, if it ever happens again in this establishment you're outta here," promised Evelyn. What a trip. She could switch from the compassionate New Testament God to the vengeful Old Testament one in a flash!

"Got it," said Sam without resentment. "It was worth it," she said as Evelyn walked away, shaking her head and smiling.

"You sure you want to stay?" I asked.

"Are you kidding? Here I get attention and sympathy tips big time. At home I get swollen, sore and depressed," she said, irrationally happy. "I'll go to the doctor in the morning," she vowed in response to my disapproving look.

"I promise, OK?" she assured me.

"What was Evelyn talking about?" I asked.

"You come buy me a drink after work and I'll tell you," she winked, grabbed a tray and yelled, "Hey Bruno, whip me up another ice pack for this abomination that used to be my face while I get to work." Everyone cracked up.

I saw Sam a couple of times during the rest of the shift, but there was never any time to talk. At closing time we finally sat down and Bruno brought over some white wine.

"So, are you going to tell me what's going on?"

"Maybe," said Sammy. "Are you going to buy me a drink?"

"Bruno, put those on my tab!" I yelled. He just shot me a what-the-fuck-are-you-talking-about look.

"Did you know I'm a body surfer?" Sammy asked coyly, sipping her wine and counting her tips. When Bruno brought her another, she slipped the first, almost untouched glass to me. I ignored it.

"What does that have to do with any…?" I said.

"Everything! You want to hear the story or not?" she asked laughing. "'Cause if you do, you need to hear the whole thing or it won't make sense. Now, what's it going to be?" Well, if Billy was a mean drunk, I was afraid Sammy was a long-winded one. But I didn't have much choice.

"OK," I agreed. "Won't happen again." Bruno brought over

another glass and Sam shoved it in my direction.

"Sam, do you know what Evelyn would do if she caught you serving someone underage!" I said. I knew. She'd fire Sam and me on the spot!

"Lighten up," she said. "It's after hours and Evelyn is gone. She'll never know."

With those words of wisdom, Sammy poured her first wine into an empty water glass and shoved it my way. Hesitantly, I took a sip of the wine as Sammy returned to her story.

"So did you know I was..." she started again.

"You mean like a boogie-boarder?" I said.

"No, not a *goddamn* boogie-boarder. I hate those *goddamn* boogie-boards!"

"Touchy subject?" I said.

"Sorry, it's just that anybody can catch a *goddamn* wave on a *goddamn* boogie board and there're so *goddamn* many of them now that they just get in the way!" she complained and trailed off into silence.

"Sorry," I said finally when she didn't continue, "No, I had no idea you were a body-surfer."

"Right, so I like to ride the bigger waves on the outside, you know, the second set where the surfers are. Get to meet the surfers, too." I didn't know, but I did know that she was incorrigible when it came to guys.

"Anyway, they don't like body-surfers getting in their way," she said.

"Like you don't like boogie-boarders?" I pointed out; starting to enjoy the effect the wine was having on me as I listened to Sam's story.

"It's different!" she said, shooting me a dirty look.

"Anyway, they were giving me a pretty hard time until they realized what a smokin' body surfer I was!"

"And?" I said on cue.

"And," she responded mischievously, "I started wearing my thong out there!"

"Sammy, you really are shameless!"

"You've never seen me in a thong! Nothing to be ashamed of," she shot back and laughed.

Bruno refilled our glasses. By this time I'd thrown caution to the wind. The story was getting good and the wine was making it better.

"So, one day I'm out there with Ray," she said.

"The plot thickens."

"And two other surfers," she said, ignoring comments from the peanut gallery. "Now, nobody likes to advertise it, but every once in a while those fins you see in the water aren't attached to dolphins." She stopped and looked at me.

"Sharks?!" I asked, delighted to play the straight man.

"Right! Well, all of a sudden three of them came out of nowhere. Not Great Whites or anything, but not babies either." She paused for effect.

"Well the surfers just pulled in their legs and started paddling on their knees 'til they got a wave and rode it in. I, on the other hand, am all the way in the water without a board, and the sharks are blocking my way in. I don't know that I'm going to die, but I do know that I'm in real trouble at this point!"

I was going to suggest that a boogie board might have helped, but diplomatically decided against it.

"They all took off except Ray?" I asked, thinking I knew where this was going.

"No! Even Ray took off and, yeah, they all saw me all right! But then Ray turned around to take another look. You should've seen the look on his face; it was pure terror and I can tell you that it did nothing for my confidence at the time!"

"So then he turned around and came out to help you?" I prompted.

"No," she contradicted, disappointing me again. "After a minute he turned and started paddling in towards shore again fast!"

I decided against trying to anticipate the outcome a third time. I realized too late that Ray's heroics, if that's where we were going, would come when Sam was good and ready.

After what seemed like an eternity she said, "But then he turned to look one more time. The sharks were circling me and I can tell you that I was totally preoccupied with them by then! But when I looked up for a fraction of a second, I saw the look in Ray' eyes and he was scared shitless!"

"But as crazy as it might seem, at that precise moment, I knew exactly what he was thinking," she said taking another sip of wine. I did likewise, waiting expectantly. "He was thinking that if he left me out there and *anything* happened, what would be the point of living? What kind of scum bucket would do that? On the other hand, if he left me and *nothing* happened, what would be the point of living?" Sammy was pretty tipsy by this time. Still, what she said made a certain amount of twisted sense.

"He told you that?" I asked disbelieving and pretty loaded myself. I wasn't used to drinking wine and it was going right to my head.

"I just know," she said with certainty.

We began to consume a third…or was it a fourth…glass of wine.

"So then he came back to help?" I asked, convinced it was the right time at last.

"Finally," she responded. "The sharks were arching their backs in that attack behavior you read about, and one started to come right at me! Out of nowhere, Ray rushed in and put his board between the shark and me and deflected it, just in the nick of time. But it still brushed me. Its skin ripped right through my wetsuit."

At that point Sammy lifted her skirt, pulled up her panties and showed me a big-time abrasion scar on her butt. This, of course, was met with hoots, howls, and catcalls from the male clientele finishing up their final drinks after last call. It was made all the more lecherous to them in that she was showing it to another girl. "You go girls!" and "Get it on!" are some of the cleaner examples of the encouragements we were offered.

Sam repositioned her skirt, even though she was enjoying the attention. "Back to your drinks, boys. Nothing to see here," she crooned, loving every minute of it.

"Good thing you weren't wearing your thong," I offered after things quieted down. "So," I said, urging her to continue.

"So," she said, "Ray was thrown in the water by the force of the attack and I was bleeding and all hell was breaking loose. And you know what that man did? That wonderful, sweet man?"

I didn't, so I kept quiet.

"He helped me onto that great big beautiful surfboard of his and started swimming us in while all those little killers were charging and bumping the board. And after he got us going, he got on the back and started paddling till we caught a nice little wave and rode it to safety!" she finished.

We just sat there drinking our wine, absorbing the story she had just told.

"Are you bullshitting me?"

"No bullshit!" Sam insisted. "He was like shaken bad. So was I, but he was starting to hyperventilate. But he didn't say a word, just walked away and, to this day, he won't acknowledge that he saved my life."

"What?" I asked. "Why not?"

"Well, I think it's partly because he doesn't want to worry people about the sharks. If he admits he saved my life, he has to acknowledge that there are sharks out there. He's in denial. And he's right. No need to scare people; I don't think there's been a shark attack in New Jersey for like about forever."

"And?"

"And," she continued, "I'm pretty sure he's embarrassed about how scared he was and how he turned tail on me…twice." Sammy never sugarcoated anything. "But I think the main reason is that he's just plain modest. Doesn't like a fuss, you know, to call attention to himself like what happened tonight with Billy."

"He's my hero," she purred. "No shit! Really! My hero."

"So what did you whisper to Billy?" I said, realizing that we'd skipped that part.

"Nothing. Just trying to calm him down," she said playfully.

"Well, that obviously didn't work," I felt obligated to comment.

"Yeah," she agreed.

"So, what did you say to him," I cajoled, knowing she'd tell me eventually, but that I was going to have to drag it out of her.

She shrugged. After another minute of pretending there was

nothing to tell, she said, "Well, first, I got him warmed up with a little pillow talk. You saw that shit-eating grin?"

I nodded.

"Then all I said was, 'Unfortunately, Ray was more of a man than you'll ever be. If he ever wanted me, all he'd have to do is ask.' That's all," she finished as if it was what anyone would have said to calm down a mean drunk.

"Sammy, you didn't!" I said. I was aghast.

"Yeah!" she laughed. Now she was rolling. "I did. Then I said to him, 'At least he doesn't need someone to stick a finger up his ass to keep it up'," she said nonchalantly as if it were the most natural thing in the world to inform a friend with a temper.

At that point, I spit out my drink and shrieked with laughter.

"That's when he whaled on you?" I asked, finally.

"No, amazingly enough. He got real mad, but that's not what made him hit me. There's more," she said after I calmed down. "*Then* I said, 'At least maybe Ray could make me come!'"

I couldn't believe anyone would have the audacity to say that to anyone!

"That's when he hit me," she explained. Everyone was staring at me after my last whoop and aerosolization of my drink, so, this time, I made a truly heroic effort to get it under control and I somehow managed to choke back my intense reaction.

After a few minutes we calmed down and I asked, "Sam, what did you say to Billy, at the end that scared him like that?"

"I'll never tell you that," she said seriously. "You don't want to know—believe me."

At that moment I saw Sam's eyes focus on someone coming up behind me. "Yo, Ray," she said, as I turned to see Ray sit down next to her.

"Sammy. Are you OK, darling?" he asked.

"I'll be OK, baby," she said with a softness that was more daughterly than womanly.

He examined her face closely until he convinced himself that the injuries were superficial. Having reassured himself that she was alright, he lifted her face to look into his and said sternly, "Sammy,

I appreciate what you did, but I can fight my own battles!"

Sammy just shrugged.

He got up and took her hands and said, "Take care of that face. And Sammy, I owe you one." With that, he tried to walk away but she wouldn't release his hands.

She didn't say anything at first. Then she uttered one word. "Even?"

"I owe you one!" he said but she still wouldn't release him.

"Even!" she insisted.

He stood there, considering the bargain she was offering. Who could tell what he was thinking, but he was thinking about it hard.

"Even," he conceded finally, kissed her on the forehead and walked away.

"You're my hero," she whispered.

"I'd appreciate it if we never discussed this again!" he whispered back.

"Never," she agreed.

"Well, I'll be damned," she said after he left. "He finally admitted it."

"He did?" I was on my fourth or fifth glass of wine by this time.

"He did," she said. "And now we better get you home. You're snookered."

"I may be *snickered*, but you took that beating for him, didn't you!" The realization had finally struck my pickled brain. "So Billy wouldn't get him later!" I concluded.

"Very perceptive, Sherlock," she said.

"You're heroic yourself you know!" I slurred.

"No, not like Ray. I've been hit before and I knew I'd live."

I didn't say anything, just looked at Sam skeptically.

"Katy, you had to be there, out in the water. It was like they were playing that heartbeat music from *Jaws*. Boom-boom, boom-boom. Ray was scared out of his skull, even more scared than I was and I was the one that was gonna to die! And yet, he still came back for me. He put his life on the line for me. That's courage! That's a hero! He's my hero!" she said. As drunk as I was, she was drunker.

"You know why he was so scared?" she asked after another sip of wine. I shook my head.

"Do you know *why* he was so scared?" she repeated loudly.

"'Cause with guys they go for the nuts first?" I said, making her gag.

"No," she replied after she recovered, "Because he was attacked before and bit bad! Real bad!"

"He doesn't have any 'bad' bite on his body!" I countered. "I've seen him at the beach."

"Oh yes he does," she informed me, leaning in real close. "He showed me one night when he was real drunk." She leaned in as if to whisper then blurted out loud enough for the whole bar to hear, "It took a big chunk right out of his ass!"

That was too much. I whooped, knocked over our drinks and fell off my stool laughing!

Chapter 12

Jersey Girls

"Katy?" asked Sam during a lull.

Every once in awhile the timing works out that all the tables are full, orders have been taken and the ones that are ready have been delivered. The salt shakers are topped off, the tables are bussed, and there is nothing more to do that would not be considered "make work". When one of those moments occurs, I've learned to take advantage, catch my breath, and embrace a little respite. Evelyn knows she has a good crew this season, maybe even a great one, and doesn't push when we take one of these moments to cool our jets. She also knows, as we do, that the price of these precious, pacific intervals will be chaotic times later in the evening when everything needs to be done at once.

"Kathleen," I corrected. She was picking up bad habits from Grandpa.

"Whatever," she said. "Listen, I've got three tickets to see Springsteen at the PNC Arts Center. What do you think?" she asked.

"What do I think? That would be awesome," I drooled, "But why three?" I asked.

"Well, my cousin Vinnie works the lights for him. One of his coworkers got four comps, but the guy he gave them to only needed one."

"Your cousin Vinnie?" I teased. "Hey, did you know Joe Pesci lives over on West Point Island?"

"Yeah, yeah, he and DeNiro were in the other night. Makes a real stir when they show up," she said unimpressed.

"DeNiro?"

"Yeah, they come in once or twice a year. They like Evelyn's Penne Vodka, I think. At least Joe does," Sam said, casually.

"So back to the question. You interested in the concert?" she asked again.

"Yeah, but who else should we ask?"

"Daniel," she said without missing a beat.

"Whoa, timeout! Backup! I thought you didn't like Daniel?"

"Have you ever seen Jacob's Ladder?" she replied, answering my question with a question.

"You mean like a stairway to heaven?" I responded, perplexed.

"No, no, that TV antennae thing with the lightning going up it?" she said.

"Yeah, I guess," I said, remembering something like that on some old sci-fi movie.

"Yeah, well that's what it's like between Daniel and you. Two antennae with sparks flying that would kill anybody that got between you!" she said laughing, catching me completely off guard.

"Oh shut up! You're so full of shit, Sam! I'm not interested in him!" I said, putting an end to this asinine conversation.

"Methinks thou doth protest too much. Besides, I already asked him. He's coming. Lit up like the fourth of July when I told him you were coming too."

"So, since you told him I was coming when you hadn't even asked me yet, how do I know that you're not telling me that he's coming when you haven't even asked him yet?" I asked.

"You know, that actually made sense?" she said.

"It's true what they say about 'Oh what evil webs we weave'. I've told so many lies lately that I can't even remember if I asked him and what he said if I did. Which, by the way, is a lie. That's easy to figure out. The truth, however, is utterly indiscernible. So, are you coming?" she asked renewing her inquiry without answering my question. The scary thing was that that made sense too.

"What if I say no?" I asked contrarily.

"Now I remember. That's the reason I asked him first! That's right, I almost forgot. Look, if you say no then I get a shot at him. And I was just playing matchmaker so if you ended up not coming, I don't look too much like a slut! If I asked you first and you refused, then I wouldn't have an excuse to ask him."

I wouldn't be surprised if this was the truth. Appalled but not surprised.

"I'm in…if just to protect him from you," I said, giving in to her machinations. It wasn't as unappealing as I was making it out to be, and it irked me that Sam realized it.

"You are, by far, the more dangerous of the two of us," she commented cryptically. "Now, I better go ask him," she finished and walked off with one of her orders, leaving me with my mouth hanging open.

The night of the concert Sammy not only supplied the tickets but also insisted on driving.

I rode shotgun, and Daniel crawled into the back.

"So, Daniel, what have you got to say for yourself?" asked Sam after we got off Route 37 and onto the Parkway.

"Nothing much," he said, unfazed by Sam's confrontational approach. "I'm shy."

"Me too," I preempted before she went after me.

"Well, I'm not," she said, temporarily frustrated. "You know, Daniel, I've been trying to fix up our Kathleen all summer but no luck. People are starting to wonder if she's gay!"

"Hey!" I protested vigorously to this new line of attack.

"That's what you say about me," Daniel said coolly, amused and above it all. I liked that.

"That's right!" Sam agreed. "But that's because you have better skin and prettier eyes than most women. Not to mention those legs. God you'd look great in spiked heels," Sam said. "So?"

My Island Beach

"Sorry to disappoint. I'm definitely 'hetero'," he replied. "But a little 'discipline' is good for everyone, isn't it?" he said.

"That's perfect! Katy gives all the appearances of a 'passive', but I'm reasonably sure she'd just as well play the heavy dominatrix type," said Sam, as if I wasn't there.

"*Hey!*" I complained again. "I'm here in the car, OK!? Maybe you two want to ask *me* what I'm into."

"So what are you into?" asked Daniel suggestively, joining in on Sam's game.

"Now we're talking," said Sam. "I'm just itching to hear!" Sam said lewdly, fidgeting in her seat.

That broke the tension which was her intention.

"I'm into quiet eroticism. Discreet and private!" I teased coyly.

"Wow, super sophisticated!" said Sam. "You know, Daniel, this is one classy Beny Bitch!"

"A rare combination," agreed Daniel.

At the PNC Arts Center we were supposed to meet Vinnie, Sam's cousin, on the steps next to the entrance to pick up our tickets. We wandered around for a few minutes, and then located him without too much difficulty. He was easy to pick out in a crowd.

"How's my favorite cousin?" came the greeting from what can only be described as a large and imposing Italian gentleman. Not outright handsome but with a dynamic face. Intimidating, very intimidating, but oozing character...until he smiled. Then you knew he was the type that saves baby birds that fall out of their nests. I wonder if he realizes how fierce he looks when he's not smiling.

"Vincenzo!" Sam exclaimed following by something endearing in Italian, "Too bad we're related. You get handsomer every day, and you are *definitely* my type," vamped Sam, giving him a big hug. "Are you sure you're not adopted?"

"I'm not, but I know for a fact that you are, darling cousin," he said, playing along. "Shall we elope, have a big wedding, or just fool around?" he teased. I was blushing.

"Vinnie, you look too much like me to be unrelated. Let's just go for it, the kids will either be idiots or 'Superman', ala Nietchze," she said.

"*Hey*!" I blurted for the third time that night.

"Oops, sorry. I brought the 'moral majority' with me tonight! Vinnie, Katy and Daniel. Katy and Daniel, Vinnie. If things don't work out between them I'll e-mail you her phone number," she said winking. We shook hands and our heads at Sam's in-your-face approach to social interaction.

"Vinnie, Katy doesn't realize that when Italians are talking about sex, they're really thinking about food and when they're talking about food, they're really thinking about sex. Gotta tone it down," Sam admonished.

"Sorry," said Vinnie. "Listen little cous'," he said, pronouncing it 'cuz' like 'buzz' with undisguised affection, "Pretty good seats, assigned, not in the infield. You know, all this talk about sex has got me starving, gotta see if I can connect with a cheesesteak or something. Enjoy the concert, all. Gotta run."

Sammy gave him a hug and a kiss, "Thanks, Hon," she said. And off he went.

Daniel ran after him, whispered something, and then handed him an envelope.

We found our seats and they were outstanding! These things never start on time, and tonight wouldn't be any different. When the warm-up group finally got started, it was 10:00. The band was called "The Good Rats". Definitely a '70s band, ala The Grateful Dead, and most definitely New Jersey, but excellent. I'm sure that if I knew their stuff I would have enjoyed it even more. Sam and Daniel and most of the people around were into it.

Then it was Springsteen! He opened with *Born in the USA,* which set the tone for the beginning of the evening. Later, he mixed in some of his more recent stuff like *Brilliant Disguise* but kept coming back to classics like *Tenth Avenue Freeze Out* and *Glory Days.*

All in all, it was a beautiful night, cool and clear. Sammy was silent, totally engrossed in the music. This was a unique condition for her and I noted it for future reference.

My Island Beach

Daniel, on the other hand, was more animated than I had anticipated based on his serene demeanor on the drive here. He was immersed in the music but talkative between songs and sets.

Daniel's father was a huge Springsteen fan when Bruce frequented clubs like the "Stone Pony' and other NJ Shore venues. Springsteen, Southside Johnny and the Asbury Jukes, and John Mellencamp (back when he was John Cougar), had been his father's signature groups. As Daniel put it, "My dad wasn't afraid to say that the best Rock came from, and will always come from, New Jersey!"

The Boss ended his last set with a rousing rendition of *Thunder Road* and exited the stage, apparently for good. His crew, including Sam's cousin, Vinnie, were beginning to break down the equipment when the crowd just plain went berserk. They demanded an encore and would not be denied. This was probably the usual series of events but I wasn't sure, since I'd never been to one of his concerts.

Eventually, the lights went down, the crew withdrew, and the crowd started chanting, "Bruce, Bruce, Bruce". After an over-long period of time, the lights came on and there they were. They launched into *Rosalita* and the crowd went wild!

When the song ended, the band started to unplug and walk off, despite the crowd's protests. "Wait a minute, guys," said Bruce. You could tell that this wasn't standard operating procedure.

"Ladies and Gentlemen," he said addressing the crowd. "There's a song, I haven't performed in a long time." The crowd was silent except for an occasional whoop of enthusiasm from some zealous fan.

"But tonight I received a letter from a special friend of the band that I'd like to share with you," and he produced an envelope from his pocket that looked suspiciously like the one Daniel had given to Vinnie.

"*Dear Mr. Springsteen, very few people understand the ambience...* I've never heard New Jersey referred to as having ambience," he mugged. After the applause died down he returned to the letter, "*...understand the ambience of the Garden State and especially the ladies...*" he stopped, waiting for the applause to stop again, *"...of this great state!"* More applause.

"*Jersey Girls,*" he continued and the crowd erupted! They knew where this was leading. "*Jersey Girls*" he repeated, "*have been maligned, libeled, and misunderstood. They have been stereotyped as easy, with big hair, and a dearth of gray matter between their multiply pierced ears.*" The crowd laughed and started to applaud again.

"Wait, wait," he said, "It gets better."

"It goes on to say, *The Beach Boys are full of shit! California girls got nothing on Jersey girls...they aren't even close.*" The crowd lost it at this point.

"*I'm here tonight with someone who not only doesn't realize she's a Jersey Girl, and doesn't even know what that means. So please, I know you know about Jersey Girls. Please...*" he continued reading this letter, "*...close your concert tonight with 'Jersey Girls!'*"

Well, at this point the crowd went totally incandescent. No other way to describe it. Just plain scary! It must have taken 10 full minutes to settle them down, and the first bass notes that eased into the song set them off again. The band had to go through the intro three times before Bruce could get them settled down enough to start the first verse so that it could actually be heard.

It was amazing. A standing ovation followed. Everyone—and I mean everyone—was so moved by this last song, that we didn't know what to do. We clapped but less than you would expect. We were caught up in something that was more than Tom Waits, who wrote the song, or Bruce Sprinsteen, who just sang it.

Even Bruce seemed a little surprised at the calm.

"Good night Jersey Girls!" was all he could say.

Chapter 13

Opposites Attract

"Too bad you couldn't stay the night," he said casually.

We were lying on the beach in the early afternoon of the day after the concert. Last night Sam dropped us off near Evelyn's where we could both find our separate ways…if that's what we wanted. Daniel offered to escort me home; I suggested we just walk. It hadn't even been a real date or anything, but there was something about this guy? We talked, a little at first, about the concert and Sam's outrageous behavior but then stopped; content to walk in silence. We ended up on the beach. When I stumbled, reaching down to remove my shoes, he caught me by the hand. He never relinquished it after that.

His touch was warm and his presence intense, in spite of the silence. Then, as we stood watching the waves break on the shore, I kissed him. Maybe I should have waited for him to kiss me, but I was afraid he might not. And if there's only one thing that I learned this summer from Grandpa, Sam and Evelyn, it's that if you really want something you'd better grab for it before it slips away.

Well, it was like Sam said—electric! Sparks flew! I've never been kissed like that! I didn't know you could, and I doubt if I'll ever be kissed that way again. Wordlessly, we worked our way to Daniel's house, well, it was his parents' house, but thankfully he had a private entrance.

It wasn't frantic but it wasn't methodical either.

We started removing our own clothes but about halfway through switched to each other's. Naked on the bed, we slowly touched each other, kissing occasionally but exploring mostly. Me him and him me, then me him again. We teased and caressed, looking directly into each other's eyes or at the parts we were touching and shared not a single word nor thought; it wasn't necessary. It was exciting but not new. We were inexplicably practiced and expert at providing pleasure to each other and to ourselves, at the same time. It was as if we'd discovered our long lost love from a previous incarnation. It was extraordinary!

Then he was ready and so was I. And the world stopped! We consumed each other, alternating between voraciousness and acquiescence! Over and over again with a fierceness that was both surrender and greed. We were luminescent, lighting up the night! When it seemed like it would never end, we peered over the edge of the pinnacle and, without hesitation, plunged headlong to complete that simple, that extraordinary biological act!

I stayed until the wee hours. I'd never done anything like this before. Truth be told, although I wasn't a virgin, I was very inexperienced in matters of love, especially physical love. But I didn't feel guilty, I felt exhilarated. Like, no matter how things turned out between Daniel and me, last night was a right thing in my life. A thing I would always cherish.

I channeled my drifting thoughts back to the here and now…sitting at the beach the morning after.

"Me too," I agreed, responding to his stated desire that I had stayed overnight. "But I don't think Grandpa's ready for that yet." A little white lie. More like the understatement of the year.

I was sitting there in my latest swimsuit. It, of course, hid nothing! When I walk around I put a towel around my waist; otherwise guys stare at my ass which is hanging out because of the way they make women's swimsuits.

My Island Beach

"What are you thinking?" he asked.

After being together in the dark last night, I was wondering if my body was standing up to the light of day in a skimpy swimsuit. He certainly liked my body last night, but did he like my *body* last night? *He* looked great in a swimsuit.

"I was thinking about that letter you gave to Vinnie for Bruce," I said. "I didn't have any idea you were a friend of the band."

"You think that letter was from me? What do you mean, a friend of the band?" he asked earnestly.

"Don't you know?" I asked, knowing as I asked that he didn't. "You didn't write that letter did you?"

"No," he answered, laughing. "That letter he read? You thought I wrote it?" he asked. "Is that why we ended up...?" he stopped before saying something he'd regret.

"Sam wrote it and gave it to you to give to Vinnie," I said.

"And made sure you saw me give it to him so you'd think I wrote it."

After a few moments he said, "You don't think I knew...?"

"Don't worry, neither of us had a chance against the intrigues of Great and Powerful Sam!" I said, furious at Sam's manipulations. What irked me the most was that it threatened to mar the memory of last night, an otherwise perfect night.

"Which brings me back to my question. Last night wasn't just because you thought I wrote that...?" He'd decided to say something he was going to regret after all.

"Do you...do *we* really want to go there?" I asked diplomatically, giving him one more chance to *not* question my motives in a morally ambiguous situation that had turned out feeling so right.

He decided not to take the easy way out. This did not bode well for any future we might have. "Look," he said, "maybe we wouldn't have ended up in bed last night if it hadn't been for Sam's ploy with the letter, but we would've ended up in there in short order, anyway. And don't waste your time being upset with Sam. Maybe she saw something we didn't. Because no matter how it came about, what happened last night was a right thing in our lives."

The exact thing that I'd been thinking earlier! "A right thing in our lives." I decided not to contest the nicest questioning of my motives I've ever heard. "Would you like to know what I was really thinking?" I asked.

He nodded.

"I was wondering if you liked being a fisherman?" I said.

"You were not! You're such a liar!" he accused.

"Then why would I say I was?" I said laughing.

"'Cause you don't want to tell me what you're really thinking. Maybe something dirty, hopefully?" He wasn't far off and I flushed!

"So?" I said, implying a return to the fisherman question.

"Sticking with your story, eh?" No response from me. "Judging from that blush, it must have been a good one."

Still no response.

"I'm not that crazy about being a fisherman, but then again I'm not one. I help out in the summer, but I'm not gonna follow in the family business," he explained.

"I don't like fishing. Too smelly. But I like being out on the ocean. You have time to think and you see cool stuff sometimes."

"Like what?" I asked.

"Like schools of dolphins riding a bow wave or flying fish sailing along. I mean, that's one hell of a cool way to escape from a predator. Leave the media and reenter somewhere else. Very Sci-Fi if you think about it."

"Or when a school of blues comes in and decimates a school of bait fish. Like piranhas. Imagine living like that. Talk about paranoia...*everyone* is out to get you! And when you go to heaven and God says, 'So what were you on Earth?' you'd answer, 'They called me bait. Apparently I fulfilled my destiny.'"

"Every once in a while you see whales migrating. Beautiful! Have you ever seen a whale up close?" he asked.

"Up in Cape Cod. Humpbacks," I said.

"So you know," he said, "you know, and I don't mean this in a bad way, but maybe they're really destined for extinction. They're so specialized in their diet, so low in birth rate, and so passive in their own defenses. Most species of whale are just traveling bags of fat waiting to be eaten." What a strange thing to say.

"So, Katy, am I really your type?" he said shifting gears suddenly before I could react. Screw the whales, what the heck was this about?

I scrutinized him trying to comprehend his meaning. "You mean, are you physically the type I'm attracted to?"

"Personality-wise, too," he said.

I took a good look up and down, laughed and said, "I'm changing types."

"Which means I'm not your type," he persisted, not allowing me to blow off his question with a joke.

When I didn't reply he said, "Was Jason more your type? Big shoulders, blond and blue eyes and what else?"

"Big hands," I offered, wondering where he was going with this.

"You know, big hands are inversely proportional to…" he started.

"And I thought they were directly proportional. All the more reason to change types," I tried again to make a joke of this. Daniel's hands weren't especially large.

"But that's right isn't it?" he asked. "I'm not your type, am I?"

I didn't like where the conversation was going, considering that this was a guy that I really liked and maybe even loved and had slept with last night. "So are you jealous or trying to pick a fight so you can dump me?" I asked testily.

"Neither," he said quickly. "Honest," he assured, looking into my eyes and finally realizing that I was taking this conversation very seriously!

"But you're usually attracted to simple, sorry, make that, uncomplicated guys? Right?" he continued. Why wouldn't he let this drop?

"I guess," I conceded, still wondering what his point was.

"And I'm neither of those." That was his point. "I mean I'm not tall, I'm fair and my butt is even smaller than yours," he said grinning.

"I'm gonna take that as an extremely back-handed compliment…I think!" I laughed.

"I know I'm not uncomplicated," he continued. "People have made that much clear to me."

"So what the *fuck* is your point?" I bristled, pissed off by his over analysis of our budding relationship.

"So what attracted you to me? You're as drawn to me as I am to you. We both felt it the first day. It was devastating! It was earth shattering!" he concluded for both of us, and he was right!

"And," he said, "You're not my type either."

"Then what was that last night?" I asked still annoyed—flattered—but still annoyed.

"The best thing that's happened to me in my short life," he said. After aggravating me yet again, he redeemed himself once more.

"Change your type!"

I jumped up and ran into the water to prevent him from screwing things up by saying something else stupid. Daniel, on the other hand, had to settle down for a few minutes (if you know what I mean) before he could join me. Talk about body language.

"Did you ever wonder why men and women can't talk like women and women?" he asked after we came out of the water.

He's right. He is complicated.

"If you heard what we talked about, you might not think that," I said.

"No, seriously. At least you can be honest with each other. When it's a guy and a girl you always have to keep up your guard, be cool and mysterious."

"Women? Honest with each other? Now I know you haven't got a clue. We are spiteful, shallow, and extremely competitive!" I said.

"Whoa!" he said, "Really?"

"No, not really," I denied peevishly. "It's just that everyone thinks it's greener on the other side. It's not. It's just the other side."

"Katy, I'm not talking about group dynamics. Hell, I'm convinced that only a group of women is worse than a group of men when an attractive female is around!" This was not going to be the easy kind of relationship I was used to.

"I'm talking about girlfriends like you and Sam. No barriers, no competition...at least one-on-one. Guys aren't like that," he continued. "And girls and guys are never like that."

"That's not true," I protested. I knew before this started that he was gonna get under my skin and he was. "I've had guy friends who I was just as open with as Sam. Closer even."

"*Platonic* guy friends," he said with an irritating certainty.

"True, but Sam's a platonic friend, too."

"So it's the sex thing, the romantic relationship, the intimacy?" he asked.

"Guys are afraid to let their guards down, to drop the cool attitude. Afraid they'll look like duffuses!" I laughed.

"You know, you're right," he agreed. "Just like women!"

"Nooo," I whined.

"Sure it is," he said. "Think of the makeup, push-up bras and bleached hair. The perfume, the teasing, the dance. And guys love it. It means you've made a fuss to look good for us. Very flattering. That's why couples make love in the dark. They don't want to spoil the mystery on that special night with potbellies and mismatched hair colors...north and south!" he said, smirking.

I slapped him hard—as hard as I could! But he didn't get angry. He just sat there, inscrutably, thinking about God-knows-what. I can't believe I smacked him but, for God's sake, can't we just be together without dissecting our relationships?

This was followed by a protracted period of silence.

Finally, I said, "You don't smile much. Actually you seem kind of stern most of the time." He didn't reply. "Except when someone slaps you," I made another peace offering when he didn't reply.

"It was dark so maybe you didn't see, but I was smiling last night." His face lit up. I tried to slap him again, but he ducked.

"What are you doing Monday night?" he asked sweetly, gazing into my eyes.

"We could do something," I said, agitated, but also relieved that he wanted to see me again. I definitely wanted to see him!

"I'll show you then how serious I can be," he said enigmatically. And with definite coooool!

Chapter 14

Close Encounters

We rendezvoused after dinner in the restaurant parking lot. I still didn't want Grandpa to know about Daniel, at least not yet.

He arrived in an old Jeep Cherokee outfitted with a pair of kayaks on the roof. Seems like everyone on this island was preoccupied with kayaking.

I got in the car and we drove into the park, back to 21 where Grandpa and I had entered the sedge previously. We unloaded and rigged the kayaks.

These were very different than the sit-on-top types that Grandpa and I had used. They were sit-inside touring kayaks. Longer and lower in the water, they were faster and required less effort to operate; less maneuverable, but much easier to keep straight.

We penetrated one of the channels in the sedge—third channel from the left and "on till morning" I thought, like Never-Never Land. It was dusk and there was no moon. Very eerie. If I lost Daniel, I'd be stuck out here until sunrise.

Eventually we escaped the claustrophobia of the channel into what, in the waning light, appeared to be open water. It went pitch black as we crossed and I was disoriented when we ran aground.

Like at the bottom of a staircase when you're expecting one more step but there isn't one.

We hauled our kayaks onto the beach and Daniel retrieved something from inside of his. We walked. I guess it was a good sign—or a horrid mistake—that I trusted him enough to let him lead me on this obscure adventure. I felt out of control, as I usually do in these situations, but somehow able to endure it with him there.

Birds, almost exclusively gulls, were everywhere, and they moved out of our way as we walked. We were literally surrounded. It felt like a scene right out of *The Birds*. I could see a little now from the lights on boats moving through what appeared to be a channel on the opposite side of this spit of sand.

Finally, we arrived at a place that suited Daniel. He kicked away the guano, which was ubiquitous, and threw down the blanket on the cleaned spot. We seated ourselves, silently searching the horizon.

"This is Barnegat Inlet," he explained, "which separates Island Beach from Long Beach Island to the South. This strip of beach that we're standing on used to be the opening from the inlet to the Snake Ditch and the Winter Anchorage. The Army Corps of Engineers, in their infinite wisdom, decided to close off this ingress using a 'geotube', which is really just a sand-filled net bag that lets water through, but not sand."

"Why?" I asked.

"Not really sure", he said. "But if you look closely you can see that it's not working that well."

In the dim light I could make out what looked like the silhouette of a submarine. It was a small breach in the barrier! The "submarine" was the exposed geotube.

"They keep sealing it off and the ocean keeps opening it up," he said, "sort of like Cranberry Inlet."

"Fascinating," I said sarcastically. In spite of my strong attraction to Daniel, my opinion of his humorless approach to life hadn't changed so far. "Daniel, is this your idea of a good time? Taking your date on a kayak tour in the dark, complete with an ecolecture?"

"Have you read about the meteor showers in the Asbury Park Press?" Looks like he was about to start on the second topic of the evening. Hope there won't be a quiz!

"Yeah, I did read something about it. Always in the same place." I thought for a minute. "In the Barnegat Inlet?" I said hopefully.

"And always when there's no moon," he further enlightened me. He started doing something I couldn't make out in the murky light.

"What are you up to?" I whispered, intrigued. Why I whispered, I'm not sure.

He hushed me, confirming my instinct to stealth. A sailboat started moving up the channel. As it approached, I could see by their running lights that Daniel had set up what looked like a series of mini water towers all in a row on the sand. And that he was gripping a stick of some kind.

Then *whoosh, whoosh, whoosh, whoosh, whoosh, whoosh, whoosh* and *whoosh* as he swung the stick and launched what I realized were golf balls towards the sailboat! He managed to send off all eight before the first one landed.

"Get down!" he whispered urgently, and I hit the dirt...or the sand...or the sand covered with *guano*! He had somehow managed to land on the blanket!

Splash, sploosh, splash, sploosh, splash, sploosh, splash, and *splash*! All eight balls landed in an approximately circular pattern around the boat. You could see that the inhabitants, who were in the midst of the cocktail hour, were startled, then excited and looking up for more "meteorites"!

After they disappeared over the horizon, I stood and faced Daniel. I was livid but he was laughing his ass off. He shined a flashlight on me and I looked down and started laughing too. What a mess! "I take it back what I said about you being serious. You're a *freakazoid*. You're the meteorites?" I asked.

"The one and only," he said proudly, "Guano Girl," he said christening me, snickering and pushing his luck *real* hard.

That earned him a handful of gull shit on his head. He retaliated but I couldn't get much shittier. He caught up with me, shit-wise, before we finally sat down in the shit, exhilarated.

"How the hell did you ever think up that one?" I said standing and starting to brush off the guano-saturated sand.

"I saw it on Seinfeld. Kramer was driving balls into the ocean, so I came out here to give it a try. I didn't realize there was a boat out there. It was running without lights, which you're not supposed to do, and there was no moon."

"Anyway, the next day, the paper had a story about a meteor shower in Barnegat Inlet in the right place and at the right time to be my creation. It was too good not to try again. This will be the third 'meteor shower' this summer," he finished vainly, like a proud father.

"Who else knows about this?" I asked.

"Just you," he replied. "Letting my cool down. Not too serious for you?"

I laughed. Any idea that I had this guy figured out went out the window then and there. He was either going to be a royal pain or an interesting person to get to know.

Meantime, we were covered with gullshit. Daniel took me to a private little area at one end of the spit and...well...my clothes were disgusting, too, so I went skinny-dipping and he joined me. One thing led to another...

It was totally different than the previous night. Then we had been intense and erotic—focused and instinctive. Tonight we were frisky, gregarious. We frolicked, we talked. Told each other what we liked, what felt good. We experimented with each other, and not all the experiments worked. And every once in a while, one of us squealed with delight—or in some cases in intense pain from the bite of the formidable green flies that stalked human flesh in the sedge. It's sometimes difficult to distinguish between pain and sex. It was delicious but totally different than the first time. It was like we were two strangers engaged in our first intimate encounter.

Afterwards we lay on the blanket not saying anything for a while, satiated but invigorated. Eventually, we talked about this and that, nothing really important. Until I mentioned that it was ecologically irresponsible to dump a couple of dozen golf balls into the bay.

"That's true," he responded, lazily getting dressed. "Might end up in a whale's spout," he said dismissively, referring to the Seinfeld episode when the feckless George saved a beached whale by removing Kramer's golf ball from its spout.

"Seriously, though," I persisted, "plastic golf balls won't decompose for about a million years. You've got to admit…!"

"I thought you were tired of the *serious* me?" he said sharply, agitated by a taste of his own medicine. "The Corps will be by in 10 years, more or less, to dredge them up."

"Is everything black and white to you?" he asked in a very insulting way, when he realized that I was getting upset.

My immediate inclination was to deny it, but instead, considered his statement and said, "More or less!"

That seemed to please him. "At least you admit it," he said. "Remember how you thought I was—how might you put it—humorless? Now you find out that I'm a little more warped than the average bear."

"Yeah, yeah, I get the point," I said, chagrined.

"What are you up to Wednesday night?" he asked.

"I'm off, why? If you're off, maybe we could get off together?" I mugged waving a non-existent cigar, doing my best, but barely recognizable, Groucho.

"Something like that," he replied. I could almost hear the wheels turning in his head. "I'll call you."

Chapter 15

Perspective

"What are you up to?" I asked suspiciously, as we approached a functional-looking boat near the end of the pier.

"You'll see soon enough," he said.

I had dressed down, *way* down as he had suggested, for our night out. After the guano incident, I tended to take Daniel's recommendations concerning appropriate attire at face value. As I feared, our destination was the aforementioned boat. When I say functional-looking, I mean no frills and it smelled funny. Daniel helped me on board.

"Yo, Danny, glad you made it! Thank God! We're really short-handed tonight. Two last minute cancellations," said a voice from inside the darkened cabin.

"I brought help," Daniel said. Oh, God, now what had I signed up for?

"Katy, right?" said the disembodied voice. As he emerged from the shadows I suppressed a small gasp. It was Billy!

"Right," I acknowledged with a sigh. I had given up on Kathleen; apparently, on the island I was destined to be Katy. Besides, Billy could call me anything he wanted and I wouldn't contradict him. Boy, did I feel uncomfortable. This was the guy who had almost taken Sam's head off in the bar that night.

"Great," he replied. "Don't worry, we'll put you to work," he assured me and lumbered off.

"OK, Daniel, that's it! You tell me what's going on or I abandon ship right now!" I demanded, feeling manipulated and completely out of control at the prospect of heading to sea with this woman beater.

"OK, sit down. Look, we have about five minutes before we cast off. Here's the deal," he said. "Do you know where Tice's Shoal is?"

I shook my head.

"Well, you know where Fisherman's Walk is in the park?" he asked.

"Yeah, about halfway in," I replied.

"Well, part of the reason for Fisherman's Walk was to give the boaters access to the beach from the bay, from Tice's Shoal. But another reason was to give them access to the bathrooms."

"You see," he continued, "Tice's Shoal is a favorite place for boaters to drop anchor overnight or even for a few nights. And when they stay awhile their holding tanks get filled. You know, for the toilets?"

"So you made it so they could use the toilets in the park if their tanks got full."

"Not me, but yeah. Only it didn't help that much. Nobody wants to launch a dinghy or wade in, in the middle of the night, so when their holding tanks get full they just empty them in the bay."

"Pretty soon there were algae blooms and high counts of coliform bacteria...*E. coli*. It was getting really disgusting," he said.

"So?" I asked.

"So now a pump-out boat goes around and empties the holding tanks so they don't have to dump them," he finished. He waited expectantly for my reaction.

When I didn't respond, he added, "Manned by volunteers," he said. I still didn't get it.

He didn't say anything else, just opened his arms expansively. "Oh no! I'm spending my free evening at sea with Billy the Babe-

Beater pumping out other people's shit!" I groaned.

"It would be the ecologically responsible thing to do," he said. My very words from the golf ball escapade. That stopped me cold. Shit, shit, shit! A setup and he had me. That settled it. The balance was rapidly shifting from "interesting person" to "royal pain" with this guy.

I took a deep breath. Big mistake! After I finished gagging from the fetid (and now recognizable) aroma I said, "Do you do this often or is this a one-time deal to make you feel better by teaching me a lesson?"

"Or are you the one that thought this thing up?" I asked.

"Not my idea. Billy's the one behind this," he said.

"Billy?"

"Yeah, Billy. He heard about the problem and about another pump-out boat program in Massachusetts. He convinced a coalition of groups interested in the bay's environment into purchasing and operating the boat. Labor's all supplied by volunteers. Billy ropes 'em in," he explained as Billy walked up.

"Not nearly enough," he added, having overheard the last part of the conversation. "The operation's plagued by people who want to *talk* instead of *do*. You know, people who want to feel good about themselves but see it more as a social contribution due to their presence, than due to actual work. Like you two, for instance! Danny, Charlie needs a hand in the engine room, and Katy, Alex needs help in the bow," he said and rushed off to tend to what appeared to be a minor emergency. There was no doubt about whose operation this was.

Alex turned out to be Alexis, and she really didn't need much help. She was casting off lines so we could launch. I assisted her and as we moved away from the dock I realized that I must have decided to go.

There wasn't much to do once we were underway. Daniel found me and explained more about the operation as we motored to Tice's Shoal. "Billy's been running this for almost three years by himself for at least three days a week."

I continued to be amazed. "You know this doesn't make up for him hitting Sam!" I said, furious with Billy for breaking character with his evil persona.

"Never said it did. Frankly, if I'd have been there that night, I might have helped beat the crap out of him. And if I were Sammy, I would have brought charges against him for assault. I still think she should," he said, confronting me with the anachronism that was Billy. At least Daniel wasn't sticking up for him.

"But nothing's ever simple," he continued. "I've known Billy for a long time and we've never gotten along. Ever! I had no use for him and he had no use for me. And I learned, early on, to stay away from him when he'd been drinking."

"Then he started this pump-out boat and I never thought he'd stick with it, but he has, these three years. He asked me to volunteer and I did, like a lot of other people. But I've stuck with it too, once a week for three summers, unlike most of the other volunteers. And so Billy and I have reached a sort of mutual respect," he finished.

"That still doesn't excuse what he did to Sam!" I wasn't about to start admiring this guy.

"Nothing excuses that," Daniel said and paused to consider how to word what he wanted to say next. "But you know he was looking for a fight with Ray not Sam?"

"That still doesn't…!" I began to protest.

"Katy!" he interrupted, "I said nothing, *nothing* excuses what he did to Sam! And I meant it. But it's not that simple," he said. I settled down a little.

"He was looking for a fight, because he was jealous of Ray's relationship with Sam, no matter how platonic. Sam took that beating to save Ray by antagonizing a guy she knew was a mean drunk!" He paused. I couldn't disagree.

"She had to have said some pretty nasty shit to get him to hit her, didn't she?" he asked. I didn't answer.

"And I bet he didn't react to her first attempt to bait him?" Another question. Another non-answer from me.

"In fact, I'll bet she went way beyond the pale to get him to hit her the way he did!" This time I acknowledged his conjecture.

"By that time the rage had really boiled up in him because, believe it or not, he cares about her so much that he held off for longer than he would have with anyone else. So when she finally brought him over the edge, there was absolutely no restraint left."

"If he hadn't responded, she would have kept it up until he did. He had two choices, to walk away or smack her. He made the wrong choice," Daniel said. "Sammy did what she had to and he fucked up big time."

"So, I'm supposed to like the guy?" I asked.

"No. I don't," Daniel responded. "And I'd never trust him when he's drunk. But I know for a fact that that's the first time he's ever hit a woman. He's actually kind of chauvinistic that way. I've seen him stand up for girls that he didn't even know if someone's giving them a hard time. Not popular girls. Girls who needed a friend but didn't have any. He's very religious. Knight-in-shining-armor type. Otherwise, he goes to Hell!"

"Then that's where he's going," I said, not giving an inch.

I sat there stewing for a minute and finally said, "You know, Daniel, I had a girlfriend who had a pit bull. Sweetest thing and great with kids. But then, one day, we were at her brother's soccer game and she brought the dog on a leash like you're supposed to. Suddenly, it spotted a black lab across the field and broke loose from my friend. It was far enough away that the dog, the six-foot-four guy holding the dog, and everyone else had plenty of warning that the pit bull was going try to kill that lab. And there was nothing they could do to stop it. Not the lab, not the big guy, not no one!"

"That little pit bull took down the lab by the throat and the guy in the process. When he got up, he pulled the lab away from the pit bull by the leash and managed to swing both animals off the ground—the lab by the leash and the pit bull attached to the lab's throat! Miraculously, the dog wasn't hurt but it took four guys to detach that dog from the lab's neck."

"Is that it?" Daniel asked.

"No," I replied and continued. "That dog had never harmed a fly until that day. And he calmed right down afterward. Our family went on vacation the next day and, when I came back in two weeks, my friend had a brand new labradoodle puppy," I said.

"Labradoodle?" Daniel asked.

"Labrador and poodle mix," I explained.

"The pit bull was gone. He'd attacked another dog and, even though it had never attacked a person, they had it put down," I finished.

"So Billy's a pit bull who will attack again?" Daniel asked.

"Don't know but you can never really trust him again, can you?" I said.

Daniel didn't disagree but didn't agree either.

"What makes you think it was so hard for her to antagonize him?" I asked.

"'Cause he loves her," Daniel said disdainfully. "And she loves him. Can't you at least see that?"

When we arrived at our destination, the fun began. I swear people bring their boats to Tice's Shoal when their holding tanks are full because the service is free. We spent the next four hours pumping human excrement. It was neither satisfying nor fun. But it provided an opportunity for me to think about things while I was performing a mindless and disgusting task.

On our way back, I was sitting on the stern by myself when Billy approached.

"Thanks for the help, Katy. I guess Danny roped you in, huh?" he asked. I nodded. "You know, I'll understand if you don't want to talk to me, but can I say just one thing?" I nodded again.

"I owe you an apology and I know you can't forgive me. *I* don't forgive me but that doesn't change the necessity for the apology."

"You owe someone else an apology, a hell of a lot more than you owe me!" God, was I out of my mind talking like this to a guy who could throw me overboard with a flick of his hand?

"Well, if you'll let me say one more thing, then let me tell you that I'm a very devout Catholic. And one of the tenets of Christianity, in general, is forgiveness for your sins."

"So you expect me to forgive…?" I began.

"Oh, God no!" he exclaimed, as if he had never considered the possibility. "I don't want forgiveness for what I did. I don't want it, I don't deserve it—ever!" he said zealously.

"You're not forgiven," I said, still angry and, apparently, still crazy.

"I know," he said.

"Something else?" I asked when he didn't leave.

"Could you talk to Sam for me?"

"What?!"

He didn't say a word and we just sat there for several, uncomfortable minutes. I could see Daniel watching from a distance, but he wasn't about to come and rescue me from the ambiguity of it all.

Finally, I relented. "What do you want me to tell her?" I asked.

"Just what I told you. That I apologize but I don't expect to be forgiven." He hesitated. "Tell her that I joined AA to deal with my drinking problem and that I've started sessions with a priest to get help…" he hesitated again, "…and come to grips with what I've done."

"Anything else?" I asked, impressed with his words, in spite of myself.

"One other thing," he replied. "I know Sam has a lot of other admirers and I'll understand if she doesn't want to see me again. Even if she somehow does, I can't. Not for the rest of the summer. Not until I get things under control. Not ever if I don't." He seemed like a balloon after the air was let out. "And," he began, and then relented. "Well, she knows," he said finally.

"I'll tell her," I said.

As he started to walk away I observed, "You're the only one that ever calls Daniel Danny."

"I know," he responded. "It's one of those annoying little things that guys do to remind each other to keep their guards up no matter how much they might think they like each other. Don't worry. He understands."

Chapter 16

Indiscretions of Youth

"Hi Grandpa," I said as I walked in the door, back early from the restaurant. It was 11:15. I was making it a point to get home early and sober after the hangover and bruises (from falling off the stool) the night of Sam's beating in the restaurant.

Grandpa was hunched over with one hand rubbing the back of his head. His shoulders were slouched forward and I got the impression was that he was tired. Old and tired. Then he stirred as if he'd just realized I was here, but he must have heard me drive up and come in the door! "Hey," he grunted.

That's when I noticed the bottle and shot glass in front of him. "Grandpa, you've been drinking!" I said. "What's going on?"

"Yes sir, I have...I mean yes ma'am," he slurred.

He looked up at me, stupefied and disoriented, "Katy!" he said and stared as if he'd seen a ghost. But for the second time during my visit, reality asserted itself and he said stoically, "Oh, Kathleen, it's you. Sorry." In his inebriated state he had mistaken me for Grandma again.

"Grandpa, I've never seen you drink hard liquor!" I said, trying to make light of it. "What's going on?"

"Someone asked me that before," he said. Boy was he in the

bag.

He poured another shot, spilling a little. He offered it to me but I shook my head.

"Down the hatch," he said as he threw it back.

"That was me that asked you before," I said. He shot me a look.

"She did look a lot like you," he agreed and returned to his reverie.

"Grandpa, what's going on?" I asked for the third time.

He looked at me and started to protest yet again, became aware of the déjà vu of it all and said, as if continuing his previous thought, "But you're so different from her. She was liberated, impulsive, instinctive, but you—you're deliberate, directed, and relentless in a passive sort of way. Different. You and her are really different!"

I didn't know what to say so I didn't say anything.

"I only do this once a year. Three shots of good 12-year-old Scotch whisky. Then a couple more but I never remember how many," he said, with visible effort.

"Why, Grandpa?" I asked, really getting concerned at this point.

"What is this, the Spanish Inquisition?" he yelled, trying to stand but falling back into his seat.

I didn't ask again or respond to him in any way. Despite his drunken state, he could tell I was losing patience.

"It's my anniversary…your grandmother's and mine. August 17th," he said.

So that was it.

"And your grandmother's birthday," he added, grinning.

"Which is it, Grandpa?" I asked, figuring it was their anniversary.

"Oh," he said pointing at me and making silly faces, "You think I'm confused. Old and confused."

"No," I replied, "I think you're *drunk* and confused."

"Well, I'm not," he said, "Well actually I *am* drunk and I was confused when you first came in," he said, confirming that he had mistaken me for my grandmother.

"But I'm not now!" he said, assertive again.

"So which was it, her birthday or your anniversary?" Having established that he was both drunk and confused, I returned to my original question.

He gave me a who-told-you look, but when he realized that he was the culprit, he said, "That's right! Her birthday and our anniversary!"

"But, Grandpa, why in the world would you get married on her birthday?" Nothing was more tedious than arguing with a drunk.

"Her 17th birthday!" he said watchful of my response.

I looked at him and considered it. "So you had to wait until she was of age. I get it, but you couldn't have just waited a couple of months?"

"Do the math, darling," he said as he took another shot.

I really didn't know what he was talking about. Then it hit me. Father's birthday was on March 15th—easy to remember—the Ides of March. I started counting backwards. August 17th was 7 months!

"Oh god, Grandpa, Grandma was 2 months pregnant when you got married. Grandpa, she was underage. You had to get married!" I was shocked.

"That's not quite right," he said deliberately. "We'd planned to get married all along. We just got married *sooner* than we thought."

"You knew she was pregnant but you couldn't get married till she was 17!" It dawned on me.

"Damn straight! Nothing gets by you," he said sarcastically, but with a smile.

"That's statutory rape, Grandpa! You could have gone to jail."

He glared at me and said, "Not in those days. Not if you married the girl. What good does it do anyone for Daddy to be doing time? Things were simpler then. Made more sense."

He smiled then laughed. "Besides, if anyone got raped, it was me! Your grandmother was a lusty one, even at 16."

With that he rambled off, inexplicably straight and steady, like he was dead sober…then slammed smack into his bedroom door! Dazed, but seemingly undamaged, he opened the door, turned to smile at me, and hit the sheets, fully clothed and hangover-bound!

Chapter 17

Del

Grandpa was hung over after celebrating his anniversary. Therefore, he was being all seven dwarfs, as my father used to say when trying to extricate me from one of my rare funks: Grumpy, Dopey, Sneezy, Stubborn, Obtuse, Arbitrary, and Intractable. Growing up, when I finally saw *Snow White and the Seven Dwarfs*, I couldn't figure out how Disney got some of the names wrong. Ironically, for the first time in my adult life, I realized where my father got his mean streak.

"Grandpa, I like the guy!" I said emphatically.

"I won't have it!" he insisted.

"But, Grandpa. You don't even know him," I said appealing to logic.

"I know the family. That's enough!"

"Since when do you judge people by their family? That's not like you Grandpa." He presented neither defense nor explanation.

We had been going back and forth for some time when I decided to appeal to his romantic side.

"I like this boy, Grandpa," I said. "I don't know if he's the one for me, but he could be. I have to find out." I knew if he understood how I felt he'd come around. How could he resist?

"*No*! No, no, and *no!*" he sputtered. His face had an irrational but determined look about it and his color was rising by the minute. It intimidated me...but not for long.

Because then I got mad.

"Who the hell do you think you are?" I screamed. It was not a question. "Would you have let anyone stand between you and Grandma? She was underage, for God sakes, but that didn't stop you because you were in love!"

I don't think he'd ever seen me like that and it unnerved him momentarily.

"Who in the hell do you think you are!" I repeated, asserting my momentary advantage and serving notice that I would not be bullied on this topic. I was getting more furious by the minute. "I don't know what you're feud is with that family, but it's not mine. And if you can't abide my seeing Daniel, then I'll be moving in with Sammy. She's been asking me to share her place since her roommate moved out a week ago!"

"Don't threaten me," he said.

I took a long cleansing breath. Then another.

"I'm not threatening you," I said minus the hostile tone. I really had been thinking about moving in with Sam. My calm tone of voice seized his attention more than the shouting had. He knew I wasn't bluffing.

"When you get angry, you're so much like you're grandma," he said. "So passionate!" I seemed to be getting through to him, at last!

"No, you can't move out. It's out of the question," he concluded unilaterally, as if I had asked and was waiting for his decision.

"You can't tell me who to see!" I said, refusing to be passive about this.

"Oh God, it's happening again! Katy...Katy, why couldn't I have gone with you?" he asked, but the "Katy" he was talking to wasn't me.

"Grandpa, you'll want to explain what the hell you're talking about or I'm outta here right now!" I said.

"Sit down!" he commanded. We were both ready to detonate.

"And show a little respect for the dead and your elders!" He was furious and it was all I could do not to lash back.

I sat and neither of us said a word for several minutes. I was trying to imagine what could possibly cause this primal hatred of someone he'd never met.

When he finally calmed down, I had too…well, some.

"Do you remember, in the dunes that first day, when I started telling you about your grandmother?" he asked.

"Yes!" I said. I was still smoldering. "You didn't get too far as I recall!"

"Watch your tone!" he warned, glaring at me. I glared right back!

"Then later you asked me about Ken Hawkins' father's brother. Daniel's uncle, once removed?"

"Yeah, Del Vecchione. I got chewed out for that one, too!" I said, a little less angry.

"Well, it's time for you to hear the story of 'My Island Beach'!" he said. "So lose the attitude and get comfortable."

"Before I met your namesake, she was dating a boy named…"

"Del Vecchione," I supplied.

"Your friend's uncle," he finished. "How did you know?"

"I know," I replied without explanation.

He didn't ask again.

"So you don't want me to see Daniel because of a rivalry between you and his uncle?" I said, not really believing it.

"Katy, give me more credit than that," he paused. "It wasn't just jealously. Del was evil! The most depraved person I ever met. Don't believe me? You know the kind of things he did? He told me he used to hamstring the stray dogs that came round to the back of the fish market for scraps. Bragged about it. I always wondered why there were so many lame dogs in the neighborhood. Limping around on three legs. Evil! That's what he was," he repeated.

I was at a campfire on the beach with a group of young kids, both locals and summer people. Del was there. His full name was Delmonico Vecchione, but everyone called him Del. He was 15 that year and small for his age. His looks were ethnic Italian, short with curly black hair and a swarthy complexion—what some people called a 'little eye-talian grease ball'. In the next few years his appearance changed drastically. His hair straightened, he grew tall and lean, and his complexion changed from swarthy to an olive-skinned Mediterranean smoothness. He became what was referred to back then as tall, dark and handsome. But that year—that night—he was just another little grease ball.

Everyone was having a good time roasting marshmallows, talking in small groups. Sometimes I'm amazed at how innocent we were. No making out, no bad language and no booze. And we still managed to have a great time.

Then a gang of 17 and 18 year-old guys showed up. Spoiled summer kids who had been giving the rest of us a hard time at every opportunity. Tonight they'd been drinking.

"So, what do we have here, a wild beach party thrown by the punk brigade?" taunted Johnny Allison, the ringleader of the gang. Nobody said anything. We'd learned the hard way not to call attention to ourselves.

"Hey boys, this sure is a quiet bunch," he said. His boys agreed. Still, no one said anything. He was searching for a target, and no one was going to make it easy for him. Finally, it looked as if we'd bored him to death.

"Come on guys, let's get out of here. These twerps wouldn't know a good time if it bit them on the ass!" he said laughing. They started to leave.

"Maybe you shouldn't come back," said Del, in a quiet but ominous voice. God, was he out of his mind? Johnny and his friends heard it in spite of the whispered quality of the request.

"What did you say?" asked Johnny. He couldn't believe what he'd heard but, more importantly, it was dark and he didn't know who had said it.

"Maybe you should leave and not come back and leave us alone for the rest of the summer while you're at it," said Del, standing up this time so that Johnny and his friends could see him.

"Well what do we have here?" said Johnny, playing to his friends, his victim now singled out.

"And <u>who</u> might you be, little man?"

"My name's Del Vecchione," said Del. Johnny must have had 25 pounds on him. Some of the younger kids started dispersing into the dark, sensing the confrontation to come.

"And does Mr. del Vecchione have a first name?" asked Johnny with mocking politeness.

"Del," responded Del.

At that point Johnny smacked him in the head. It was one of those smacks that didn't do a lot of damage but must have stung like hell. And was totally humiliating.

"I asked you for your first name, del Vecchione!" he demanded, smiling. "Smart ass!" Now he kicked Del in the stomach. He was really enjoying where this was going.

"His last name's Vecchione. His first name is Del," I jumped in, doing the bravest or stupidest thing I'd ever done up to that point in my life.

Johnny glared at me for a second and I got ready to run. I wasn't *that* brave or stupid. Then he smiled. That seemed even more dangerous. He was getting ready to move on me.

"Johnny," said one of his friends, "I think you really hurt the little guy. Maybe we'd better just get out of here?"

Johnny looked at Del, then at me, then at his friend. "Why didn't he just say so? Stupid wops with their stupid names. How am I supposed to know how their names work," he *said*, sneering and sauntering off with his friends, apparently satisfied with the quantity of abuse he had doled out.

Del was in pretty bad shape but starting to come out of it. Without any warning he shot up and lunged at Johnny, landing a sucker punch in his kidneys. Johnny went down like a sack of potatoes. I was amazed that Del could even walk.

Johnny's friends moved to help him but the rest of us "little" kids placed ourselves, as a group, between them and the fight. "Let 'em fight," I said, "or can't Johnny take care of one little Italian kid?" I said, knowing that I had gone way beyond brave all the way over to stupid! They backed off. I got the distinct impression that some of them had been on the receiving end of Johnny's bullying and weren't averse to being provided with an excuse to *leave him to fend for himself.*

Well, Del, all bruised and bleeding, looked like he'd been in a war by the end of the brawl. But Johnny was hospitalized with two broken ribs, several broken teeth, and with one eye nearly gouged out. Later, we heard he had internal bleeding and almost lost the kidney that Del injured in the initial attack.

We finally ended the fight by pulling Del off of Johnny. Del was throttling him even after he lost consciousness. That he would have killed him if we hadn't stopped him, I had no doubt. That he would have killed anyone trying to stop him if there weren't enough of us to overcome him, I likewise never questioned. He was totally possessed by his rage.

Johnny's friends shared a common goal with us of preventing Johnny's execution. Del was out of control and there was no way he was going to calm down quickly. He broke free and ran off into the night when he realized that we wouldn't let him complete his attempt to murder Johnny. No one went after him.

Johnny never returned to Island Beach after his hospitalization and, needless to say, his friends never bothered us again that summer. And Del...well, we all became wary of him after that.

"But, later, Katy told me that Del would go over and take care of his grandmother for days at a time. Brush her hair, change her bedpan, and run her around town for hours. A real saint."

"So which was he?" I asked.

"Both, as near as I can figure," he said.

Chapter 18

The Story of Island Beach

"I think that's enough for now," said Grandpa, already pulling back to be alone with his thoughts.

"No way, Grandpa," I said. "You're not getting away with that again! You'll be in a funk for the rest of the day and won't want to finish this for another month."

"Finish it! Now! Let's go!" I insisted when he didn't respond.

He shrugged and continued out the door.

"*Now!*" I yelled.

He looked at me, sat down and didn't say anything for several minutes. This silent war of wills went on for so long that I was starting to zone out when he abruptly rejoined his narrative.

But the real story began two years later at the blowout in the dune. The rangers were pissed at us. They said we screwed up the dune by using it as a hangout. This weakened the vegetation so the dune would blow out when a storm came. They're probably right. Once it started it got worse and worse. We stayed away after that and they made sure we did.

After Katy and I got married, we were living here in my parent's summerhouse year round' til we got on our feet. Of course in the summer my parents lived with us since it was their vacation house, after all. The upside of the arrangement was that we had live-in babysitters for your father. So we could enjoy the beach more than most couples with a newborn could, and we even went out at night once in a while. The downside was that we didn't have much privacy, what with four adults and a newborn baby in this little place.

One evening Katy came back from the beach and asked if I wanted to go for a "walk". We went out for our "walks" fairly often to be alone so it wasn't particularly suspicious. She was acting nonchalantly for my parent's sake, but I could tell that she was excited about something.

When we'd gone about a block she guided me towards a parked truck, and who do you think was sitting inside but Del!

"Don't do anything. Just get in and shut up," she said before I could protest.

Well, I wasn't about to get in that truck with that bozo who I knew had history with my wife!

But she pulled me aside and whispered, "I don't know what you think this is but, whatever you're thinking, you're wrong 'cause you can't know! I'm with you, I'm for you, that's what I was put on Earth for. But if you don't get in the truck right now," she stopped and raised her eyebrows threateningly, "the season will be over before I'm 'for' you again, if you know what I mean!"

Grandpa sat there like a love-struck teenager rehashing past conquests.

"So you went!" I said, interrupting his reverie.

"Of course I went. No heterosexual male really has a choice," he said good-naturedly.

In the truck she sat between Del, who was driving, and me. "So what's it all about?" I asked her as we started into the park.

She didn't respond verbally, just handed me a coin. Now I don't know a doubloon from a piece of eight or a Spanish Real, for that matter. But what she handed me was one of the above or something like it. I just sat there inspecting it and considering the possibilities.

We drove to the beach access road, stopped to let air out of the tires and flipped the four-wheel drive lock hubs. Then we headed down the beach 'til we reached the blowout.

You couldn't see it from the beach but, when it came into view, I was stunned. There had been several n'oreasters since I last saw it and the effect on the dunes had been devastating. What had been a thriving primary dune community was now stripped of vegetation and eroding badly. And something new—the remains of a moderately sized, very old sailing vessel—had been exposed if you looked closely. A stump from the main mast and weathered ribs were evident. Most of the vessel was still buried.

I looked at Katy and Del, wondering how they knew that the ship was here. All I could think of was that it must have been a private place for teenagers before the dune started to deteriorate and the rangers chased us off. It wasn't visible from the beach. That's what we liked about the dunes, the seclusion.

They saw the way I was looking at them. Del smiled, and then laughed! That bastard!

She finally got the gist of what I was imagining and what he wasn't refuting with his sleazy look. "Phil, don't be a jerk. I was on the beach <u>alone</u> when I caught the glint of something in the dune. When I came to investigate, I found the coin I showed you."

"Lucky find," *I said unimpressed and unconvinced.*

"Along with these." *She opened up a cigar box with 15 or 20 ancient coins of different sizes and denominations.*

"Jesus! All lying loose?" *I asked.*

"Just picked them up lying there," *she said.* "Yesterday," *she explained.*

"Yesterday?" *I asked, wondering why she hadn't told me until today, and after she'd already told Del! She didn't respond to my one word question and all its implications. She knew I'd ask her about it later so I let it drop for now.*

"Today I made some discreet inquiries and found out that the state will take almost all of it when they find out," *she said.*

"In the library and talking to some state flunkies," *she added in answer to my quizzical look.*

"So?" I asked.

"So we don't tell them, Dorkwad!" exclaimed Del.

"Hey!" I said, shoving him into the sand.

"Cut it out!" said Katy.

She pulled me aside and whispered, "Go along, I know what I'm doing!" Then she acted as if I had said something stupid and yelled, "Don't be an asshole. Let's see what we've got and then decide what to do," she offered as a compromise.

We silently agreed and started working on a plan.

"It's a full moon so we can work at night without lights. It's isolated so we'll work it for a few nights and see what we've got," Katy suggested.

Del and I agreed, reluctantly, and got to work. As we exposed more and more of the ship's ribs, you could see that the deeper we went, the better preserved they were. That first night I found two more coins. Del found one, at least one that he told us about. Katy made the most interesting discovery, though. It was a box that contained what must have been a strand of pearls rolling around loose after the string rotted.

Not to mention cutlery, pulleys and even a cannonball.

It was exhilarating but, as dawn came, we disguised our digging as best we could, loaded up our tools and left. As we were departing a fisherman drove by in his Jeep Wrangler. Luckily, he didn't see what we were up to.

"Guys," said Katy, "having the truck parked here all night is like sending up smoke signals. It can't be spotted here two nights in a row or someone will know something's up."

"Tomorrow," she said, "Phil, you drop Del and me off, take the truck out to the road and hoof it back out here. Del, right before dawn you can go get the truck and pick us up." I could tell that this wasn't a spur-of-the-moment idea. She had it all figured out. I didn't like her being alone with Del, even for a few minutes, but her plan made sense.

When Del dropped us off near the house, we walked together with her clutching the box that contained the night's find. Neither Del nor I questioned her right to hold on to the booty.

"Why the hell did you bring him in on this?" I asked as he drove off.

"He had the truck and the tools, we need the help, and he knows how to keep his mouth shut!" She knew that this wouldn't be enough. "And he was there when I found the coins," she confessed. She knew I would accept that as a reasonable explanation for including him and at the same time that I'd be totally pissed off that she had been there with him.

"You said you'd found it <u>alone</u>!" I said, deranged at the thought of them alone together.

"Because that's what I told him I'd tell you," she said as if that was a totally reasonable explanation for her behavior. "Nothing happened—nothing ever will between him and me."

"You still haven't explained what you were doing there with him," I said, reassured that she was claiming nothing had happened, but still unsatisfied.

"You'll just have to trust me, Phil," she said looking me straight in the eyes, expecting me to do the right thing and trust her. Or maybe she was just trying to shut me up. The explanation was lame at best; but, the subject was closed and I'd acquiesced for the present.

She added, "I just hope we don't go to jail!"

The next night we uncovered more paraphernalia, a few coins and some bones which, I swear, were human. Even a few pewter and silver dishes. I realized later, much later in my life, that this was an important archaeological find and should have been investigated systematically. But back then it was treasure!

"You're serious, aren't you?" I asked as he paused. "You really found pirate's treasure?"

"Who could make up a story like this?" he asked in response to my skeptical look.

"Not even me," he shrugged when I didn't respond.

Chapter 19

X Does Not Mark the Spot

"OK Grandpa, let's wind it up," I said. I could see he was getting emotionally, if not physically drained. "Cut to the chase."

He looked up at me. He seemed defeated. It took less effort to comply than resist, so he proceeded.

The third night I was digging some distance from the ship at Katy's suggestion. The ship was lying on her side and Katy felt that some of the contents might have been thrown in that direction. In fact, I found a skeleton with a dagger intermingled amongst the bones, suggesting larceny. And several more mundane articles of commerce and hygiene! Is the evidence of our murderous nature always so closely juxtaposed to the trappings of our routine existence?

A couple of hours before dawn and, at a large distance from the ship, I scraped against something metallic. It was some kind of large box. As it was exposed I realized it was a chest of some sort, facing downward with a hinged lid that was open.

I shouted to Katy, and Del, of course, trailed along. After we dug out around the sea chest, Del and I turned it over, expecting to find the contents underneath. In fact, there were five or six coins and a jeweled necklace of some sort. As exciting as this was, it was disappointing, judging by the size of the chest.

"Dig!" yelled Katy after a moment's hesitation. "It's probably drifted down into the sand."

So we dug. Five, six, seven feet down. Two more coins but nothing else.

It was getting close to sunrise by now. We sat, tired and frustrated.

This was very unsatisfying, this incremental discovery. A few coins here and there. A cup or a dish then several hours without anything. We were kids; treasure hunters not archeologists. I jumped up in frustration, climbed to the top of the dune and surveyed the area, looking for inspiration. Nothing. Nothing and Del obviously more interested in Katy than the search which had become tedious after the initial novelty wore off.

Then, suddenly, I knew but I didn't. Almost but not quite. It slipped away and wouldn't come back. Finally, exasperated with the search and Del and especially Katy, I yelled, "Katy, where did you spot the coins on that first day?" She pointed and went back to talking with Del, but I shook my head and told her to go stand where she was pointing. At least I'd get her away from Del.

"Del," I somehow managed to say civilly. "Go stand where we found the coins the first night!" At first it seemed that he would refuse but then reluctantly complied.

Well, now, two points define a line but three random points should form a triangle unless they accidentally fall on the same line. And four points on the same line were not coincidental. Looking down, I knew. They sensed that I had figured something out and yelled, "What?"

"Stick a shovel where you're standing, both of you and come on up here!" I said. Del grumbled, but Katy realized I was on to something. So did Del.

The sun was just coming over the horizon as they reached the top of the dune. The two shovels (the two points) and the chest (the third point) and the ship (the fourth point) all fell on a perfectly straight line.

"The chest was thrown from the ship with such incredible force that it opened and almost everything flew out before it landed here," I whispered. "Whatever was in the chest will be found in the sand along the line between the ship and the chest."

They looked at the line, then at each other, and then at me. They knew I was right.

"We gotta go!" said Katy, indicating signs of life on the beach as the sun began to rise.

"We can't leave now!" I protested.

"Have to," she said.

"No," insisted Del, agreeing with me.

"Look, I've got an idea," Katy said. "You guys make your way to the truck; I'll head for the beach. Go back home, get blankets, an umbrella, chairs and food. I'm starving. And come back with the truck. Make some kind of excuse to your folks. I'll keep an eye on things while you're gone. We'll take shifts all day, sleeping and guarding."

Del got a stubborn look on his face and started to protest.

"Don't be stupid!" said Katy. "If somebody knows what we're doing, we're already in trouble. If they don't—and they don't," she continued confidently, "then the safest thing we can do is to go home and come back tonight." She stopped, waiting for it to sink in.

"But you're nervous and I'm nervous. So we'll have a picnic and sleepathon and keep an eye on the treasure from a distance," she said. "Now get going!" she ordered without waiting for a response. We did.

That night we returned and dug a ditch from ship to chest, fully 100 feet...maybe a little more. The final take, which we didn't tally until the next day, was as follows: 687 gold coins of various denominations; 483 silver coins; 43 items of jewelry including gold, silver, pearls and precious jewels such as diamonds, emeralds, sapphires, and rubies; and finally, four jewel-encrusted goblets. We placed them all back into the ancient chest which regained its functionality after lubricating the hinges with a little 3-in-1 oil.

We covered up as much as we could that night. At Katy's

suggestion, we stayed away from the wreck for a fortnight. But, later that year, we returned for two nights to police the area for more treasure—not to be greedy but to prevent anyone else from finding it and calling attention to the site.

Chapter 20

The Conundrum

A few nights later, after we'd had caught up on our sleep and put in some home time to calm down the parents about the constant "late night partying" we got together again at the beach.

"Any idea what this stuff is worth?" Del asked greedily.

"One to two million dollars," Katy said. "Maybe twice that to a private collector."

We both gaped at her.

"Library," she said. "You can find almost anything in the library if you know where to look." She produced a volume on pirate treasure including a chapter on the value of specific pieces.

Del was ecstatic and even I was thinking of what one-third of that kind of money could buy.

"Do you guys know who owns Island Beach?" I asked.

"The Phipps family," Katy said. "Technically the treasure is their property."

"So, not only would the state take most of my treasure, but the Phipps would probably take the rest," grumbled Del. Suddenly, it was his treasure!

"Didn't I hear that the Phipps were trying to develop Island Beach into a resort like Atlantic City?" asked Katy.

"Actually, like Coral Gables, Florida. They bought it in the late twenties but then the stock market crashed and it all fell apart," I said.

"I heard that the Feds are trying to raise money to make it into a park," Katy said.

"Fell through too," I said. "Couldn't get the bucks together."

"The Phipps heirs aren't going to part with it without getting their money's worth," Del remarked cynically. "Well, so much for the park. So what do we do now?"

No one said anything.

None of us, at least not Del or I, had really considered what to do at this point.

Legally, the treasure wasn't ours, at least not totally ours. And you couldn't just put an ad in the New York Times saying, "Several million dollars worth of pirate contraband for sale!"

"What we do," said Katy "is think about it long and hard until we figure out the right path forward." Uncharacteristically, she didn't seem to have a plan either.

"What do we do with the treasure until then?" I asked. Right now the treasure was covered with a tarp in the back of Del's pickup, where it had been for the last two days. Even Del felt uncomfortable carrying it around in his truck. I know I did, since I trusted him not at all.

Finally Katy said, "Look, we're in this thing together. If word of this or one single coin or artifact gets out, we're sunk. I know you two don't trust each other but you both trust me?"

We agreed reluctantly.

"I'll put the treasure in a place that's safe..." she said.

"Like you're not going to tell your own husband where you're stashing the loot?" Del questioned, and rightfully so. I wouldn't tolerate her trying to keep it a secret from me and she could see that from the look in my eyes.

"Fine," she said, ticked off. "I'll put it in the shed at your parent's house. They haven't gone in there in years. We're the only ones that use it. Now you both know, and if you want to rip each other off you can," she finished and stomped off.

"You know Katy, I suspect we all left that meeting with different ideas in mind for the treasure," Grandpa said.

"Del, I'm sure in his mind, was rich beyond his wildest dreams. Your grandmother was confused, I think. I, on the other hand, had some very definite ideas to explore over the next few days."

Chapter 21

My Island Beach

"Before I tell you more, you need to know a little bit about the history of the island," he said. He seemed to be gaining a little momentum so I just nodded.

In the early 1900s, Island Beach had two hotels, the Reed and the Haring, used mainly by sportsmen who came to shoot the waterfowl. At about the same time, bay men started settling the island, realizing that they could support themselves by hunting for muskrats and birds, catching striped bass and blue fish, and collecting oysters and clams.

Then in 1926, Andrew Carnegie's partner at Pittsburgh Steel, Harry Phipps, purchased Island Beach.

He planned to develop it into an exclusive resort with expensive summer homes. He actually built the Ocean House, the Bay House, and the Freeman House. The Phipps' cottages are now the Governor's summer mansions located within the borders of the park.

Francis Parker Freeman was a World War I cavalryman who signed on as estate manager for the island in 1926. Two years later he married Augusta Hueill Seaman, an author of children's mystery books.

But then, thank God, the Depression struck and the endeavor to develop the island into a resort foundered. In 1933, Freeman, his wife, and a retired Coast Guard Captain founded the Borough of Island Beach. They continued to manage the Phipps' Barnegat Bay and Beach Company which administered approximately 100 leases and issued passes to visitors. His rules were simple, "Leave things be, don't trample the sand dunes, don't pick the flowers and don't disturb the osprey."

Those rules, as you know, are pretty much still in effect today. Francis Freeman was the heart and the soul of the island and the first real caretaker for 22 years. And the effects of his legacy are still felt today, like the absence of those horrible rock jetties in the park. Obviously a man ahead of his time.

In 1945 the National Monument Committee attempted, but failed, to raise enough money to buy Island Beach for the National Park Service. Former President Herbert Hoover was one of the fundraisers. They did, however, honor Francis Parker Freeman with the following epitaph, "He measured the assets of this borough not in numbers of paved streets, of new cottages or in the number of feet of boardwalks, but in acres of heather and holly, in sand dunes left as god made them, in beach grass holding the drifting sands and offering a haven to numberless birds, rabbits and other wildlife. No jetties, bulkheads or other beach protective devices mar the beautiful shoreline." Francis Parker Freeman died in 1948.

Which bring us to 1953. The island was building up quickly, since times were good and getting better after the war. People were doing well enough to start thinking about luxuries like summer homes. Of course, Island Beach was a tempting target with almost ten miles of undeveloped ocean and bay front property. There was nothing like it on the Eastern Seaboard. It was irresistible and worth a fortune!

"And you just happened to have a fortune!" I said. "Are you trying to tell me...?"

"Let me finish," he said, interrupting my interruption.

My Island Beach

As we neared the end of his tale, Grandpa seemed to be getting a second wind. Maybe it was the relief of getting it off his chest after all these years. Maybe it was just seeing the light at the end of the tunnel. Anyway, after a biobreak, he continued, with a new zest, with the final installment of this bizarre tale.

"*I found a buyer,*" *Katy told us matter-of-factly.*
"*What!*" *Del and I said in unison.*
"*I found a buyer,*" *she said.*
"*Who?*" *we asked, to our mutual discomfort, in unison.*
"*My father has a friend who is an art dealer in Manhattan. A very discreet individual. Deals in pre-Colombian art and French Impressionist paintings of dubious origins. From the War, I think. Nazi booty. Risky business but profitable,*" *she said.*
"*He's interested?*" *Del asked. I remained silent this time, tired of parroting my rival's questions.*
"*No,*" *answered Katy.* "*But he has a client whose passion is pirate-based antiquities from the Americas.*"
"*Did you tell your father's friend how many 'antiquities' we're talking about?!*" *asked Del.*
"*No,*" *Katy stated.* "*We'll deal with the client anonymously through a fourth party and try to gauge his interest and ability to pay, before informing him of the extent of the collection.*"
"*Fourth party?*" *asked Del, confused.*
"*I'll explain later,*" *she said. Del accepted it for now.*
"*Ever play poker?*" *I asked, impressed.*
"*Only for money,*" *she said, winking at me.*

Kate eventually cut a deal for half the loot with one collector. She didn't make him aware of the other half of the collection. But honestly, he was ecstatic to get what he did. Another independent party acquired the rest. Neither party was aware of the other, thanks to the discretion of Katy's art dealer friend. Total price for both halves was $3,000,000. And they wanted to give us cash!

"Grandpa, you don't expect me to believe that a 17-year-old girl negotiated a multimillion deal with a private collector?" I said.

"She was almost 18 and she was no girl. She was a wife and a mother. She was a woman—and quite a woman at that!" he said.

"Big whup!" I replied, unimpressed.

"But that was only part of the deal. The other part was my idea," he continued.

I told Katy and Del that we should use the money to buy Island Beach. Del didn't want to be a property owner even though he knew the property would someday be worth a bundle. He wanted the cash and he wanted it now!

Katy wasn't that receptive to the idea, either. She said that, first of all, we would never see the cash because we were all under age. And how could we hide it? She didn't come out and say it but the idea of Del being discreet with that kind of money was inconceivable. Likewise, we couldn't publicly buy Island Beach because who would believe a bunch of teenagers would have that kind of cash.

To answer your question, no, a 17-year-old does not negotiate a multimillion-dollar deal by herself. My father had a lawyer who was the epitome of respectability and discreteness, especially for a price. He, along with the art dealer, brokered the deal but Katy issued all instructions and bargaining strategies. She was a formidable woman, even at 17.

Anyway, when I suggested we buy Island Beach, my idea was to preserve the park, not become a real-estate developer...Katy's vision, too, eventually. In fact, after some initial skepticism, she warmed up to the idea fairly quickly. But Del wanted nothing to do with that. One way or another he wanted his share of the money.

Our lawyer knew a state administrator who had been involved in the failed National Monument Committee's attempt to purchase the Phipps' estate for the Federal Government. She suggested that an anonymous donation to the state might be arranged with the money specifically earmarked for the purchase of Island Beach. At Katy's insistence, our lawyer did not make the state administrator aware of the source of the money, just the amount. This state administrator was interested but skeptical that there would be enough money for the purchase. The lawyer was also aware, based *on her previous involvement, that the Phipps heirs were not interested in philanthropy and wanted a fair price for the property. She also knew that Phipps had paid $2.5 million in 1925 for the 2,000 acres known as Island Beach and was certain they would never accept less than that. She estimated that it could be purchased outright for $3.3 million.*

We were actually aware of that figure before we began negotiations, again through my father's lawyer, with the private collectors. The negotiations were very complicated. We, that is, Katy thought the lawyer had to trick our first buyer, as I mentioned before, so we could get a second buyer so there would be enough money to buy the island.

Of course, smart as we were, we were only kids and didn't consider the ancillary expenses, mainly a significant commission to the lawyer and to Katy's art broker for acting as intermediaries for a couple of kids unloading stolen property.

Del was furious! Livid! But Katy got tough and told him that, first of all, the treasure was not legally ours, second of all it was not morally ours, and third of all it just wasn't in the cards for us to get the money. And if he didn't keep his yap shut, we'd all end up in jail!

"That's what was supposed to have happened," Grandpa said, sighing deeply.

"So what did happen?" I asked.

"I don't really know," said Grandpa cryptically.

"What do you mean, you don't know?" I asked, surprised at having to pry information out of the consummate storyteller.

"What I mean is…" he started then faltered. This time he really looked like he was going to fold up and leave me hanging. He looked so pitiful that I would have let him get away with it this time.

"Two days before the deal was supposed to take place, your grandmother disappeared!" he exclaimed.

"Del?" I asked the obvious.

"Disappeared too. No trace. Neither was ever seen again," he said and the story was over, I thought. A tragic and unresolved mess like real life usually turns out to be.

As I was preparing to leave Grandpa to his thoughts, he unexpectantly continued.

"The next day, I got a letter from your grandmother." He had me again—he was still telling the story!

The letter said that, no matter what happened, I should go through with the deal! No matter what! It was quite emphatic. It described all the arrangements and contacts I would need to close the deal.

She said the park was her legacy. That and our child, your father.

So I did the deal without knowing what happened to Katy or Del or when they might turn up. Which they never did.

"So what do you think happened to Grandma, and Del, for that matter?" I asked.

When he didn't respond, I demanded "So?"

"When I was young, I had no patience for the method of age. When I was old, I had no patience for the impetuousness of youth. It seems my impatience was ageless."

Where the hell did that come from? "Shakespeare?" I asked, unfamiliar with the passage.

"Only me, I'm afraid," he apologized.

I waited, having had enough of his sage wisdom.

"So," he said, "your grandmother died that night."

"How do you know?" I asked.

"I know it in my heart," he answered without anguish, apparently having long ago extinguished the rendering passion it must have evoked. "Some people say they went off together, but she would have at least let me know she was OK. And she would have never have left our baby," he reasoned, "even if she'd left me."

"No! She's dead and, somehow, he's responsible!" he said. "And in some ways, so am I."

"Grandpa, I'm sorry—really, I am. But do you seriously expect me to swallow all this?" I asked, sympathetic but skeptical, nonetheless.

He stood and pulled out a small drawer from his desk. He flipped it over and detached a miniature zip-lock bag taped to the bottom. From that bag he removed a large gold coin, irregular in shape and stamped with an epigraph in an unfamiliar language, and handed it to me.

Looking up from the coin, this doubloon or whatever it was, I now fully accepted his explanation and wondered aloud, "How did you cover the shortfall?" He looked at me quizzically, uncomprehending.

"You had $3 million, but the Phipps heirs wanted $3.3 million. Where did the other $300,000 come from? Pocket change?"

Grandpa laughed. "Oh that," he said as if $300,000 was a minor detail. "Our state administrator's estimate was high. The state purchased the park for $2.7 million. The rest went to pay off the various dealmakers guaranteeing their silence by making them paid accessories," he explained.

"And you think that because Daniel looks like Del and I look like Grandma..." I started to protest. But he wasn't listening.

I let it drop for now. But something else occurred to me and I asked, "And that's why you call it 'My Island Beach'?"

"A small vanity," he murmured and shuffled away, consumed by the consequences of past events.

Chapter 22

Sea Glass

Walking along the beach, I moved from South Seaside Park into Island Beach State Park unaware of crossing that artificial demarcation. Recent events and their consequences were occupying my thoughts more and more. Grandpa's explanation of the circumstances surrounding the disappearance of Grandma Katy did *not* ring true. Nothing I could put my finger on, but I just didn't believe it. There it was. I believed my beloved Grandpa was lying to me which was the underlying source of my despondency!

What were the motives behind Ken Hawkins' request that I mention Del to Grandpa? To break up things between Daniel and me? There had been nothing to break up at the time he mentioned it. A preemptive strike to prevent any romance that might develop? Too farfetched. But why, then? And what was Evelyn's part in all this? She was as bad as all the rest with her little intrigues and 'let's-never-speak-about-it-again' philosophy. She was totally unforthcoming with regard to my inquiry about Ken Hawkins and Del. She knows, but she just won't say.

But the most frustrating individual, the most infuriating one, was Daniel—even more galling than Grandpa. There were things he wasn't telling me. Things that might change my opinion of him, or maybe of Grandpa. Maybe he was trying to spare me. But I couldn't see it as a virtue, at least not at the moment. I needed to know what was going on. I needed facts. I needed information.

What I knew—what I really knew at the moment was nothing! I didn't believe that any of them were telling me the truth. The only person in my life who didn't seem to have an agenda was Sam. As flaky as she could be, and she could be way flaky, I trusted her above my family, my lover, and my employer. I could confide in Sam without fear that she would have a stake in my perception and act with prejudice as an advocate for one view or another.

But there were things I couldn't even tell Sam, in spite of her lack of bias. Feelings I was experiencing that I couldn't explain to her. I would not expose myself to the ridicule that Sam would not have any choice but to react with. If the situation were reversed, I would! Not to mention the suspicion and distrust I was feeling towards Grandpa, who I loved so dearly. I couldn't tell her about that. That was family stuff and not for outsiders.

The most terrible things were the worst-case scenarios that were brewing below the surface of my consciousness. I had only recently become aware of them. Not yet fully baked, these scenarios were not confined to any specific resolution or definitive point of view. And in not committing, they avoided prevention by masking their intentions.

As I was contemplating these sinister designs, I was walking with my head down scanning the flotsam and jetsam strewn along the high tide line, beach-combing as humans seem instinctually compelled to do.

That's when I spotted it. A small piece of sea glass, that matte-finished textile of the ocean that was no longer a bottle but not yet returned to sand. It was a delicate green color and as fine a specimen as I had ever seen. Derived from the bottom edge of a bottle or glass, a corner piece bisected by a right angle. Very rare!

All the sharp edges had been worn and smoothed to a fine patina. Which brought to mind my collection. My sea glass collection!

Why hadn't I remembered it before now?

R. E. Salter

Two summers ago, when I had spent most weekends and two full weeks with Grandpa, I became fascinated by these small collaborations of man and sea. At first it was because they were rare. There were lots of shells, thousands of shells, millions of shells, but very little sea glass. At the present moment, however I was thinking about them more as little insights into the life cycle of sand. Like fossils of the dinosaurs or early humans, small hints that survived the vagaries of time on their inevitable journey back to dust.

These articles, this glass, started out as sand processed into fine grains by the ocean, crushed, abraded, and refined into a relatively constant particle size. This sand was then transformed into glass by the industriousness of humans. It had a life and existence as an article of commerce before being discarded and somehow finding its way back to the sea. Its recycling into sand was underway, the rubbing, polishing and eroding to create new beaches.

But, by removing it for my collection, I had stopped the process, interrupted the recycling and prevented the completion of the circuit.

As I returned to the house I recalled that collection of sea glass. It started with a piece here and there that summer, two years ago. Ranging in size from large irregular chunks, perhaps one to two inches along their longest dimension, to miniscule round dots. It's a wonder we ever discerned the small ones against the background of real sand.

As the collection grew I asked Grandpa if he had a suitable container to keep it in. He provided a long-stemmed wineglass. It was not a fine piece of crystal, by any means, but a cloudy, rose-tinted artifact. I realized then that it was old—very old. "A 'Sea Glass' for your sea glass," as Grandpa put it. Something he found on the beach one summer a long time ago. It was perfect—it had a primitive elegance—I loved it. I objected that it was too fine a piece for something as common as a sea glass collection, but he insisted.

I realized now that it was a relic from the wreck in the blowout. A valuable, but non-precious piece of the treasure. It was too undamaged to have survived in the sea for any extended period; it had to have been preserved in the dunes with the other artifacts of the wreck.

As I mentioned, it was cloudy, but not from the grinding that provided the matte finish to sea glass. It was perfectly smooth, not worn. The haziness of the glass was derived from the primitiveness of its manufacture, not the nature of its surface. How the rose tint was accomplished, I cannot guess.

I graciously accepted the goblet and made it the home and residence for my burgeoning assortment of glasses. It was, as I expected, perfect.

Returning to the beach house, I sought out Grandpa to ask about the location of my collection. It never entered my mind that he might have discarded it, or more fittingly, returned it to the sea, wineglass and all, to complete its journey back into sand. Grandpa, unfortunately, was nowhere to be found.

The glass was no longer displayed on the hideous green-painted dry sink that Grandpa still owned. I scoured that cabinet to see if it had been tucked away, but to no avail. I perused the closets of the bedrooms, thinking it might have been exiled there. No luck.

Finally, I worked my way through the dark and convoluted recesses of the kitchen cabinets and spotted it in the rear of a high cupboard that required a stool to investigate. I recovered the collection in the "Sea Glass" and examined it by emptying it onto the counter. An inventory indicated twenty-nine pieces of various sizes, shapes and colors. I added the corner piece I had found today to make it an even thirty.

It was the middle of summer, my last vacation before becoming a full-fledged adult. Upon consideration, I felt like a piece of that sea glass in my collection. I'd been plucked from the continuity of my life, my karma. I'd become a part of this collection of people, this summer colony, to contemplate what was to become of me.

How would my life evolve, what would I accomplish? Was this interlude at the shore a respite or a cusp that would profoundly affect all my future endeavors?

I had no idea. How could I?

I considered the pieces of sea glass. The pieces were covered with dust from their long storage in the back of the cabinet. It was impossible to say if a given piece was derived from a common beer bottle of recent vintage or a fine decanter from a ship of the Spanish Main. I replaced them into that ancient rose chalice and added water to rinse off the dust. I was about to decant the water and spread out the newly washed pieces onto a paper towel to dry when I noticed the sun setting into the bay.

I held up the water and sea-glass-filled goblet to observe the refractions of the sunset through that unique medium.

I still had no inkling as to my destiny—my future. Nothing had been resolved or clarified in any way. But, in spite of that, I was awash with a feeling of optimism from the splendor of that vision of a sunset through wetted gems. So encouraging was that singular diffusion of light that the uncertainties and ambiguities of my prospects were shelved, delegated to an obscure file cabinet in the deep recesses of my mind.

At least for the time being.

Chapter 23

Undercurrents

"Thanks, Katy, I appreciate it," said Sammy as I picked her up and started driving.

"No problem," I assured her.

"It's just that I don't like to bother other people if I can help it," explained Sam.

"Don't want to be a burden?" I said.

"Hell no, I don't mind being a burden. I just don't like being beholden," she replied.

"Kind of selfish," I said.

"You bet," she admitted. "Like most people."

"Well, I'm pretty sure you can't pull out your own wisdom teeth or drive yourself home on anesthetic."

"'Well' yourself!" she said, sticking out her tongue. "The doctor gets paid and, as for you, 'well' I'll just have to make an exception."

Leave it to Sammy. I was taking her to the dentist and she was making the sacrifice.

"Very noble of you," I said sarcastically.

"Think nothing of it," she said. "In fact…" she paused.

And we said together, "Let's never speak of it again!" and

laughed.

These things never go on schedule and this time was no different. The procedure, which lasted about 15 minutes, started over an hour late and we were both getting pissed off. I remember once waiting over two hours in a waiting room to see a doctor who had actually left to go to the hospital. If I hadn't said something to the receptionist I'd be sitting there still.

Afterwards they ushered me to the recovery room where Sammy was laid out on a table like a slab of beef. Standing next to her was the stereotypical "mother" of all nurses. She was big, enormous in fact, but not fat. She had a stern look that did not soften as she spotted me entering the room. I'm sure there was a good reason for her surliness, and I'm likewise sure that I didn't care to know what it was.

"She'll be coming out of it in a moment. Keep her on the table lying down until she's stable," the nurse decreed and left. That might take a while, I thought, as I had never known Sam to be "stable" before.

Sam looked like she'd been in a prizefight. Her cheeks were bruised and yellow, as was one of her eyes. Her eyeballs were rolled back so that only the whites were showing, like a vampire or werewolf. Something didn't look right, in fact, it looked very wrong!

Suddenly her eyes rolled back down, she grabbed me by the lapels, pulled my face very close to hers and said in an intense whisper that scared the hell out of me, "Gotcha!"

I started to get angry but it was impossible with that smile of hers. "Admit it!"

"You got me," I said grinning. "Now get your grimy hands off me!"

"Not till you tell me a joke."

"Sammy, I don't know any jokes," I protested, but she didn't let go.

"Yes you do. Think back. I need a joke and I need it now," she said with that mischievous look on her face. "I'll be forever *beholden* to you—that's what you want, isn't it?" she vamped in her best little Southern Belle voice.

"Sammy, that's just the laughing gas talking," I said.

"Damn straight and it's a rush. And I need a joke to fully appreciate the experience," she said. "Now cough one up."

Now, I couldn't tell a joke to save my life. Didn't have the timing. And the only joke I could remember was a long convoluted number. Exactly the kind Sammy didn't need and I couldn't tell. But at least it wasn't politically correct. Sam would like that.

She still had me by the lapels and showed no signs of releasing me. She pulled my face an inch from hers and whispered ominously, "Joke!"

"So a priest is looking for a bell ringer for the church steeple," I began with trepidation. "And the only applicant is a young man who, unfortunately, has no hands or arms." At that, Sam finally released me.

"'So, young man' began the priest. 'Don't tell me you're here for the bell ringer position?' 'Yes Father, I am' said the boy. 'But how will you ring the bell without hands or arms?' asked the priest. 'Why don't I show you?' he replied." Sammy was totally rapt.

"Up they went, to the belfry, where the boy refused the offer of the bell cord from the priest and proceeded to slam into the bell with his head. Bong! He made it ring loud and clear, convincing the skeptical monk. 'Very well, son, you've persuaded me. You have the job if you want it,' said the priest."

"The next day the boy went up to the tower and at one o'clock rang the bell by whacking it with his head once." With that, I snapped my head forward and said loudly, "Bong!" Sammy giggled.

"At two o'clock—Bong! Bong! At three o'clock—Bong! Bong! Bong!" I illustrated each bong with a snap of my head. "And so on until…"

"No, no, no. No, no, no! Do them all," insisted Sammy. "Tell it right." I had a feeling she'd heard the joke before as it was a very old joke. But I humored her and 'Bonged' factorially, 4, 5, 6, 7, 8, 9, 10, and 11 times all the way up until midnight.

"At midnight he went Bong! Bong! Bong! Bong! Bong! Bong!

Bong! Bong! Bong! Bong! Bong!" snapping my head for all 11 Bongs! "But on the twelfth Bong, he was so dizzy that he missed the bell and fell to this death in the courtyard below!" In fact, I was getting dizzy just "Bonging" my way through this joke.

"People gathered around the fallen bell ringer, murmuring until the priest arrived. 'Father, who was this poor unfortunate lad?' they asked."

"'I don't actually know his name,' answered the priest thoughtfully, rubbing his chin, 'But his face rings a bell!'"

At the punch line, I stopped to see if Sammy got the joke. It was a delayed reaction. Her mouth opened but no sound came out. She slapped both hands on the side of her head and started rolling. Then came the inevitable delayed-reaction hoot, followed by a screeching howl.

I was both gratified and mortified! No one had ever laughed at my jokes before. I tried to hush her but she would not be subdued.

The nurse rushed in and was about to start giving CPR when she realized that Sammy was shrieking with laughter. She gave me a withering look and barked, "Try to keep her calm! Do you think you can manage that?"

I got the message loud and clear but she really pissed Sammy off. In her present, more uninhibited-than-usual (if that's possible) condition she screamed, "Oh yeah, Nurse Ratched! Well, my panties are on backwards! What do you think about that, huh?" We, the nurse and I, looked at each other in a moment of common befuddlement.

Sam continued her tirade. "Tell the dentist that I'd like an explanation! What kind of an operation is this! I want—no, I demand an explanation!" The nurse just walked away shaking her head. They knew Sammy here.

"What's the hell is wrong with you Sam! You can't talk to people like that!" I was appalled and embarrassed.

"What do you mean? Look, they are on backwards!" she insisted.

The she showed me the waistband sticking out of the top of her jeans with the tag in the front. They were on backwards! "Samantha, what the hell is going on?"

She looked confused. Then enlightenment registered on her face. "Oh yeah," she said sheepishly, "Now I remember. I put them on backwards this morning. Never mind."

"No, Sammy, you're not going to get off that easy. You put them on backward... why in the world would you put your panties on backwards?" I asked. I wasn't amused.

"In case they molested me while I was under," she said as if a reasonable person would understand her motivation. When she realized that I didn't, she explained, "I figured that if they molested me they'd put my panties back on frontwards and then I'd know," she explained earnestly. Then she started laughing her ass off at the whole situation.

"Just because you're paranoid doesn't mean everybody's not out to get you!" she said. Even I was laughing, now.

But when I thought about it some more, I wondered aloud, "Sam, has anyone ever molested you?"

She became solemn for a fraction of a second. One blink and I'd have missed it. Then she caught herself and continued, laughing. "Tell me another joke. You're a riot, you know, like my mother. Told two jokes in her whole life. But when she did, no one saw it coming and we were on the floor for days just repeating the punch line over and over again and laughing. Something about a banana in her ear."

"Tell another!" she pleaded.

"I don't know another," I said. Her face fell. God, I felt powerful!

"I don't know another...but that wasn't the end of the first joke," I said. Sam beamed. I continued.

"So...the priest still needs a bell ringer and another young man with no arms shows up to apply for the job. And he looks just like the first bell ringer. 'You're not applying for the bell ringer job are you, son?' asked the priest. 'Don't worry, Father, I can do the job in spite of my condition. I believe you knew my brother?' 'Oh, I believe you,' said the priest, and gave him the job.

"The next day at one o'clock..." I went through all the Bongs again for Sammy's sake.

"And on the twelfth Bong at midnight he was so punchy that he missed the bell and fell to his death in the courtyard below."

"The people gathered around and the priest ran out. The crowd asked again, 'Father, do you know who this unfortunate young man is?' to which the priest, scratching his head pondering this turn of events, answered, 'Actually I don't know his name,' he replied scratching his head pondering the recent turn of events, 'But he's a dead ringer for his brother!'"

Well, that was too much for Sammy and she laughed so hard that she rolled off the gurney which went flying across the room and out the door. It slammed into our nurse's keister, causing her to throw a tray of something biological and herself, onto the floor. Sammy, rolling on the floor shrieking with laughter and gasping for breath, was uninjured.

The nurse was furious! The dentist stuck his head out and yelled, "She's stable enough. Get her the hell out of here!"

As we exited, Sammy turned to the dentist and yelled, "Doc, I haven't forgotten about my panties," trying to show him how they were on backwards as I hustled her out before they called the cops on us.

In the car Sammy said, "You really need a third part to that joke. That would slay anyone."

Realizing that I could be a great comedian if only they'd gas the audience, I continued, "So the priest still needed a bell ringer." Sammy clapped her hands together with glee.

"But he, like the others, ended up in the courtyard, dead as a doornail," I continued. Thank God this part didn't have any Bongs!

"Did he have arms?" asked Sam.

"He did, which the people in the crowd noticed immediately. 'Oh he had arms all right,' said one of the two exceedingly stupid steeple painters who had spent the last several days in the belfry with the latest bell ringer. 'That's right' said the other dull-witted painter. 'Two arms and two assholes!' he informed the crowd."

"'Two assholes?' they asked skeptically. 'Yep,' confirmed the first half-wit. 'How do you know that?' asked someone in the crowd."

At that point I pulled the car over to the side of the road, turned

My Island Beach

to Sam and delivered the punch line, "'Because every day when we come to work with him the priests say, 'There goes the bell ringer with the two assholes!'"

Unfortunately, Sammy was sound asleep. Oh well, it was a good run while it lasted. She'd never think it was funny if she were straight.

As we pulled up to Grandpa's house, I went around the car, shook Sam awake and helped her into the house. Grandpa wasn't around.

"You're not just funny," she said giving me a peculiar look, "You're very complicated!" she said as I covered her in bed.

"And you're simple?" I asked.

"I'm very simple," she insisted. "If you're my friend I'll jump off a bridge for you," she assured me, "and if you screw with me you better watch you're fucking back!"

"Simple," she finished with that beatific smile that belied her passionate approach to relationships.

"But you're complicated," she repeated. "It's like there's more than one of you in there."

"In where?"

"In there! In your head," Sam clarified.

"What like a multiple personality?" I asked.

"No, just the two of you," she said without missing a beat.

I laughed. "This from the girl with her panties on backwards."

Startled for a second, she looked down at her crotch, then remembered and chuckled. "Yeah—OK, I remember. But you're two people, I think," she said and dropped off to sleep for the second time that night.

Chapter 24

Simpler Times

"Katy!" Grandpa shouted as I approached the house from the beach where I had gone when it seemed that Sammy would never wake up. "Do you know anything about a strange girl in my house?" he asked laughing.

"Oh Grandpa, I'm sorry," I said. "You must've come in after we were asleep," I explained.

"Not that I'm complaining, mind you, but we introduced each other on the way out, in my case, and on the way in, in hers, to my bathroom. Does she, by chance, have any clothes with her?" he asked roguishly. I wanted to giggle like he was doing, but I couldn't bring myself to. The thought of Grandpa and Sam!

"I gather she's had some kind of dental surgery. Wisdom teeth, if I'm not mistaken? I'll go down and whip up some nice soft scrambled eggs. Don't be too long," he said and took off.

At that moment Sammy appeared in my half robe, which was only about a "third" robe on her. "Hi sugar!" she said to Grandpa, giving him a wink.

"Hello, sweet darling!" Grandpa crooned.

In spite of the fact that I knew they were yanking my chain I couldn't let this pass, even though ignoring their little game was undoubtedly the best way to defuse it. "OK, we're going to put a stop to this nonsense right now!" I said. "So cut it out!"

They looked at each other and laughed. "Maybe," said Grandpa, "you should tell me when you're going to bring a young and nubile lady friend into the house?" he teased.

"Grandpa!" I warned.

"Nubile? I like that Philip," Sam teased out his first name. "And maybe you should take me where you're supposed to, home that is, when I ask for a favor," she said. "Right, Philip?" she asked, as if he were her spouse.

"I have to agree with Samantha," concurred Grandpa.

"Grandpa! Sammy! Cut it out!" I exclaimed as Grandpa headed off to start breakfast. They just laughed, enjoying my discomfort immensely. I guess I was laughing a little too. Inside. Deep, deep inside.

Sam sat on the bed, toweling off her wet hair. Then she turned to look at me with a confused look on her face.

"Katy, I don't know how to tell you this but someone...I really don't know how to tell you this" she hesitated. "Someone climbed into bed with me last night," Sam said, finally.

"Sammy, enough teasing," I said, tired of the little innuendo-job Grandpa and she had been doing on me since I got back from the beach.

"I'm not kidding, Katy," she insisted.

"You must've been dreaming," I said dismissing her allegation. "There's no one in this house but Grandpa and me."

"Nevertheless, someone crawled under the covers with me last night," she reiterated, raising her eyebrows, suggestively. She was really upset.

"And did anything happen when this person crawled in beside you?" I asked disturbed by her implication.

"Nothing really. They just 'snuggled' me. It actually felt really good," she said, raising her eyebrows questioningly this time.

"Sammy, Grandpa would never do any such thing. You were probably just hallucinating from the anesthesia," I said.

"I was a little out of it but I've learned to operate pretty effectively when I'm out of it," she insisted. "Someone crawled into bed with me last night and I don't think it was your Grandpa."

I didn't say anything.

It must have been evident to her that I would not be responding to her ridiculous implications. "I think it was you," she accused, fishing for a reaction.

Which I duly furnished. I turned bright red and felt panicked, wanting to flee!

"It was you!" she said, surprised even though she'd surmised on some level that it must have been me. "Come on Katy, 'fess up now and let's get this behind us! What's going on?" she asked guilelessly.

I still didn't say anything, hoping the situation would simply disappear. "Katy, the longer you wait, the weirder it looks. Tell me what's going on. I guarantee you it's no worse than what I'm already thinking," she tried to reassure me.

"Fine!" I said, angry at being compelled to confront something I wanted nothing more than to forget about. My friends and I, in our youth, referred to this type of response as a "Fuck you, Fine!"

"Fine!" I repeated with the same implied meaning. "You were shivering, Sam. I mean violently shivering, probably some kind of reaction to the anesthesia. I gave you a second blanket but that didn't help. All I could think of was to crawl in with you to try to warm you up. You were absolutely frigid—chilled to the bone!" I said. "You wouldn't stop…and you were starting to scare me…" I started to cry. "You scared me. I didn't know if you were going to be OK or not. Grandpa wasn't home yet and I didn't know what to do!"

"You were crying last night, too," Sam whispered, starting to mist up herself. With that, she came over and gave me a big hug and we started in on a really good crying jag.

"You scared me!" I repeated. At that moment Grandpa wandered in with a pan full of eggs, probably to announce that breakfast was ready. Seeing what was going on he had the good sense to do a quick u-turn without a word and headed back to the kitchen.

"Not many people do things like that for me," Sammy confided after we settled down. "Taking me in and taking care of me."

Still embarrassed about the whole affair, I didn't know what to say so I changed the subject. "You were also speaking in tongues!" I accused.

"What are you talking about now?" she asked, amused.

"After you warmed up and stopped shivering, you started to relax. Then you started talking in some other language—Greek or something," I told her.

"And what was I saying in this other language?" she asked skeptically. "You're not just busting my chops for flirting with your beloved granddad, are you?"

"You were speaking in tongues," I insisted. "God, Sam, sometimes it's really hard having you as a friend."

"But worth it," she assured me, without taking offense at my candor. "But seriously, Katy, what was I saying in this other language?"

"Well I was half-asleep myself but it sounded like 'Semper Scooby Dooby your Booby' or something like that," I said and giggled. "'Semper Scooby Dooby your Booby', 'Semper Scooby Dooby your Booby'. Over and over again," I laughed. "Sounded kind of kinky!" I said, not sure I wanted to know, but intrigued.

She lost it. After several minutes she managed to stop laughing and gasped, "Wait—wait—stop! I'm gonna pull out my stitches!"

"So tell me what's so funny?"

"That," she said, finally.

"What's that?" I asked.

"'That' is what I was saying. '*Semper ubi sub ubi*'." Which she pronounced lyrically "semper ooby Sue booby".

"Great, that clears it up," I replied sarcastically.

"It's Latin," she explained. "Semper means 'always', ubi means 'wear' and sub means 'under'. So it literally means…"

"Always wear underwear! But I don't believe that translates to any such thing in Latin," I protested.

"Only literally. We made it up, pulling an all-nighter studying for a Latin test," she said. "We were punchy as all get out. But if you think about it you gotta admit it has a certain onomatopoeia about it. I think that's what appealed to us. And not only is it sage advice but also my subconscious recognized it as being apropos to my situation yesterday. You know my underwear situation. God, I haven't thought about that night since it happened."

"*Semper ubi sub ubi,*" I repeated as we entered the kitchen.

Grandpa had the good sense, yet again, to ignore our swollen eyes and incoherent babbling as we entered the room. That's why he's my favorite.

In spite of her difficult night, Sam was starving and not cautious about filling that need—literally. In between shovelfuls of eggs she asked, "Mr. Brace, do you remember what this place was like before…?"

"Samantha, darling child, if you can't call me Phil then you'll not eat my food," Grandpa declared and reached out as if to take her plate. To which Sammy replied, "Phil," wrenched back her plate and stuck out her tongue which was covered with eggs. Not the most delightful sight first thing in the morning—or any other time for that matter.

"Thank you," he said and laughed. "Now, I think you were asking what it was like before—what? Before Christ? Before dinosaurs? Before the planet cooled?"

"Before," she said without elucidating, flirting again. She stuck out her tongue again and this time I think it was jelly and an English muffin, at least I hope that's what it was.

"And delightful table manners, too. I'll take it as a compliment that you're enjoying my cooking so much that you feel compelled to display it to the world," he teased. She laughed.

No kidding, if it weren't for the age difference, I'd be seriously concerned about the chemistry here.

"Well, 'before' encompasses the first time I came here as a child. That would have been 1945, near the end of the war. I was nine," he began. I hoped Sammy wouldn't be sorry she asked.

My parents didn't have much money and this, I think, caused them to fight a lot. Or maybe it was the disappointment of observing the reflection of your own shortcomings in your mate.

My Island Beach

Whatever the reason, they were constantly on each other about everything and nothing.

That summer, my father came home with a couple of roof racks for the car, a bunch of plywood, a tarp and a can of ugly blue paint. Sounds like the beginning of a joke, doesn't it? But this was something very different for him. Firstly, he hadn't consulted Mother and, secondly, she did not instantly insist on knowing what he was up to. She just figured he was wasting money and time on a project that she not only had not preapproved but was also unaware of until it was well underway.

He built a big open box, painted it with that ugly blue paint and mounted the box to the roof racks. He attached this construct to the top of the old Plymouth station wagon, which was our only mode of transportation in those days. The one with the floorboards rusted out so we had to stick some plywood down there to keep from getting splashed <u>inside</u> the car on rainy days!

The following Friday he said we were going to the beach for the weekend. Predictably, Mother protested, dismissing it based on the implied expense. He replied that it would only cost us the gas needed to get there and back and the food we'd eat anyway. So, on one of the few occasions I can remember, Father insisted and Mother actually agreed. I think she was curious—maybe even hopeful—and if it didn't work out she'd have fodder to belittle him with for months.

We drove down Route 9 to Tom's River and then worked our way over to Island Beach. No Garden State Parkway then...not until 1959 or 1960, I think. Anyway, we arrived after dark on that Friday night and pulled into a little alcove near the beach, totally isolated from everyone else in the whole wide world. My sister, Barbara, and I wandered down to the water, *trying to imagine what it was going to look like in the morning. Meanwhile, Mother and Father prepared our camp.*

Father emptied out the big blue box and laid out a double sleeping bag for Mother and him in the back of the station wagon with the backseat and tailgate down for more legroom. Father had bought a second-hand Coleman white-gas camp stove and Mother used it to make soup. She also broke out sandwiches for a late supper when we returned from our explorations.

After dinner we made a small campfire and wordlessly absorbed the sounds of the seashore. After we got ready for bed, Father asked Barb and me if we'd like to sleep on the ground in sleeping bags or in the now empty, big blue box on top of the station wagon!

Well, if there is a Heaven on Earth for a nine-year old kid, it is sleeping on a cool summer night under the stars, perched in a big ugly blue box, watching and listening to the surf on a barrier island on the eastern seaboard of the United States. For several years after that, I sincerely could not see the sense of sleeping indoors, which caused no end of aggravation for my mother!

The next day I woke, watched the sun come out of the water and got my first glimpse of what this earthly cathedral looked like in the light! It took a combination of having to pee and the smell of bacon and eggs to finally convince me to come down from my perch.

I wasn't the only one that felt that way. Barb was as enthralled as I was. We went beachcombing after breakfast and returned with a pair of crabs in our bucket. The little crustaceans were all over the place, easy to catch in the flats and tide pools. After the first day, we had steamed crabs every morning for breakfast with our eggs.

Katy, your great-grandparents didn't fight at all that first weekend or almost any other time when they were here. Mother, who wasn't a happy person, never complained and rarely sighed when she was here, despite the unstructured lifestyle and Spartan conditions.

"Mr. B...Phil, I mean," stammered Sammy, as Grandpa raised his eyebrows at the formality of the Mr. "I wish I could have seen it then. It must have been wonderful," she said.

"If you'd have been there back then, you'd be old and decrepit by now, like me," Grandpa pointed out.

"One less barrier to a meaningful relationship," Sam said suggestively.

"Jesus, I give up," I thought. "If they want to play games, let them play."

"Besides, Island Beach isn't much different now than it was then," he said, "But…"

That first summer, there was one experience a couple weeks after our first weekend that I'll never forget. We slipped past the access gate as we usually did on Friday nights, since no one manned it at that late hour. Dad knew a way through the back roads to avoid the roadblock. He'd go out and get a permit the next morning. Anyway, about midmorning the next day, Father was under the hood of the Plymouth working on something or other. He told me he didn't mind working on the car here, unlike at home where car repairs where too often peppered with vocabulary that a nine-year-old boy shouldn't be exposed to.

Barbara was in the outhouse and Mother was taking a nap in the shade of the tarp which Dad had rigged to be a sort of canopy. I hadn't seen anyone at the beach all weekend and I believed we were the only Benys, and maybe even the only people on the island that day.

"Time out Grandpa. Time out!" I interrupted. "What's a Beny? I hear people calling the tourists that at the restaurant and usually not in a very complimentary way."

"A Beny? Well, you are," said Grandpa, at which I frowned. "So is Sammy!" he continued. "So was I when I first came that first summer. Basically, it's a term that locals use to describe the tourists that invade the shore in the summer."

"OK, but why 'Beny'?" I asked.

"No one really knows for sure. The best explanation I've heard is that it stands for <u>B</u>rooklyn, <u>E</u>lizabeth, and <u>N</u>ew <u>Y</u>ork, BENY, which is where a lot of tourists jumped on a train to come to the shore in the old days."

At any rate, everyone but me was preoccupied when, all of a sudden, a rocket ship shrieked across the sky—very low, very close and very, very fast! It woke Mother but she didn't see it and went right back to sleep. Dad and Barbara heard it but didn't see it.

But I was a nine-year old boy enamored with Flash Gordon and Buck Rodgers. It didn't matter to me; either Ming the Merciless was attacking or this was just plain Never-Never Land with pirates, Indians and rocket ships!

When I came hurtling over the dune hollering that I had seen a rocket, my father laughed and complimented me on my vivid imagination. He said it was probably just a low-flying Air force plane. Barb refused to acknowledge that she had even heard the roar in the outhouse since she'd missed seeing it. I told her it was because she was farting too loud! But Mother, instead of disciplining me for using "language", silently mouthed "Momentous!" to me in an exaggerated fashion when Father wasn't looking. I got upset, at first, with my father's and sister's skepticism and with Mother's irrational acceptance. But then I told myself that it didn't matter—this was heaven—not to be questioned, for fear that it would disappear or that I would be banished from this enchanted place forever!

"Operation Bumblebee!" declared Sam.

"That's what some people think," said Grandpa. "In fact, we were hustled off the island by some military types later that day, told to forget what we saw and not to return for the rest of the summer."

"Operation Bumblebee?" I asked, feeling left out.

"In 1945 scientists from Johns Hopkins University came to Island Beach to test the world's first supersonic, anti-aircraft missile," said Samantha.

When we both gawked at her, she said," It's in The Island Beach History Pamphlet. I like that kind of stuff," she said defensively.

"Operation Bumblebee was a success, traveling over one and a half times the speed of sound. This RamJet Rocket was the prototype for the 'Man-of-Iron' missile system that became the primary weapon of the Navy's light cruisers. It also launched the United States into the missile age and, in a very real sense, into the Space Age." She finished shrugging her shoulders. When we continued gaping at her like she was an alien, she said,

"Photographic memory. So sue me!"

"By the end of 1945, Candice Everly, leading a group of the Garden Clubs of America members, forced the rocketeers off the island because of the destruction they were causing to the flora and fauna," added Grandpa.

"So Grandpa," I asked, "Did you ever convince them that you saw Operation Bumblebee?"

"*They* eventually tried to convince *me* of that. However, I remain positive that it was Ming the Merciless or maybe Flash himself!"

"You know, Phil, in all seriousness, if you were seven or eight hundred years younger we'd be exploring the island together this summer!" said Sammy winking shamelessly at my Grandpa whom she had only met today.

After breakfast I shuttled Sam home. Her apartment décor was—how can I put it? Ultra feminine. Lots of stuffed animals. Who would have guessed? And a gorgeous 4-poster bed. I can understand now why she'd wanted to get home, just for the bed alone. And neat as a pin, when anyone who knew her would have predicted that she lived in squalor. Matching quilt and curtains, for God's sake.

We didn't say much but, before she started unpacking her overnight bag, I made a proposal. "Sammy you're invited for dinner and I think you should stay one more night. You still look a little peaked."

"Thanks, Katy," Sam said sincerely. "It was really great of you and your grandfather but I think I'll pass."

"Actually, I'm insisting. Let Grandpa and me take care of you one more night?"

"It's OK Katy; I'm ready to be back in my own digs. You know what I mean, don't you? Thanks again," she said nicely, but firmly, and gave me a hug.

"I do, Sam, but here's the thing. Grandpa ordered me not to come back without you and not to tell you that it was his idea," I confessed. "I can't go back if you don't come!"

Sammy started to protest then stumbled and fell. When I went to pick her up, she was sweating and had that deer-in-the-headlights look. "Sammy—Sammy—are you OK!" I cried.

Her color returned gradually and, at length, she looked up at me like she'd just come out of a trance. She didn't know where she was.

"Sammy, talk to me. Are you OK?" I implored.

She shook her head, getting her bearings and finally said, "I'm OK now. I haven't been eating that well lately, plus I got my period this morning. I'm not sure what that was all about," she admitted.

"That was a sign. In case you didn't catch the gist, it suggested that you spend another night in the care of friends!" I said pushing my agenda.

"Help me inside?" she asked, which I did. After a glass of juice, she acquiesced. "Well it was probably just low blood sugar but OK. Let me put together a few things."

Chapter 25

Look Who's Coming to Dinner?

Sammy lounged around the house reading a book, taking a long shower and sleeping a lot. Having only observed her in the context of the restaurant and partying, it was strange to see this introspective Sam. It made me wonder if she was like this when she was alone, or if this was an artificial persona forced upon her by the presence of Grandpa and me. It's hard to imagine anyone forcing themselves upon Sam, so I suspect that this is simply a side of Sam that other people rarely see.

By dinnertime she was refreshed and back to her perky self.

"You know, I think I'll head home after supper. I'm really fine now," she said, testing the waters.

"*One more night*" I decreed, leaving no room for negotiation.

"OK, OK...OK!" she said. "The trouble is that the living is too easy around here. It's gonna be hard to go back."

"So what's for dinner?" she asked, embracing the hardship.

"Teriyaki chicken, grilled the way only my grandpa can. Seawater potatoes, fresh asparagus and homemade onion bread," I recounted like the waitress I had become.

"Jesus, I'm gonna get fat here and love every calorie!" she commented. "What are 'seawater potatoes'?"

"Basically…seawater potatoes! You boil new potatoes in ocean water with a little bit of a certain kind of seaweed. They're soft and salty with a bit of a bite from the seaweed. You don't need butter or anything on them, you just eat them like apples when they're cool enough."

"Sounds like it's worth a try," she said.

As we entered the patio the smell of the chicken was overwhelming. "What's this?" asked Sam. "Place settings for four? Hope you didn't invite one of my beaus. I'm not looking my best."

"Hello, Samantha," said a voice from behind. It was Evelyn on Grandpa's arm. "Sorry to intrude on your convalescence but Phil and I made this date a while ago and it's difficult for me to arrange a night off, as you might imagine," she said. "How are you feeling?"

"How do I look?" Sam asked daring Evelyn to be candid.

"Honey, you know you don't look great but you don't look that bad either," said Evelyn, unprovoked. I couldn't help thinking, "Better than when Billy put that beating on you," but kept that thought to myself.

"Would you like me to get you a glass of wine?" Evelyn asked.

Sam glanced at her suspiciously. "It's not that vinegar you served to Katy's gourmet the other night?" she joked. That seemed to break the ice.

"No, that's for Phil and me. I brought some of the really cheap stuff for you since you probably wouldn't know the difference," she cracked back, accepting the opening Sam had graced her with.

Grandpa looked to Evelyn before offering me a glass. She said, "I don't care what you do in the privacy of your home as long as I never hear of anyone underage being served in Evelyn's." Sam and I silently agreed to comply with her request and never mention my drinking incident the night Billy hit her.

Having Evelyn wait on her was an enlightening experience for Sam. Evelyn could stare down the bulls at the running in Pamplona, but when she waited on you, you sincerely felt you were her only concern! She must have been one helluva of a waitress in her day! It wasn't hard to see what Grandpa saw in her.

After two or three glasses of a truly exceptional wine, Sam and

Evelyn were gossiping like old friends. Watching them I had a sudden insight that Evelyn was very much like Sammy when she was young, and that, sometime in the future, Sammy would be very much like Evelyn is now. I carelessly shrugged off that notion; it must've been the wine talking.

Anyway, dinner was delicious. We cut up Sammy's portions so she could chew them. She loved the potatoes.

During dessert, a beautiful fruit tort from the restaurant, Sammy said, "You know, Evelyn, Phil was telling us about the old days on the Island and made it sound like the Garden of Eden. Do you remember it being that wonderful?"

"Everyone's youth looks wonderful viewed through the telescope of time," she said, pretending to be cynical.

But after considering the question for a moment she asked, "Do you remember when we were 14? Well, you must have been 15 or 16, Phil?"

He nodded. "Eddie's," he said.

"Eddie's," she agreed.

"So what's Eddie's? I asked.

"And why was it so special?" said Samantha.

"What was special was that it ever existed..." said Evelyn, "...on the Seaside Boardwalk."

"It was built over the sand on the beach between Seaside and Seaside Heights, pretty much where the Boardwalk is today but a lot smaller," said Grandpa. "It was truly a sight to see. As brash, crude and pure American—make that pure New Jerseyan—as you can get! There was nothing subtle, or sophisticated about it. It was heaven!"

"There wasn't much to this part of heaven. The walls just folded down to reveal an open-air pavilion looking out on the beach. There was a changing room with those numbered wire baskets to lock up your clothes and things. And a concession stand inside where you could get a decent hamburger, fries and a Coke, or an ice cream and..." Evelyn paused.

"Pins!" exclaimed Grandpa. "That's what drew all the guys here. And the guys drew the girls, who drew more guys. Eddie piped music over loudspeakers out to the beach. God, I haven't thought about Eddie's in 40 years."

"You know, Evelyn, it wasn't much to look at but it was pretty cool. Tacky, but cool," he said.

"Oh, oh!" exclaimed Evelyn. "Do you remember that one pinball machine? What was it?" she asked, excited.

"I know the one you're talking about. I think it was Mermaid, or something," he said.

"What was so special…? Sam started to ask.

"It wasn't really special," said Evelyn. "Remember, Phil, three games, five balls for a quarter?"

"So *you* played pinball?" Sammy asked Evelyn

"Oh, she was better than most of the guys," Grandpa said.

"Better than you," she teased.

Shooting her a mock dirty look, Grandpa continued, "There was one machine, one of the better ones, except that it was always shorting out and gave you a shock every time you hit the right flipper…or maybe it was the left," he said. "So they put a wooden pallet in front of it to insulate you from the ground, especially if your feet were wet, so you wouldn't get shocked."

"So let me guess," said Sammy. "You moved the pallet so people would get shocked and leave without finishing their game?"

"I like the way you think, Samantha," said Evelyn. "It didn't hurt them, really, but it was annoying as hell. Usually they didn't get past their second ball."

"Then you'd move the pallet back and claim their games," said Sam.

"Or just wear rubber-soled sneakers," Evelyn confirmed. "We took turns so we didn't draw attention to the scam."

"Phil, do you remember that one game, that one extraordinary game?" Evelyn asked.

"You know I do," confirmed Grandfather.

"A special machine?" I asked.

"Yes, a special machine but what I was talking about was a particular game that your grandfather played," explained Evelyn. "Do you remember the name of that machine, Phil?"

"You know I do. So do you." he said.

"You still don't like to talk about it, do you?" asked Evelyn.

My Island Beach

"Well," he sighed, "to tell you the truth, before I was kind of embarrassed about it. Now kids just don't get pinball. Now that they have video games and computers," Grandpa said petulantly.

"C'mon Grandpa. Stop whining and tell us about it," I said.

"Phil, why don't you stop being coy and tell us about it. Or tell Evelyn to buzz off," said Sam, cutting to the heart of the issue.

"Yeah, Phil," agreed Evelyn, ganging up with the rest of us. "Shit or get off the pot!"

I've never, ever seen Grandpa shy away from talking about himself or from telling a good tale, but he was definitely reticent about this one. I figured he was about to refuse outright when he said, "OK, OK, OK, I know when I'm outnumbered!" And in that instant you could observe the metamorphosis from kindly old grandpa to P. T. Barnum himself.

Well, if you must have the story, then you must have it. There was something in the air that day, you can ask Evelyn.

I had one thin dime from returning two 32-oz. Crush bottles for the deposit. I'd spent most of the morning scavenging for them, which is how I generated most of my pinball money, and 'Knockout' was open. This was what, 1951 or 1952? It was the best machine of the day but primitive compared to the pinball machines today. If you can imagine, it was built in a wooden box, not the painted press wood used to make modern machines but an oak box on stilts with a garish picture of fighters in a ring surrounded by all kinds of mayhem, including medics carrying away an unconscious fighter and a scantily clad cigarette girl. The backdrops didn't even having scoring wheels then—not mechanical ones, anyway. You lit up 100,ooo, 200,ooo, 300,ooo boxes until you got to a 900,ooo. After that it was 1, 2, 3, 4, 5 MILLION! Imagine, for one thin dime, even though a dime was actually worth something back then, you could get up to 5,900,000 points! If that isn't a bargain, I don't know what is!

Inside the box, it had the usual two flippers which, by the way, was a relatively new innovation at the time, bumpers, and some targets to aim at. But this game was special—a technological marvel. Inside of a diamond-shaped area in the center of the game were two mechanical boxers that duked it out in response to your success with manipulating the little metal ball. Nothing spectacular by today's standards, but to us it was the pinnacle of pinball technology, an electronic/mechanical game with bells and whistles like we'd never seen before. I don't think I can convey to you how really novel that was. And, as far as I'm concerned, for all the hoopla, things have gone downhill since then. Shows what an old fogey I am.

Anyway, I'd usually save up a quarter because you got more for your money, one game for a dime, but three games for a quarter. But the prospects of putting together another 15 cents didn't look good and I had a feeling...a feeling that I was going to do something special that day and it wouldn't wait until tomorrow.

I inserted my dime and, on the first ball, I knocked out the other boxer and lit all the Specials. We were so fascinated with these amazing devices that, when we didn't have the funds to play, we'd read the complicated rules that outlined how to get the higher scores. That was most of the time.

You didn't get any real points until you lit the Specials. A good player might work hard and get them lit on the fourth or fifth ball. Evelyn, who actually was a much better player than me, occasionally lit the Specials on the third ball. On Knockout, it was usually took her until the fourth or fifth ball or not at all.

People started to gather around. On the second ball I won my first free game. That puts the number 1 on the inconspicuous little wheel located in the basket of the backdrop's sexy cigarette girl. But it also makes a little chunking kind of sound. Like a hammer on a piece of lead. No reverberation. You got a sort of gratifying, Pavlovian feeling from this not-too-pleasant sound, which is the advantage of a mechanical device over an electronic one!

At that point a lot of people were gathering around.

By the fourth ball, I had four free games. I was in the zone like I'd never been before. It was like I couldn't lose!

But the fifth ball, the last ball—it was like it was part of me. Not only could I anticipate it like I was reading its mind, but I actually felt like I could control it. It was positively metaphysical.

I won five more free games on the fifth ball—chunk, chunk,

chunk, chunk and chunk! That's as high as the wheel goes, up to nine, since it was only a single digit indicator. After that I was just showing off. I took it up to 5,500ooo, 5,600ooo, 5,700ooo, 5,800ooo.

At that point, I whispered to Evelyn, 'Play my free games but don't let anyone—not no one—touch this machine till that ball drains.'

I was looking at Grandpa with SKEPTICISM written in large capital letters all over my face. A big word for my little face. This was the tallest of tall tales he'd ever tried on me. Evelyn, seeing my cynicism, took up the tale at this point.

"Kathleen, I was there and it was weird beyond comprehension. It was like a primal struggle between your grandfather and that machine for control of the ball. And your grandfather won every time. He made shots that I know he wasn't capable of...hell, nobody was. I know your granddad likes to tell his stories but this is no tale," she insisted. Evelyn continued the narrative.

On the last ball though, when he was almost to 5,900ooo, your grandfather did something that made him a legend at the ripe old age of 15. After he whispered to me to use his free games, he gave the ball one more hard flip and walked calmly out of Eddie's, went down to the beach and dove into the water! Never even looked back. Never asked me how it ended, not then, not later, not to this very day!

Well, the crowd, and it was truly a crowd by this time, gasped. But the ball went to the top and kept hitting bumpers and bands for probably a minute. It kept causing the defending fighter to be knocked down. That's a long time for an old-fashioned pinball machine not to drain. It was like a perpetual motion machine. Bumper to band to bumper to bumper to band again. When it finally did drain, one guy lunged for the flippers but changed his mind before I would've stopped him. And I would've! You could almost read his thoughts, 'What's the point? Everything's pegged. You can't do any better than this.'

Your grandfather made a score that could be tied but could never be beaten on that machine—5,900,<u>ooo</u> and 9 free games.

"Was something wrong with it? Was it broken?" I asked skeptically.

"Of course not!" said Sam. I was beginning to think that Sam the Cynic was a closet romantic. I really didn't know this girl.

"I played all nine of those free games and only won two more, playing at the top of my form! Nothing was wrong with that machine!" Evelyn said.

"You're wrong about my motives, though," Grandpa said, having remained silent during Evelyn's telling of the story's conclusion. "That wasn't a calculated move on my part…walking away at the end."

"But that's what you always told me," Evelyn said.

"Because I didn't think you'd believe the truth."

"And you do now?" she asked, confused.

"I'm not sure. But if you don't believe me now, it's OK," he said philosophically. We all waited impatiently for the explanation.

"The reason I walked away was because it was so pure. I owned that ball, that day, on that machine. I could have kept on going for another 6,000<u>ooo</u> if I wanted. I knew it, you knew it, and everyone else knew it too, Evelyn. And nobody who wasn't there will ever believe it."

"I left that ball up there because I knew it would peg at 5,900<u>ooo</u>! There was nothing left to accomplish, nothing left to prove. It would have been wrong not to walk away and, instead, to try and milk it," he concluded.

After a pregnant pause he said, "And if you ever ask me about this when I'm sober, I'll deny it all. Everything!" he vowed, trying to make a joke of it. But it wasn't a joke to him.

"Momentous," Grandpa mumbled, barely discernible to me and unheard by the others. After dessert and coffee, Grandpa escorted Evelyn home.

Chapter 26

Seeds of Discontent

After they left, we started doing dishes, then looked at each other and said, simultaneously, "Morning!" and left them. We'd had a pretty easy day, lying around, napping and, in general, accomplishing nothing of substance. So we weren't ready for bed yet even though it was late.

"Wow, Katy, your grandpa's really out there," said Sam, laughing but impressed. "It must've been cool to have someone like that around to talk to?"

"Still is."

"No kidding. Cool story," Sam said. "Do you believe it?"

"I sorta do," I said. "I want to, don't you?"

We finished up Evelyn's wine and made small talk until Grandpa returned.

After sitting down next to Sammy, he said, "You know, Sam, Evelyn really likes you."

"Did she say so?" Sam asked.

"No," answered Grandpa truthfully. "But she does. I can tell."

"I know," Sam said.

"She does?" I asked. I was under the distinct impression that

Evelyn didn't approve of Sammy's wild lifestyle.

"Well, Sam's a lot like Evelyn was at that age," observed Grandpa.

"Really?" I asked, surprised that someone as self-possessed as Evelyn could ever have been as wild as Sam, despite my similar feeling earlier in the evening.

"I'm not surprised," said Samantha.

"You know, she's thinking about retiring?" said Grandpa.

"She is?" we asked in unison. It was hard to imagine Evelyn's without…well…Evelyn.

"But she needs someone to take over the business," said Grandpa. I had a sneaking suspicion this was leading somewhere.

"Have you ever thought of going into the restaurant business, Samantha?" he asked.

So this was where he was going. I was afraid that he had me in mind. Which left me relieved but ever so slightly insulted. But it was too ludicrous to even consider. "You think that Sammy wants to be a waitress forever? A lifer! God, Grandpa, what are you thinking. Get a grip!" I blurted.

"Evelyn's not a waitress," he said, giving me a scathing look! "And I can think of several worse things to be. Insensitive, thoughtless and blundering come to mind." I was flustered by his rebuke.

Sam piped in. "Mind your own business, Katy," she said, dismissively, momentarily reminding me again of Evelyn. Turning to Grandpa, she said, "To answer your question, Phil, I was thinking of staying on after the season and asking Evelyn for more responsibility. Do you think she'd actually consider selling the place? Did she put you up to this? Did my name come up?" she asked in rapid succession. I couldn't believe what I was hearing, but I didn't dare say a word.

"Nope, your name didn't come up. In spite of the fact that she likes you, she thinks you're pretty flaky," he said.

"Yeah," Sammy said resignedly, giving up on the idea.

"But if you proposed the idea to her with a realistic business plan, she might change her opinion." he counseled.

"And where the fuck am I going to get a business plan?" she

asked caustically.

"First of all you need to change your attitude, clean up your mouth, and stop thinking like a flake!" Grandpa snapped back. This was getting very heavy.

I had expected her to lash out again but, instead she waited expectantly for him to finish, unperturbed. "Good," he said. "Now, I can probably get my accountant to help you develop a plan. She owes me a couple of favors. But don't waste her time and my favors if you're not serious," Grandpa warned.

"You think she'd do it?" asked Sam.

"You mean my accountant or Evelyn?" Grandpa asked.

"Both," she asked, pensively.

"Yes and no, respectively," he paused. "Doesn't mean you shouldn't try." On that ambiguous note he went to bed.

Upset by Grandpa's reprimand and Sam's dismissal and embarrassed by my own lack of perceptiveness, I had been silent during their exchange. "Sam, I'm sorry." I apologized.

"Huh? Oh, get over it, Katy," she said, distracted by the possibilities Grandfather had just paraded in front of her.

"No, it's just that I know you're going to college and it never occurred to me," I fumbled, trying to defend myself but only making it worse.

"You know what, Katy? I worked hard in college and I got good grades. But it's not for me. You know what something like owning Evelyn's would mean to me?" A rhetorical question. "It means I'd have a place where people know my name and not because I slept with them all—or they thought I did. It means I'd have a place in the world where I belong, a home…control over my life." She paused.

"It's not for you Katy, that's why you couldn't see it for me," she said.

"You're right," I confessed, fighting the urge to defend myself and starting to cry.

"Damn straight!" she said. "Now get over it. Right now I need a friend to talk to."

We talked into the wee hours, not just about the restaurant but also about boys and aspirations and sex and world issues and, well, sex.

Finally, from out of nowhere, Sam said, "You know, you're like two different people."

Having already started to doze off, I perked up at that remark. "You said that before. What the hell do you mean?" I demanded.

"When?" she asked.

"You said it when you were coming out of the anesthesia."

"Really?" she asked. "Boy, I gave away all my deep, dark secrets, didn't I? First, *'semper ubi sub ubi,'* and now this."

"But you are," she reiterated. When her sudden switch back to the original topic didn't register, she rephrased it. "Like two people in one body."

"What do mean, like Sybil? Like two different personalities that are unaware of each other?" I asked.

"No," she replied, thoughtfully. "More like twins. You know, the kind that finish each other's sentences and get pissed when their parents make them wear different clothes. Like Siamese twins, really, joined at the hip," she said.

"If we're so much alike and in the same body, what makes you think there are two of us?" I asked logically.

"Don't know." she replied flippantly, flopped down on the bed and promptly went to sleep.

As unsettling and unsatisfying as her response was, I did likewise.

Chapter 27

When You Wish Upon a Star

Morning was overcast and uncharacteristically cool for what had been an almost picture perfect summer. It seemed ominous. While Sam was still sleeping, since she hadn't yet recovered fully from her surgery, Grandpa and I sat down to breakfast. Grandpa was reading the paper and I was silently revisiting the events of last evening.

"You're just sitting there trying to figure out what my angle is in all this, aren't you?" he said. I hadn't been, but now that he mentioned it, I did wonder what his motives were.

"I was," I lied.

"You never considered that I might be completely altruistic in this matter of Sammy and Evelyn and the restaurant?" he said.

"Not for a second," I said cynically.

"And you can't figure it out?"

"Not a clue."

"And you're going to badger me mercilessly until I 'fess up, aren't you?" Apparently he wanted to get something off his chest.

"You know how I can be Grandpa," I warned.

"And sooner or later I'll buckle under your relentless inquisition and spill my guts," he said, continuing our little vignette.

"Sooner," I said.

"So here it is," he began with the prototypical sigh that precedes a confession.

"Before your grandmother, there were feelings between us, Evelyn and me, that is. But we were only kids. Then Katy came along and eclipsed any feelings I might have developed for Evelyn." He paused. "After Katy disappeared, well, Evelyn would have taken up where we left off before Katy, even though we both knew it wouldn't have worked." He sighed again.

"As we grew older, we became extremely close but in a platonic way. Evelyn never married, though I know she had several offers, and I never remarried. However, in recent years, some of the old feelings started blossoming again."

"So what made you start feeling differently towards each other?" I asked.

"Nothing really, nothing definite. Maybe the realization on my part that the passionate, all-consuming relationship I had with Katy would never be repeated. I'm not really sure I'd want it to. And that what I was feeling about Evelyn was valid and certainly not what one friend feels for another. Much more, but different than the passion I felt for your grandmother. So we've become romantically involved."

"And is it wonderful?" I asked.

"Yes, but in a totally different way than with Katy. A soothing, encompassing warmth of love. Stable, dependable, but not in any way routine or boring. Something, no offense, a 17 year-old could appreciate."

"So there must be some conflict," I said. He didn't respond.

I thought about it. He watched.

"The restaurant!" I reasoned.

"Evelyn's," he confirmed.

"Pretty selfish of you, Grandpa."

"You know, you're a real ball-buster in a quiet sort of way, but that's exactly right. I'm not interested, after all these years, in sharing her with that surrogate husband of hers."

"In my defense," he argued, "I sympathize with her reluctance

My Island Beach

to hang it up. It carried her through a tough part of her life and made her someone in this town. It provided stability and a reason to get up in the morning. I know that's hard to give up so I didn't ask her to. I told her that when she was done with it, when she was good and ready, I'd be waiting. I wasn't going anywhere. And if she got out of the business before she or I died, I'd marry her the very next day!"

"Oh Grandpa, that's wonderful. Selfish, but wonderful," I gave him a big hug and kissed him on the cheek. "I take it she's ready?" I reasoned.

"She is, but only if she finds a suitable buyer. She's way too attached to the place emotionally and financially can't afford to just close it down. She won't sell it to anyone she thinks will destroy what she's created. She's had two excellent offers already, one with a major restaurant chain who she turned down flat!" he revealed.

"And you think Sam has a shot?" I asked.

"Do you, Phil? Do you, Kate?" demanded Sam, walking in at the most inopportune moment.

"Sam!" I exclaimed. "I wasn't trying to imply that you couldn't run Evelyn's. All I meant was that if she was turning down pros, I doubt if she would consider anyone without experience."

"Got it Kate," she snapped. "Excuse me for not being as coldly rational as you are!"

I wrote it off as the reaction of someone who had indulged her wildest hopes last night, probably for the first time in her life. Now, in the cold light of day, she realized that her chances were near zero.

"You didn't mention last night that she'd turned down other offers, Phil," Sam accused. "From pros!"

"You wouldn't have taken the idea seriously if I had," rationalized Grandpa, unapologetic about his duplicity.

Samantha didn't say anything but you could see she was angry. Not so much at Grandpa, as she was at herself…for allowing herself to hope.

"Samantha, Katy's wrong!" he said. "In case you haven't figured it out yet, this here is a magic place. Eden and Never-Never

Land all rolled into one. Where marshmallows grow on bushes and aliens invade in their rocket ships. Where pirates bury treasure and men walk the plank. Where animals are named after spies. And conflicts between Man and nature, or even Man and machine, are simple, basic—fundamental. Things are right or wrong; there is very little gray here."

Sam remained unconvinced. But I was starting to be. I wanted to be!

"If its right for you to own the restaurant, which we all know it is, it will happen despite any rationalizations to the contrary!" Grandpa insisted. He reminded me of Burt Lancaster in "The Rainmaker," the ultimate con man who ended up believing his own spiel.

"Sam, as perceptive as my granddaughter is, she hasn't figured that out yet," he continued. "Has she?" he asked Sam.

Sam considered his perspective for a moment and said, "Have you got the number of your accountant handy?"

Chapter 28

Losing Focus

I wasn't expecting to get a Saturday night off but Janie, who was sick a lot, was feeling good for a change and wanted the time. So I got bumped.

Which didn't bother me much. I hated to lose the money but I hadn't seen Daniel all week. He was busy with a visitor from out of town…and he'd invited me to a party.

We decided to meet at the party since he was still preoccupied with his visitor. I was about forty-five minutes late, so things were already hopping when I arrived. I wandered around for a while, but there was no sign of Daniel.

"Katy," said a voice from the next room. It was Billy.

"Hi Billy," I said, especially wary of Billy in a drinking situation. Then Jason appeared from around a corner. The combination really made me feel uncomfortable.

"Hey Katy," he said, all warm and familiar.

"Hey Jason," I replied, non-committally.

"Can I get you a beer?" he asked.

"No thanks, not right now," I replied.

"You're not still pissed off about the other night?" he asked. I could see Billy grimace at the mention of something he'd rather forget.

"No, I'm not Jas," I said. "But I'm meeting someone else tonight, thanks."

"Not the D-man? You aren't serious about him, are you?" he asked derisively.

"It's none of your business, Jason," I said, "But yeah, I am meeting Daniel here tonight."

"Buzz off, Jason," said Billy, out of character, at least the character that hit Sam in the bar that night. That got him a very dirty look from Jason, who stalked off.

"He's not too happy with me since I went on the wagon," Billy laughed. "God, I must have been one miserable prick to be around when I was drunk."

I didn't know what to say to that so I changed the subject. "Sam's working tonight, Billy."

"I know," he said. "If she wasn't I wouldn't be here."

"Did you give her my message?" he asked.

"I did."

"Good," he said sincerely. He didn't ask how she responded. Apparently he didn't want, or need, to know. She'd reacted better than I had expected her to.

Her understanding and surprisingly insightful response was, "In spite of what everyone who was there thought, once that scenario started to unfold, it was all destiny, preordained, especially for Billy. I was the only one with a choice and I'm happy with the one I made." Pretty much what Daniel had said.

None of which I revealed to Billy that night.

"You know why I don't want to see her?" he asked.

"Billy, that's none of my business," I said.

"I won't see her because I'm pretty sure I can't do it. If I hit someone that I care about as much as Sam, then there isn't much hope for me," he confided, disregarding my lack of curiosity. He was making no attempt to defend himself to me.

"She didn't leave you much choice," I rationalized. Wait a minute…what the fuck was I doing defending this misogynist from himself!? "She told me what she said. She would have said worse if she had had to. She would have said anything to keep you from putting a beating on Ray," I said, sympathetic towards the Billy I had seen on the pump-out boat but confused about what I felt about the Billy I had seen in the bar that night.

"Can you imagine someone doing something like what she did for Ray? God, she's one terrific lady," he beamed, then soured. "We both know I could have walked away. Katy, don't let me off the hook. It'd be too easy. Right now I need a conscience, not a cheerleader!"

Then I remembered what I could never forget, in spite of everything! "You should have walked away from her, you son-of-a-bitch!" I spewed, meaning every word of it and crying a little. "If Sammy *ever* finds it in her heart to forgive you, *you* had better not, ever forgive yourself!" With that I marched off to find Daniel.

Daniel was just arriving with someone who I presumed was his visitor. As I approached I noted that his friend was blond-haired and fair but somehow bore a vague resemblance to the Mediterranean-skinned Daniel.

"Katy," said Daniel when he recognized me. "There's someone I want you to meet," he said, turning towards his guest.

"Katy, this is my brother, Jon."

Well, that explained the vague resemblance. Still, I would have never have put them together as siblings...not even cousins.

"I can see my brother's taste in women is impeccable, as always," he said, shaking my hand.

"And I can see that his brother is as silver-tongued and insincere as he is," I said. What kind of crap was that? At least Billy was sincere, if flawed.

"Whoa, guess I had that coming," he apologized, again a little too smoothly. He then stuck his tongue out as if trying to see if it were silver-colored. Cute. "I've been living in L. A. where straight talk is considered poor taste," he said.

"Which is the truth, but still sounded a little calculating, didn't it?" he asked, sincerely this time.

I nodded in agreement.

"I wish I was going to be around a little longer to get to know you," he said. "I could use a reality check and I've got a feeling you'd provide one. My little brother is very impressed with you, in case you haven't noticed." he said, realizing he'd gone a little too far.

"And now I'm going to shut up and get a drink. Would you two like something?" he asked.

"Beer," said Daniel.

"Nothing," I replied. Off he went.

"That's your brother?"

"That's my brother," he confirmed. "A little hard to take, lately, but really a good guy."

"You know, I got that feeling," I said sincerely. "But I never would have picked him as your brother."

"Twin brother," he said.

"You're kidding?" He shook his head.

"No shit!" I said. "You know, one of our neighbors, when I was growing up had twin girls. One was short, slender and fair—platinum blond. The other was tall, built, and dark. But so similar in personality that I don't think they realized they didn't even look like they were related. They even wore the same clothes. Truly weird!"

"That wasn't how it was for us," he started cryptically but changed the subject when Jon reappeared with our drinks.

The remainder of the evening was uneventful.

Chapter 29

Smoke and Mirrors

"Look at this," I said, as I handed Daniel an old National Geographic.

"Oh, so you found it," he said. "What did you think?"

"Cool," I replied. "I actually remember reading about this a long time ago when it first came out."

"Yeah, it was pretty wild at the time. Have you met Pete McLain?" he asked.

"No, but Grandpa talks about him all the time. So it was your brother who worked with him on this?"

"Me, too," he added, warming up to the topic. "But it was all Pete's idea. We just supplied the muscle."

"He made arrangements with a group of conservationists in Alaska to get hold of peregrine falcon eggs. But not before we built the hack tower in the sedge. Pete had a stellar reputation, after his successes with the osprey program.

"Grandpa showed me the hack tower when we were out kayaking. So how many eggs did he bring back?" I asked.

"I don't remember," said Daniel. "Does it say in the article?"

"No."

"But it really got wild when he decided he didn't want the

chicks to imprint on humans," said Daniel. "Which meant they couldn't see us."

"So that's when you started doing the puppets?" I said.

"Yeah, he had these really lame peregrine puppets made up and, after the chicks were born, we'd climb up to the hack tower and pretend to regurgitate food from the puppets. Some of the kids thought it was nuts."

"Did you?" I asked.

"Nah," he said. "It was definitely worth it."

"So they put your brother's picture in the National Geo?" I asked.

"No," he said, and then hesitated.

"Yeah, I saw they put your name on the caption but it was your brother in the picture," I said.

"Katy," Daniel said quietly. "That's me in the picture. It was labeled correctly."

"No, this picture here," I said, pointing to the picture of a blond 15 or 16 year old, reaching onto the platform with a peregrine puppet on his hand. "Is there a picture of you here too?" I asked.

"Katy, that's me in the picture," Daniel insisted.

"Then I'm blind—that's your brother." I hated it when people didn't pay attention to me.

"Katy," he said, patronizing, but not meaning to be, "That's me—be quiet!" he commanded when I started to disagree again. "That's me. Let me explain," he said, calmer now.

"I used to look like Jon, two or three years ago," he began.

"Nobody changes that much. That fast!" I said.

"I did," he said. "It was very disorienting."

"Your hair color went from blond to dark brown?"

"Katy, my eyes went from deep blue to brown, my eyebrows started coming in heavily and I went from shaving every 2 or 3 days to being able to grow a full mustache and beard in a week. Katy, I'm telling you it freaked everyone out but especially Jon and me!" he explained.

"One of the reasons I decided to go out of state to college was to get a fresh start, away from people who knew me before I changed so radically."

"Wow!" I murmured, unable to come up with anything better.

"That's not all," he said.

"Jon, our folks, and I always figured we were identical twins," he continued.

"Before you changed." Ah, reality check.

"That's right," he said. "So, after I changed, we went in for genetic testing."

"Let me guess," I ventured. "You're not even brothers or cousins. You're not even related." I laughed. I couldn't ignore the evidence before my own eyes.

"No!" he objected upset, I think, by my frivolous take on something that was troubling him deeply. "Genetically, we're identical twins! Clones!" That was even more twisted than my improbable explanation.

"You can't be," I protested. "You're barely the same species!"

"Nevertheless, we are identical!" he insisted. "The outfit that did the test figured they must have mixed up the samples so they reran them, no charge."

"This time they made sure the samples went directly from us to the lab. Same result—we're identical twins."

"No—that can't be!" I protested again.

"All the same, we are," he repeated. "They were so freaked out that they contacted one of those 'Nature vs. Nurture' twin research groups without our permission."

"Isn't that unethical?" I beseeched.

"Sort of," Daniel replied. "But they didn't release our names."

"And?" I asked.

"And, the research group agrees with you. It's not possible."

"So, they repeated the test a second time. We came in at different times and they made sure neither of us was palming a phony blood sample!" He seemed relieved to be dumping all this on me. I was certain that no one but his immediate family was aware of this.

"Still identical?" I asked already knowing the answer.

"Still identical," he confirmed.

"That's not the worst of it!" God, there's more!

"People don't realize it but being a twin, especially an identical one is a two-edged sword. Most twins don't even realize it," he stated. "The pros are that you have someone you can depend on, absolutely. Someone who knows how you think, understands how you feel, likes what you like. A true soul mate, so to speak, an extension of yourself, closer than most married couples. It's like having a second 'you' to help, to talk to. Someone you don't have to compete with."

"The flip side," he continued, "which most twins never discover, thankfully, until one of them dies, is that a twin is a dependent. That you tend to compromise to conform to each other. Since you've done it from birth, you don't even realize you're doing it. Like being a Borg, you know, on Star Trek. You don't know you're not fulfilled until you're free of the Collective. Or, the other possibility is that you can't cope with your newfound freedom." He paused, waiting to see if I understood.

"And you…which were you?" I asked, indicating that I at least comprehended the dilemma.

"I was liberated by the separation. I went through a period of personal growth that I know I never could have experienced as part of a pair," he said.

"And Jon?" I asked suspecting I already knew the answer.

"Jon was lost, muddled. He had a difficult time coping," Daniel continued. "Even though I was having the time of my life, I also knew exactly what he was going through!"

I was trying to absorb this weird set of circumstances.

"It got so bad that our family doctor suggested counseling. Jon was getting extremely depressed," Daniel said.

"So you went to a shrink?"

"We did, but only for one session. He, the shrink that is, suggested a marriage counselor!" Daniel said.

I laughed so hard I snorted through my nose!

"Which was exactly my reaction to his suggestion," he said laughing, too. "Jon just got angry."

"But we tried it and it really seemed to help," Daniel continued. "He got me to focus on the positive aspects of an unconditional partner," he said, "and he got Jon to appreciate his newfound space, and privacy, and unrestricted choices."

"It helped a lot. Especially Jon," Daniel said.

"But even the marriage counselor and shrink were freaked. The shrink even asked to see the DNA test results," Daniel said.

"It still doesn't explain how that could be," I said unsatisfied, but intrigued.

"No it doesn't," Daniel agreed. "I doubt if we'll ever know!"

Chapter 30

Putting it on the Line!

"Wish me luck," said Sammy as she went over to talk to Evelyn.

I did. She was going to need it.

"Evelyn, can I talk to you?" Sam asked.

It was the shank of the evening. In fact, it had been a quiet night in the restaurant. The ocean breeze had abated; there was enough wind to keep the insects from being a problem, but it was subdued as the evening progressed to its natural conclusion. We weren't seating anyone new. We just had to take care of the customers that were still finishing up their meals.

"Sure, Sam. What's up?" asked Evelyn.

"Could we go sit down? Over at your table?" Sam asked. "This will take a few minutes."

Evelyn's eyebrow went up. People, especially employees, didn't ask to go sit at Evelyn's table. It wasn't a rule she'd made, just something that had evolved. Evelyn didn't answer at first.

Finally she agreed. "Alright, Sam, let's go sit down and talk." Maybe it was just that no one had ever asked.

They seated themselves and Evelyn said, "What is it you wanted to talk to me about?"

"I'm interested in buying your restaurant," Sam proposed, as if was the most reasonable request in the world.

I expected laughter or derision. Instead Evelyn was shocked. "My restaurant?" she asked as if she'd misheard.

"Evelyn's," Sammy confirmed.

That induced the laughter, finally, followed by wonder and then enlightenment.

"Philip put you up to this!"

"He put the idea in my head," she confirmed, "but I was already planning on asking you to take me on full time and teach me the business."

"But, now you've decided you'd like to take over?" Evelyn asked.

"Yes," Sam replied.

"I don't think so," Evelyn said, rising from her chair, signifying the discussion was over.

"Hey, I know it's a long shot, Evelyn, but at least have the decency to hear me out," Sam challenged. No response from Evelyn and she didn't sit down. I don't think anyone had ever spoken to her in that way.

"Didn't anyone ever take a chance on you?" Sam asked when Evelyn didn't comment.

Evelyn hesitated, and then sat down without responding. "Before I hear your pitch—and I will hear it if you still want to make it—I want to ask you a few questions. Fair enough?" asked Evelyn.

"Fair enough," agreed Sam. Like she had a choice.

"Sam, you like to party, right?" asked Evelyn.

Sam nodded her head.

"Running this place doesn't leave much time for partying," said Evelyn.

"I know."

"You know but are you really prepared to give it up?" Evelyn said.

"Evelyn, who was the all-time biggest party-animal when you were a teenager?" Sam asked.

"That's easy," replied Evelyn. "Joey Diligi."

"What happened to him?" asked Sam.

"Let's see, divorced, disabled on the job…his back or something. An alcoholic, and moved back in with his mom."

"With his mom?"

"It's an Italian thing," Evelyn replied impatiently. "What's your point?"

"My point is that I've never heard of Joey Diligi but I've heard of you. Everyone knows Evelyn's and Evelyn," Sam argued.

"So you want everyone to know your name?" asked Evelyn.

"Everyone already knows me. 'The easy waitress at Evelyn's with the smart mouth'," said Sam.

"So you want respect?" asked Evelyn.

"Yeah," said Sam. "Is there something wrong with that? And a place to call home. My home where people know me. Should I apologize for that Evelyn?"

Evelyn looked at Sam, sizing up what she'd said. "No, there's nothing wrong that," she finally concluded. "But can you do the job?"

"Do you think I can't?" Sam replied cockily.

Evelyn didn't reply.

"Evelyn, I don't want to belittle what you do here. It's important and it's hard. But I can do almost anything I put my mind to, and I can do this." Sam said. "And we both know it!"

"What about school?" Evelyn asked next.

"What about school?" Sam asked, confused by Evelyn's question.

"Don't you want to finish your degree?" asked Evelyn.

"I finished."

"In three years?" Evelyn was obviously impressed.

"I didn't know you were counting," said Sam, surprised. "Yeah, in three years. *Summa cum laude*. Evelyn, I'm actually pretty smart.

Chapter 31

Let's Make a Deal

"Any more questions?" asked Sam.

Evelyn was about to ask another, then thought better of it. "Nope, you've got the floor, Sam, just hold on one minute," said Evelyn.

Evelyn followed the last customer of the night to the door, said "Goodnight" and locked the door behind them. We would be another 30 to 45 minutes, cleaning up the place to make it presentable for tomorrow.

"OK, Samantha, you have my undivided attention," said Evelyn as she settled back down at her table where she had left Sam. Bruno and the waitresses were hanging around, their curiosity about Evelyn's uncharacteristic behavior, transparent.

"Ladies and gentlemen," Evelyn announced. Staring at Bruno, she continued, "and I use the term loosely. Please see to the cleanup and leave Sam and me to our business. Katy, you might as well join us," Evelyn said to me, "Since you've eavesdropped on everything else up to this point."

Then to the others, "Ladies, the two girls will tell you everything tomorrow, if they wish and take on the cleaning chores to make up for tonight."

Evelyn had spoken!

"Sorry, Sam," said Evelyn. "You're on."

"OK," said Sam, "Here's my proposal. For one year, I'm your slave. I take over as much of the hostessing, presumably all, as soon as you think I'm ready. You pay me a salary and leave the day-to-day stuff to me."

"After I've taken over the hostessing, you gradually train me in the other aspects of the business, hiring…"

"And firing," interrupted Evelyn.

"And firing. Scheduling, buying, menus, the books, *etc*. At the end of the year, I make a down payment and you loan me the rest of the money to purchase 51% of the business at that time."

"Really," said Evelyn, skeptically.

"That's my proposal," said Sam, unfazed by Evelyn's unenthusiastic response.

"So I'm a silent partner, with *my* money on the line and you have *total* control?" asked Evelyn, finding it difficult to believe what she was hearing.

"That's right," confirmed Sam, still confident.

"And what do I get for the privilege of risking everything and having control over nothing?" asked Evelyn incredulously.

"Forty nine percent of the profits. And monthly payments with interest against the principal for the unpaid balance of the fifty one percent. And a rest, with the peace of mind that your life's work is in good hands," said Sam smiling.

"What if I'm not happy with the arrangement before the year is up? Before I put my future in your hands," Evelyn asked.

"Then the deal's off," said Sam simply.

"And what do you get for your year of slave labor?" asked Evelyn.

"I think the technical term for it is 'squat'," said Sam without a touch of sarcasm.

"You know you'll have to pay rent on the use of the building which I also own?" asked Evelyn.

"And for the use of the name 'Evelyn's'," added Sam. "Even if I decide to change it."

"You're going to change it?" blurted Evelyn, flustered but

giving the first indication that she was even considering Sam's proposal.

"Not planning on it, especially since it's probably the most valuable thing that you'd be selling me," said Sam. Evelyn seemed to find this both complimentary and reassuring.

"Sam, who's the most important employee in the restaurant?" asked Evelyn.

"Oh, a quiz," replied Sam. "You mean besides me...I mean you?" said Sam answering the question with another question.

"More important than me or you," said Evelyn.

Sam hadn't thought about this. "To my mind, the cook," she concluded, thinking on her feet. "You've got a great location and a good reputation but, if the cook checks out, you might as well cut bait. Word gets around fast."

Now Evelyn was impressed.

"And what kind of clientele do you need to keep this place afloat?" asked Evelyn, trying to stump Sam.

This was tougher. She deliberated several minutes before answering.

"Well, you need the kids and the adults at the bar. The bar tabs at the tables are probably about as important. And to fill the tables," she was thinking out loud, "you need the families and dates, both kids and adults again. You'd probably be hard put if you didn't get the summer blast of tourists."

"Basically, you have a broad-based clientele and, if you lost any major category, I'd guess you'd be in trouble," concluded Sam.

"Right," agreed Evelyn, "But what's the most critical part for turning a profit?"

"The bar. Your liquor license," said Sam.

"Right again! Good. The booze pays for the good food and the good food keeps them coming here to pay for the booze," said Evelyn.

"Right," confirmed Sam, realizing what she already knew instinctively.

"And?" asked Evelyn.

"And...I don't know," said Sam.

"The liquor license is critical!" said Evelyn.

"I get that," said Sam, still not understanding what Evelyn was getting at. I'm afraid I *did* understand.

"So?" Evelyn persisted.

"So," ventured Sam, "Don't serve underage kids, not even the summer tourists?"

"Of course," said Evelyn impatiently, "but what else?"

"Evelyn, I really don't know what you're getting at," said Sam, confused and exasperated by this guessing game. Unfortunately, I *did* know what she was talking about now.

"Your reputation has to be beyond reproach," said Evelyn.

"Of course," replied Sam, still not getting it.

"Your professional and *personal* reputation! That's what you're getting at, isn't it Evelyn?" I said.

Sam could have gotten seriously pissed off at this point. I would have, if she had insinuated that about me. Hell, I was pissed for Sam's sake. I was about to say so when Sam, without looking at me or saying a word, placed her hand on my arm and silenced me.

"Right," said Sam, again inexplicably unfazed.

Again, Evelyn was impressed but said nothing.

"You know, Evelyn, you're not going to offend me. I have to clean up my act. Point taken. I also know that running this place isn't just about hard work. You have to be smart too. But I'm smart and a hard worker and when I decide something is really important to me, I can move mountains!" Sam said.

"And you'd never do anything as stupid as, say, serving a minor?" she asked.

Sam didn't flinch. "I guess you know about that night that I served Katy? You're right. I screwed up, Evelyn. I don't have any excuse," she admitted.

"No, it was my idea, Evelyn," I confessed. "Sam was depressed and wasn't paying attention, and I started snitching her drinks after she got drunk. My fault, not hers."

"Is that the way it happened, Sam?" Evelyn dismissed my confession and returned her attention to Sam.

"The truth is I encouraged her to have a few glasses of wine.

And once I got her started she became a willing accomplice." Sam confessed. "But my responsibility, not hers," she concluded.

"But I…" I began.

"Shut up, Katy," Sam ordered.

"Shut up, Katy," said Evelyn. Apparently Sam was the only one allowed to be noble around here.

"I know the truth," said Evelyn. To me she said, "If it wasn't for your grandfather I'd have fired you the next day. And you," she said addressing Sam, "I cut you a break because I felt sorry for you after that nasty thing with Billy that night, but you risked my liquor license and my establishment without a thought, and now you're asking me to risk everything on your good word."

"There're really two questions," Evelyn continued, after considering for a moment. "First, can I trust you and, second, can you can make it work? My future, my financial future would be in your hands." She paused. "The first of the two questions is the one that bothers me most!"

"Regarding the first question, I don't know how I can convince you of that. All I can tell you is that when I get serious about something, then you can depend on me absolutely. And I'm dead serious about this. Regarding the second question, my people would have to see your books to determine that," said Sam, like the CEO of a Fortune 500 company.

"Your people?" replied Evelyn, snickering at first…then turning serious…then becoming hopeful?

"We ran projections and scenarios based on what we believe your financial situation is," said Sam, astonishing even me. She produced an imposing document of approximately 100 pages from her backpack. "But we'll have to see your books before we'll really know if I can make it work."

Now Evelyn was definitely impressed. "Now I'm definitely impressed," she said to Sam and sat back in her chair considering seriously, for the first time, the possibilities.

At this juncture, the cook, waitresses and bartender, Bruno, were heading out. "Goodnight," they said.

"Goodnight," said Evelyn. Sam never took her eyes off Evelyn.

"Do you have a formal dress?" asked Evelyn.

"Sure," said Sam, momentarily confused by the change of topic.

"Wear it tomorrow. You'll be hostess. I'll give this document to my accountant. I'll give you my decision the day after tomorrow night. Don't worry about my books. I'll show you everything if I decide to. This place is a gold mine."

With that, Evelyn got up, ushered us to the door and locked the place down.

Chapter 32

Acid Test

As soon as Sam walked in the door, you pretty much knew it was right. As much as I loved her, I had never thought of Sam as classy. But when she walked in that restaurant, well, there was a sort of rough elegance that I don't think anyone suspected she possessed. I mean, God, with her hair up and that sleek dress, she was Classy with a capital C.

Of course, Evelyn didn't concede the transformation. She looked Sam over and muttered, "That should do," as if she ought to teach her to do her makeup, or something. To her credit, Sam did not react.

Evelyn gave Sam a couple of rudimentary instructions and then withdrew when the doors opened. We didn't understand the dynamic then, but Sam figured it out later that night and explained it to me. "Evelyn got me just pissed off enough with that, 'That should do' remark to give me the edge I needed. Then she booked so I could get started without 'Der Fuerher' skulking around. Which was probably the smartest and hardest thing she could do for me. The really scary thing is how much alike we are. If she would have given me the 'You look great, now knock 'em dead' routine instead, I would have tanked, for sure."

Anyway, she didn't tank. She was a natural. I can't believe that I thought this was beneath her. This is what she was born to do, and I was jealous. Not just of her grace but of the confidence and poise with which she was running this complex operation.

The tourists loved her but the regulars, the locals, seemed disoriented at first. Grandpa told me later that whenever Evelyn couldn't be there, the restaurant went without a hostess, which didn't happen often. To his knowledge, no one had ever subbed for Evelyn.

It didn't take them long to warm up. She flirted with the old, harmless guys and ganged up with the wives that didn't approve of such shenanigans, against their husbands. And those husbands appreciated the good-humored attacks almost as much as the flirting. She knew everybody by their first names from waitressing the place for the last two summers. She could even recite their favorite dishes, from her photographic memory, and told them if it was good, bad or not available that night.

She befriended the little kids who liked going out to a restaurant and made it interesting for the bigger kids who were bored and could turn a meal into an ordeal, especially the young, angst-ridden boys of 15 or 16 who were completely subdued by Sam's simply acknowledging that they existed. The parents loved it because they got to *enjoy* an expensive meal for a change.

Sam had the cook make her a double order of crab-stuffed mushrooms which she gave away to the predominantly singles crowd at the bar. Orders for hors d'oeuvres tripled.

Everything was as running as smooth as silk until seating started to back up. There was almost an hour's wait now. That was the usual on a Saturday night in the summer, but people were beginning to grumble. Mainly about whether Sam knew what she was doing. And Sam, for the first time in her life, was—I don't know—actually showing fear. It was the combination of rowdy teenagers with lots of body piercings and several groups of middle-aged, grumpy 'Boomers'. Not only were they upset with Sam, but they were also getting on each other's nerves. Especially when one group appeared to them to be getting special treatment, as people always seemed to think was the case. At one point tempers flared and it took the combined efforts of Sam and Flo to get things under control. But that didn't relieve the tension...just contained it for awhile.

"Katy," pleaded Sam, "what should I do? You can only move the people through here so fast."

"I don't know, Sam. Looks like they're getting ready to go at each other. Where's Evelyn?" I asked.

"Don't know. She left me to sink or swim," Sam replied, frustrated.

The friction between the two groups continued and there was still no sign of Evelyn. Sam tried to settle them down. She was consulting with Flo when I walked up. "I don't know, Sam," I heard Flo say. "Evelyn just kind of handles people. I don't know how she does it." That didn't help.

"Sam, I've got an idea but I'm not sure if it'll work. You game?" I asked.

"Katy, anything. Nobody's leaving and we're just getting more and more backed up! I have to do *something*!" she exclaimed.

"Here's what you do," I said outlining my idea.

"Donner, party of four. Your table's ready," said Sam over the intercom system used to announce seating. Nobody claimed the table.

"What? What's that? There aren't four? OK, OK. Sorry." The intercom was still live for everyone to hear.

"Donner, party of three, your table's ready?" she stuttered and paused.

Still no response.

"Hmmm? What? Oh alright! Not even three? OK!" Again this private discrepancy was 'inadvertently' made public over the loudspeakers.

"Donner, party of two, your table's ready," she announced tenaciously. Still no takers.

"What? What—oh, alright, alright, I got it," she continued, faking irritation. Apparently, to the crowd, some serious miscommunication was occurring.

"Donner, party of…oh, hello, Mr. Donner. What's that? Only you? And you're not hungry any more? Fine."

"Donner, party of one—never mind!" she finished.

The patrons looked at her and then each at other, as if to say, "What the hell was that?"

Then a select few of the more astute customers realized that the Donner Party was a reference to the ill-fated American pioneers that got stuck in the Rocky Mountains for the winter and resorted to cannibalism to survive. A reference in extremely poor taste in a restaurant full of hungry people. They were either going to laugh their asses off or burn Sam at the stake.

Those that understood the allusion looked around to see if anyone else did. When one of the *particularly* be-studded teenage girls locked eyes with one of the *particularly* conservative middle-aged men and raised her eyebrows, questioningly, his demeanor indicated that he, likewise, understood the reference.

They began to giggle.

Then to laugh.

Then to howl!

Their respective friends and families asked them what was so funny and when the reference was explained, they started laughing too. Pretty soon, some of the teenagers were explaining the joke to some of the adults, and vice versa, and the laughter continued to build throughout the restaurant. Until, finally, the whole restaurant was in stitches. It would periodically die down, but then snickering would break out again and everyone would laugh a little longer at the sheer audacity of what Sam had implied to a restaurant full of extremely hungry people impatient to be fed.

That broke the tension. And, as often happens in these situations, its darkest just before the dawn. Several large groups of satiated customers got up and left the restaurant *en masse*. Tables were bussed instantly and waiting customers were quickly seated and complimentary cocktails flew out of the bar to the newly tolerant patrons. Even without the risky little amusement that I'd suggested and Sam had delivered, everything would probably have been OK. 'Probably' being the key word. It sometimes amazes me how thinly covered our natural aggressiveness can be.

"Katy, you saved my ass. Thank you, thank you," she said bear-hugging me.

"I just suggested it. You're the one who delivered. I never could have pulled off something like that," I said.

"Where the heck did that come from, anyway?"

"I saw someone do it in another restaurant once. Had about the same effect to diffuse the tension, but the woman who did it got fired for her trouble!" I informed, causing Sam to give me a sharp look.

She was starting to fabricate a nasty response when Janie suddenly approached.

"Sammy...Samantha," Janie corrected in view of Sam's new position of authority, "there's someone here to see Evelyn and...well...I think you'd better have a look."

I followed Sam over to the front entrance where Janie pointed out a guy who looked a little down on his luck. Not quite homeless but barely one step above. Two days' growth on his face and a generally disheveled appearance. Greasy hair, yellow teeth, and a bad attitude.

Sam approached him. "Can I help you, sir?" she asked.

"I need to see Evelyn," he replied brusquely.

"She's not here at the moment. Perhaps I can help?"

He stared at her, realizing that something must be wrong if someone was taking Evelyn's place.

"Is she OK?" he asked.

"Sir, why don't you let me take you to the..." Sam started.

"Is she OK?" he demanded and tried to grab Sam's shoulders and emphasize his concern by shaking her. No one touched Sam aggressively if she didn't want them to. Sam deflected his assault, which caused him to stumble. She helped him regain his balance.

"Sir, I was just going to suggest that you let me buy you a drink in the bar while I go find Evelyn who, I can assure you, is fine," Sam promised.

He became unexpectedly passive as Sam escorted him to the bar, fixed him up with a martini and retired to the kitchen where she instructed me to find Evelyn while she kept an eye on him.

"Make sure you bring her back here, not to the bar!" Sam ordered.

"Here first!" she emphasized.

I complied.

A few minutes later I returned with Evelyn, who had been inventorying stock in the storeroom.

"Hi Evelyn," said Sam, still distracted by our visitor. "Do you recognize the guy at the bar?" Sam pointed him out.

Evelyn responded by heading through the door. Sam physically restrained her, shocking us all. I couldn't conceive of anyone, much less an employee, detaining Evelyn that way. Evelyn smoldered. "You might not want to just run out there," Sam warned, ignoring Evelyn's menacing reaction.

"Why not?" Evelyn asked indignantly.

"Well," said Sam, "first of all because he's using—heroin, I'd guess."

Evelyn was nonplussed.

"And second of all, he's carrying," warned Sam.

"Carrying what?" Evelyn demanded.

"A weapon!" said Sam.

"Now, how would you know that?" said Evelyn sarcastically. This bravado was followed by a subtle shudder of doubt from Evelyn.

Sam retrieved a gun from her knapsack. "At least he was," she said triumphantly.

At that, Evelyn cracked a smile, and then started laughing.

"He's a cop, right?" asked Sam.

"Sort of," said Evelyn. "Street crimes unit. Undercover. War on drugs. And, oh yeah, he's my brother," she said, snickering. "Sam, why don't you ask him to come back here?"

He followed Sam to the back of the kitchen where Evelyn was waiting. They hugged, and then Evelyn produced the gun, from which the bullets had been removed. "Lose something?" she teased, handing the gun to him along with a handful of bullets.

"Yeah, yeah," he acknowledged, grudgingly. "I know. Your girl took it off me when I stumbled."

"You didn't stumble," corrected Sam.

"When you tripped me then," he agreed good-naturedly. "I

didn't realize it for a second or two. She's good," he admitted, "But then I'm not exactly at the top of my form."

"You didn't let her take it, Ronny?" Evelyn asked.

"No, I didn't," he said, embarrassed. "But I did let her keep it."

"You knew she took it but you let her keep it?" asked Evelyn.

"She was trying to protect you," he said, "and I'm pretty sure it would have been dangerous to try to get it back," he concluded, looking approvingly towards Sam. "So I waited until you showed up. Good person to have around."

Evelyn didn't respond to his statement but instead asked casually, "Staying for awhile?"

"Yeah, Evey, if it's OK?" he said affectionately, looking to her as if he and his sister were the only two people in the room.

"Yeah, Ronny. You know it's OK," said Evelyn tenderly. "Go settle down at my table and Janie will bring you some food."

"Sam...Samantha," said Evelyn, after her brother and Janie left. "The accountants may have to get creative but they'll work it out. If you're still interested, we've got a deal," she said extending her hand. "You have my word on that, which is better than any goddamn contract."

"Because of what happened with your brother?" Sam asked.

"And because you can do the job," Evelyn assured her.

"Deal," beamed Sam, taking Evelyn's hand and pumping it.

Chapter 33

Oil and Water

It wasn't easy to arrange, but one night it came together like the planets were aligned. It was my turn to lock up the restaurant, and everyone else was gone but Janie. Daniel was cooling his heels at the bar, waiting to drive me home, while Janie was putting on a sweatshirt and heading for the door.

At that moment Grandpa arrived. Janie let him in and started to leave but then looked at Grandpa and back towards the bar where Daniel was sitting. She started backtracking as if she'd forgotten something.

"Goodnight, Janie," I said firmly, steering her back towards the door. She was just being nosy and I didn't need a witness to the first meeting of the two important men in my life.

After she departed, I locked the front door and pointed Grandpa towards the bar where Daniel, oblivious to what was happening, was watching a South American soccer match on ESPN.

Grandpa spotted Daniel just as Daniel turned and saw Grandpa. Daniel seemed OK with it, but Grandpa reddened immediately. To his credit, he succeeded in keeping it under control.

"Looks like you got your wires crossed, honey. I thought you needed a ride home tonight," he said deferring to Daniel, unwittingly admitting that he was aware of our relationship. He didn't, however, acknowledge Daniel's presence. Better than I expected, but not as good as I hoped for.

Daniel didn't flinch.

"I do need a ride home, and you two can arm wrestle for the privilege after we talk for a while," I said.

"So this is a setup? Are you as ignorant of the situation as I am, or were you in on it?" Grandpa asked Daniel. This was a major improvement, acknowledgment of his existence, and without recrimination. And with a common foe—me!

"I don't know anything," said Daniel, looking questioningly towards me, "about any setup."

Grandpa shot up and headed for the door in what can only be described as a controlled panic attack! He was stymied, however, by the door which was locked and no longer bore the keys.

"Mr. Brace, it occurs to me that Katy went to a bit of trouble to orchestrate this," said Daniel, "on neutral ground."

"You!" exclaimed Grandpa. Then hesitating and no longer in control, he stammered, "You...kindly refer to my granddaughter as Kathleen!"

"Are you OK, Grandpa?" I asked, concerned about the stress this meeting might have on his health.

"I'm not sure I am," he whined, petulantly. "Especially if I have to stay here. Is it your intention to hold me here against my will?"

My worry turned into exasperation.

"I know about Del, Grandpa. I also know this is hard, very hard for you. *Too* hard I guess," I finished and handed him the keys to the door.

"I'm not Del, Mr. Brace. Just like Katy's not *your* Katy. You've accepted that, haven't you?" Daniel asked.

"Kathleen is my granddaughter and very dear to me and, therefore, worth the effort to understand the difference. You, I do not know and, frankly, you're not worth the effort!" he said.

"Maybe you do think you know me because of who I look like. Maybe if you didn't think you knew me, you'd make the effort for

Katy's sake?" he argued, taking the keys from my grandfather who was too agitated to operate the door lock. Daniel opened the door to allow him to leave.

And leave he did. Without further adieu.

Back at the bar I sat down dejected, when Daniel sat down beside me.

When he didn't say anything, I said, "I really do know how hard it must be for him, but I thought he'd have the courage to confront it."

"Apparently I'm not worth the effort," Daniel said, a little petulantly himself.

"Oh, that's not it. It has nothing to do with you. It's an almost primal hatred for your Uncle Del. You resemble Del too much for Grandpa to ever believe that you aren't at least partially like him. There is nothing rational about his response to you. It's strictly instinctual," I told him.

"I'd just hoped that if anyone could get by it, if anyone could have the courage to control their overwhelming id, it would be my grandpa," I lamented. "Let's get out of here."

After I locked the door, we started towards the car. Abruptly, a shape materialized out of the shadows. We both pulled back, startled.

"Your mistake, my dear," spoke the shadow, "was trying this on neutral ground. No matter how irrational, I am the offended party, not Daniel. I'll meet you back at the house, on *my* turf, and listen to what you have to say if you still want to talk."

With that Grandpa faded into the darkness. I wasn't sure he'd actually been there, but Daniel assured me that I hadn't imagined it and drove me home.

Chapter 34

Truth

As we entered the house Grandpa was going through the e-mail that was sent in response to his web site, MyIslandBeach.net. Not only did he not look up, but he was also going to great lengths to ignore our presence. So much for the mature approach.

After standing there for several minutes without acknowledgement, I said, "Grandpa?" but he raised his hand to hush me before I could continue. Looks like the subtle approach wouldn't work either.

"Grandpa, you lied to me," I accused.

"On many occasions," he said, still not paying attention.

"Grandpa, I'm *serious*!" I said.

"I also," he responded, looking up from the monitor to confront my irate demeanor. "I lied when you were thirteen and you asked if your pimples made you look ugly. You looked hideous but it would have destroyed you if I'd agreed," he said. "And don't forget about the marshmallows," he added, grinning as he returned to his computer.

"Grandpa!" I yelled, demanding his attention.

"Katy," he said, "The Truth is highly overrated. If everyone told The Truth, the world would come to a screeching halt.

Lawyers would be out of a job, politicians would be murdered. And, Katy, the institution of marriage would be abolished in less than 24 hours, I guarantee it!" he said with a snicker.

"Grandpa, you can be as cynical and facetious as you like, but the fact is that you've been caught in a lie. And it doesn't have anything to do with politics or marriage, and you need to take responsibility for it," I insisted. At last, he got up from his computer and sat next to me. He still hadn't acknowledged Daniel's presence…but one step at a time.

"Katy, people sometimes lie because they're lazy, but sometimes…rarely…but sometimes," he repeated for emphasis, "they lie because they'd rather take responsibility for the consequences of the lie than hurt another person with The Truth. Sometimes a lie is an act of courage."

"Grandpa, you can rationalize it any way you wish, but maybe we should deal with your lie, in particular, and leave the discussion of the morality of lying for another time!" I said.

"So we should," he replied resignedly. "Tell me what's bothering you."

"Grandpa, I know the truth…" I started, when he interrupted.

"Truth is relative," he said.

"Grandpa!" I moaned through gritted teeth.

"Sorry," he said, chastened.

"I know The Truth…" I repeated softly. I hesitated then continued, determined to have it out, "about what happened to Grandma!"

That stopped him dead in his tracks. This was no longer academic for him. No longer playful bantering.

"I know almost everything," I said.

What followed was a silence that threatened to go on forever until he finally said, "Alright, tell me what you *think* you know."

"I know, Grandpa," I assured him, feeling very sure of myself.

"How could you know?" he yelled in frustration.

"I *know*," I said firmly. Was he finally starting to believe me?

"Then tell me what you know," he demanded, fortifying himself for the worst.

"Not yet. First, I have to talk to you about other things," I said.

"Your lies," I said in response to his questioning look.
"You never did receive a letter from Grandma Katy telling you where the treasure was hidden, did you?"
Direct hit!
Now I had his full and undivided attention. He was now considering how much of the precious Truth he was going to have to tell me. Little did he know that, as they say, it would have to be The Truth, The Whole Truth and nothing but The Truth.
"Right?"
"Not with him here!" He made it clear from his tone that here would be no negotiation on this point.
I didn't stop to consider either, since I'd already sensed what was coming. "OK, Grandpa, we tried. We're outta here. C'mon Daniel, let's go."
Appalled to have someone stand up to him like that, he decided to change tacks and reasoned, "Look, you came to introduce me to your boyfriend so we can make nice. We can do that and, after he leaves, we can talk about the other," he conceded.
"No, Grandpa, the reason I broached the subject now is that it has everything to do with you *and* Daniel," I said, just as reasonably.
"And you know about this?" he said to Daniel, acknowledging him for the first time but still unable to use his name.
"If you mean, did she tell me what she's up to, then no. I do have a sneaking suspicion where she's headed but not because she told me anything," he said.
"So you never received a letter from Grandmother after she died?" I repeated the original question. He didn't answer. I continued, "We won't be talking about this later when he's gone, because, first of all, I won't be coming back. Grandpa, it's time to get everything out in the open!"
I really thought he would call my bluff. But it wasn't a bluff and maybe he sensed that. He considered his options, which he didn't have, and then answered.
"That's right," he said finally. I must have looked confused because he clarified, "I mean, that's right, I never received a letter from Katy after she died."

"I'm guessing that you followed Del everywhere the day after Grandma went missing?"

"Right again," he replied grimly.

"Grandpa, I'm on your side," I implored, hoping to find a sympathetic aspect to what I knew, without question, was The Truth.

"Maybe you shouldn't be," he said more darkly than before.

After a moment I resumed. "You followed him because you thought something happened to Grandma Katy?"

"I followed him for a while but I didn't have to. I knew he was coming back for the treasure. Damn the treasure! That goddamn treasure. I didn't give two fucks about the treasure!" he railed.

In due time he calmed down and continued. "I thought—no, I knew that he knew what happened to Katy. In spite of the rage that was eating me up inside, I knew that if I confronted him I'd probably kill him or be killed. And then I'd never find out what happened," he said.

"Eventually, he came for the treasure in my parents' shed. That was too much for me. I'd finally realized that Katy was dead and he wouldn't be leading me to her. And now he was stealing the treasure!" He paused, considering how to continue. I saw the shadow of fear, succeeded by a wave of relief, cross his demeanor.

"I confronted him. I accused him of hurting your grandmother. He said that he didn't know what I was talking about. He said that Katy was going away with him of her own free will and that I could have my share of the treasure but to fuck off!"

"Katy would never have done that!" Grandpa said impatiently, when I didn't react.

"Then he confirmed my intuition by lunging at me with a fishing knife. He caught me in the leg! Not enough to cripple me but enough to rouse me. I was enraged!"

At that point Daniel shot up and leapt for the door but his escape was thwarted by the coffee table. Sprawled on the floor, he had a terrified look on his face. His stunned demeanor matured into a grimace and then he threw up violently, several times. When he was done, I ushered him into the bathroom, while Grandpa got a mop and bucket and cleaned up the mess.

"Are you all right?" I asked.

"I'm OK, I guess," he whispered, as his color returned. "I was just overcome by what happened to my uncle," he explained.

"I know," I replied.

After everyone and everything were cleaned up, Grandpa continued, glancing ambiguously at Daniel.

"I grabbed Del's wrist...the one with the knife in it...and slammed it against a four-by-four with all my strength. His arm broke. I slammed him in the midsection which busted him up bad enough that he would have died of internal injuries if I decided not to throttle him to death. And I would have choked him to death if the hatred hadn't been so strong," he said.

"Grandpa," I said urging him to continue.

"I finally got my temper under control and my first rational thought was that I'd never find Katy if I killed him now. But then he came at me with a second shiv! I don't know where it came from but he stuck me bad this time, in the gut!"

"I was hurting. In a lot of pain! It turns out that he missed all the vital stuff but I was rabid by this time, totally out of control. I broke his neck before he could stab me again. He died instantly," he said. "And I'd do it again!" he said, challenging Daniel to comment.

"I know," I said. "Grandpa, it was self-defense," I told him when he didn't respond. Still nothing.

"But what would you have done if he gave it up, confessed that he'd killed Grandma Katy and was ready to suffer the consequences? Would you still have killed him?" I asked the unanswerable.

"He would never have taken responsibility for what he did," Grandpa replied emphatically. "But if he had, I'm not sure what I'd have done," he said starting to calm down. "I'm glad I'll never have to find out. Do you think I'd have murdered him?"

I just shook my head and shrugged my shoulders.

"What about you?" he asked, turning to confront Daniel.

"I don't know either," Daniel replied. "Maybe," he said unconcerned about Grandfather's mercurial temper. Grandfather didn't react.

"Because, if there was a trial," Daniel continued, "the existence of the treasure would have come out and the park would have been lost to developers. Since he deserved to die for what he did to Katy, I think you might have killed him before he could screw up the deal to create the park," he finished, staring into my grandfather's eyes.

"You're wrong," Grandpa responded, equally calmly and coldly. "I might've believed the same thing if the situation had been reversed but even if the park was lost and I had to go to jail for grand larceny, I wouldn't have murdered him," Grandpa maintained with certainty.

"But you're right about him deserving to die. If I knew he *wouldn't* get the death penalty, it might have been a different matter," he said, looking for all the world like one of those old men who decides to die and manages it shortly after their spouse passes on. "But I didn't."

"Are you all right?" I said, concerned about how the shock of his confession was affecting him.

"I'm fine, Kathleen," he said, "It's just that I've never told anyone about this. I never intended to."

"I know," I replied.

"Damn it, Katy, how do you claim to know…" he protested but I interrupted.

"What about his body Grandpa? I presume it was never found."

"You don't want to know and please, don't ever ask me about it again." Back to the "never-mention-it" culture of this place.

"Katy, what happened to your grandmother?" he asked weakly.

"Not yet," I replied, putting him off again.

"What now?" he asked with exasperation.

"I have more things to tell you. Are you going to be OK?" I asked, again uneasy about his health.

"Katy, I'll be all right. Now what do you know about your grand…" he demanded.

"No!" I bristled. "If you want to know then you'll just have to listen."

"Quiet!" I commanded, startling him when he started to interrupt again.

"Good, that's better," I said, establishing my dominance, at least for the moment.

"I know about the girl," I said after he settled down. Daniel didn't say a word. In response to the question, "What girl?" that I saw forming on Grandpa's lips, I preempted him. "Caitlin, Grandpa. It wasn't Cecelia or Katy or any of the other aliases in your little beach story. It was Caitlin. I know about Caitlin!"

Bulls-eye! He gave up and listened.

"Grandpa, there must have been a family history or a diary that survived?" I said, fishing for corroboration.

"Diary," he replied confused. "In a locked chest, wrapped in several layers of oilskins."

I remained silent, hoping he would continue. I think he needed to.

"It was remarkably well preserved. It was her mother's diary. Described everything up to and including the beginning of the pirate attack," he explained.

"So your little pirate tale is true?" I asked.

"Yes," he confirmed. "Except..."

"Except that the little girl, Caitlin, was really sixteen or seventeen, not eleven?" He gazed at me, completely surrendering finally, silently acknowledging that I knew things that I couldn't possibly know. "Why change the age of the girl for your story?" I asked still ignorant of a few details.

"To help the children identify. Better if she was their age," he justified. "Made a better story."

"Katy, how do you...?" he asked.

"I *know*," I replied, calmly.

"How the fuck do you know!" he demanded.

"Grandpa!"

"Sorry. How the fuck do you know?" he asked quietly, as if using a calm tone made it OK to use bad language. I laughed.

"Grandpa," I continued all business now, "You've seen Daniel. He's the spitting image of Del. Why didn't you say anything?"

"I've only seen him once before," he replied passively. "He changed so much. He never looked like Del before, like how you became your grandma. So sudden…"

When I didn't respond, he confessed, "Evelyn warned me after she saw him at the restaurant."

I pulled out a copy of an old newspaper clipping. It was a picture of Del and Grandma Katy going to the Prom; it could have been a picture of Daniel and me.

Grandpa looked at it. Then he looked at me. "I'll never know what she saw in him," he said more to himself than to me. "This was taken the spring before we met."

"I do," I said, meaning I knew what she saw in him and answering the question he never meant to ask. He started to speak but held himself back.

"Don't you think Daniel and I should have known about this?" I asked.

"I don't know, Katy. You tell me. I don't know what's right or wrong anymore. I don't know what the hell is going on!" After a beat he continued, "I know. *You* do and you'll tell me in your own goddamn time. I'll be patient," he said, stoically.

I handed him another black and white photo. "God, Katy, I miss you so much," he spoke wistfully to the picture.

"No, Grandpa. That's not Katy! That's Candice Everly, the Garden Club of America member who chased the 'Bumblebee' rocket scientists off the island in 1945."

"That can't be!" Grandpa said. "She's Katy's twin. I would have noticed her or somebody would've," he asserted.

"The photo was taken 20 years earlier in 1925," I related. "She probably looked very different by the time you might have known her." He believed, barely, even though it was beyond belief.

I handed him a photo of a lithograph. "Not Katy?" he asked, dreading the answer he already knew.

"Katherine Gray, from Lavallette, in 1892."

"Others?" he asked.

"No more pictures," I responded. "But there were others."

He considered these facts silently. Finally, after a very long silence, he looked up at me. "There's more, right." he implored.

I didn't answer his question just continued. It really wasn't a question, anyway.

"Grandpa, Daniel, there was a painter…" I started. Grandpa nodded, even though he had no idea where I was going with this. Daniel remained impassive.

"On the island—in your story." I said. He still didn't get it. "Caitlin," I repeated. "In the Caribbean."

"Vargas," he said triumphantly after considering my assertion.

"That's right!" I confirmed, realizing for the first time that, as fantastic as it was, what I believed to be true might actually *be* true. "Alejandro Vargas."

"Yes, her mother mentioned him several times in the diary. Alejandro. That's right," he confirmed, checking it against his memory.

"Her mother didn't like him much, didn't like him at all, in fact. Didn't trust him around the children," he said.

"And rightfully so. It turns out that he was from an aristocratic family in Spain which is what saved him. His style of painting was realistic and he was an excellent artisan. Technically flawless," I said.

"So why 'Rightfully so'?" Daniel asked.

"Because he was also a pedophile. His paintings were subtly erotic and often involved children with older men. Even though they were never truly explicit and, individually they were ambiguous, when taken as a group, it was unmistakable. That's what finally got him exiled from Spain!"

"Sounds like a delightful character," Grandpa said.

"That's why he ended up in that Caribbean colony," I continued. "When he got there, he used his artistic skills and aristocratic position to ingratiate himself with Caitlin's family and other families on the island! The family didn't interest him but he was totally obsessed, not unexpectedly, with Caitlin."

"He painted a few official portraits of her that were very proper, without any hints of his prepubescent inclinations unless you knew what to look for. But in the privacy of his studio, he painted over a hundred studies of her—some subtly erotic, others downright explicit. Caitlin's mother evidently sensed this, in spite of his unreproachable behavior in the children's presence, and held him at bay," I continued.

"I'm surprised I've never heard of him if he was such an accomplished artist," Grandpa said. "Even if he was a pervert."

"That's just it. His family and the Spanish government suppressed his work until recently. A treasure trove of his studies was discovered a few years ago, when his descendants started parting with anything that would bring in cash. Apparently they had fallen on hard times as aristocrats sometimes do. And the newfound tolerance for historical eroticism, demand in fact, made his work all the more desirable. Like Balthus and his obsessive fascination with the sexuality of young girls," I said with undisguised revulsion.

"There was a showing of his work at..." I started to say.

"The Art Institute in Philadelphia," Grandpa finished my sentence.

"That's where you went last week," Daniel deduced, as had Grandpa.

"That's right. Not only has his technical brilliance been recognized, but also his immature sexual preference," I said. "In fact, he and his works have attracted a cult following among pedophiles on the Internet. He supports their contention that an appreciation of the eroticism of youth and innocence is a sophisticated, artistic choice, rather than deviant sexual behavior!"

With that said, I looked Grandpa in the eye and warned, "Prepare yourself for a shock, Grandpa." I opened a book of color plates I had purchased at the showing.

His eyes grew wide then looked up and inspected me. "It's you," he whispered.

"No, Grandpa, its Caitlin," I said.

"I know, Katy, but it's you, too. And your grandmother. You are going to tell me what's going on eventually, right?" he asked, shaken to his very foundation at this latest revelation.

"Me too?" Daniel mumbled, also disturbed by what he saw.

"I will," I assured them, "but a few more things first."

Grandpa shook his head, grudgingly accepting the necessity to tell the story in the correct order. Otherwise, the case for the implausible had no chance of being fairly considered. He was, after all, a consummate storyteller himself. Daniel, on the other hand, remained uncharacteristically dispassionate.

"When I arrived at the gallery, there was a crowd of conspicuously unescorted, middle-aged men viewing the exhibit. At first, nobody noticed me but then a murmur crept through the crowd, which slowly built to a gasp. Remember, I wasn't aware of the Internet photos and hadn't seen the paintings of Caitlin yet. I had my suspicions but no hard evidence. The patrons, the cult, parted for me like the Red Sea for Moses, and the curator of the exhibit came rushing in saying, 'Where is she? Where's the girl?'"

"But why did you go to the exhibit? How did you know?" interrupted Daniel, unable to let this incongruity pass.

"She just knew," supplied Grandpa, with resignation. I didn't contradict his explanation and continued.

"When the curator spotted me, he flushed, turned ashen and fainted dead away!" I took a breath. "Grandpa, do you have any idea how disconcerting it is to constantly have that happen?"

"No, darling," he said. "I couldn't begin to comprehend."

I looked up sharply at him to see if he was being sincere or sarcastic. He appeared sincere, so I continued.

"When he, the curator that is, went down, he hit the corner of a table and cut his head badly. He ended up going to the emergency room for stitches. I went there too because I needed to talk with him."

"That was a pretty stupid thing to do considering what you must have suspected about him," Grandpa said. I could see Daniel preparing to defend me, when it occurred to him that, coming from him, it would only make things worse.

I ignored the remark. "When he found out I was there he insisted on seeing me and became frantic when the doctors advised against it. He became violent, at which point they finally gave in. My presence had an instantaneous, calming effect on him and, after exchanging pleasantries, I asked if he'd tell me about the exhibit. He started telling me about it in great detail."

"About halfway through his discourse, he asked me casually if I would tell him my name," I said.

"Katy!" exclaimed Grandpa, alarmed.

"You didn't—she didn't!" exclaimed Daniel, denoting

trepidation followed rapidly by confidence in my judgment.

"Of course not!" I assured them. "I gave him the name of a sadistic gym teacher I had in the fifth grade. I laughed but neither of them even grinned. I continued.

"After I found out what I wanted to know, I attempted to leave. Grandpa, Daniel…he fawned over me, took my hand and very subtly tried to detain me by refusing to release it. The need in his eyes was disturbing. Then," I trembled momentarily, "I had the sudden epiphany that I would be the object—the graphic object—of his unfilled desires for days, weeks—years! And all the other pervs at the convention."

"And I'd let him touch me. Oh, Grandpa!" I cried.

He crossed the short distance between us and gave me a silent and wonderful grandfatherly hug. After I'd calmed down, he returned to his chair and I continued.

"That's when I wrenched my hand free, fled from the ER, ducked into the ladies room and retched! And retched again. And kept retching until there was nothing left. After that I came home, in a roundabout way, making absolutely certain no one was following me."

We sat quietly. While I was catching my breath, Grandpa was absorbing what I had told him, and Daniel was still looking non-committal. Grandpa got up and poured us glasses of wine. "Go ahead, we'll all need a rest after this and it'll help you sleep," Grandpa urged when I started to refuse.

As I sipped the wine, I considered Grandpa's reaction to the perverted curator. His face had cycled through a succession of anger, disgust, and then something unexpected. A flash of sympathy? Not really…but what?

"Grandpa?" I asked. In that one word I voiced, I think, my need for reassurance. I realized that, while on the one hand I was his granddaughter, on the other hand I was the identical twin to the love of his life at exactly the same age she had been when he lost her.

"Darling, as I told you before, though it requires considerable effort, I have never, and will never confuse you with your grandmother in the realm of everyday life," he assured, displaying remarkable insight into my unspoken concerns, "Nor in the privacy of my own thoughts." End of subject. Another topic that will never be discussed again…this time to my infinite relief.

"Now, you have to tell us what's going on, if you know!" he ordered.

"I know," I assured him, "and now it's time."

Chapter 35

The Devil You Say!

    He waited expectantly. I had primed him with the facts, the uninterpreted data gleaned from my sleuthing. The circumstances leading up to Del's death by his own hands went uncontested by Grandpa. And the discovery that my uncanny resemblance was not only to Grandma Katy but also to a series of women dating back to Caitlin, the protagonist of Grandpa's pirate story. The photos of Katherine Gray and Candice Everly, not to mention the corroboration by Caitlin's mother's diary and the Vargas paintings, were undeniable. Now comes the hard part. As unbelievable as the facts were to accept, the interpretation of those facts—the interpretation that I knew to be true—would be impossible for any sane individual to accept. Nevertheless, I had to try.

    "I'm sure Daniel understands some of what I'm about to explain," I began, not knowing where to start. "Grandpa, you have to understand. She's a part of me…" I blurted out, obfuscating rather than elucidating.

    "I can see that Katy, in more ways than you know. The way you move, the way you…" he interrupted.

    I interrupted back, "Not Grandmother, Grandpa. *Caitlin!*"

    I could see that he couldn't comprehend this. "What do you

mean? You're related to Caitlin, somehow?" he asked.

"Not that I know of. I even tried to track down a genealogical connection," I explained. "None of us were related to each other except Grandma and me."

"So then what?" he asked, bewildered. "How is she a part of you? Are you possessed?"

"Not possessed," I said but hesitated, thinking about what I really wanted to say. "Host to her presence—more like her essence, if I really had to describe it."

He searched my face skeptically. "I don't believe you. What kind of crap is this?" he demanded, so abhorrent was the concept that he turned to Daniel, of all people, for support. Daniel shrugged, failing to proffer the support that might have brought Grandpa and him a few inches closer. But Daniel didn't support my contentions either.

"The most obvious manifestation of her presence is my physical appearance. She was rather vain, and with good reason, I might add," I said, going for the laugh or even a smile.

But Grandpa wasn't amused. He was all business. "And the others? Your grandmother?"

"Yes," I confirmed. "She also took on Caitlin's physical appearance. But Grandpa, you have to try to understand this before you judge anyone!"

He thought about it for a minute and then indicated a willingness to listen further.

"She's not a dominating presence, more of a collaborative feeling, or feelings, and a few selected specific recollections. The strongest feeling is a love—make that a passion—for this place, Island Beach."

"And other feelings?" he questioned, skeptical and what—insecure?

"Just one," I said. Grandpa waited.

"Grandpa," I hesitated momentarily then continued, "There was someone else on that ship, someone that her mother was not aware of, so it's not in the diary."

"No more storytelling," he said. "Tell me!"

"No, Grandpa!!" I stood my ground. "There was someone else

on the ship."

He was furious with me! But as I remained silent, he considered what I said and comprehension slowly emerged on his face.

"The boy!" he said triumphantly.

"The boy!" I concurred. "Except that he wasn't a boy. He was a handsome young man!"

"He was a stowaway on the ship. Caitlin was feeding him and helping him stay concealed. The mother, the crew, no one was aware of his existence on the ship, all the way 'til the end," I explained.

"Diego," I supplied when Grandpa, lost again in thought, didn't respond.

"Diego," he repeated, zombie-like. "That's right!" he agreed, recalling the name of the troublesome native boy in the mother's diary.

"He was one of the reasons they took the girl away. Part Spanish, part Negro, part native—it wouldn't do. It wouldn't do at all, not for a proper English girl," he murmured, thinking aloud. "What could those two have been planning?" he asked, referring to Caitlin and Diego. "How could they have thought they could…?"

"I doubt if they were planning anything, Grandpa. Caitlin was pure impulse, like Grandma, totally instinctive, elemental. I know, I can feel it," I testified.

"When the pirate attack came, she went to be with him in his hiding place. That's probably why they were the only two to survive!" I said.

"That's the other strong feeling that 'possesses' you from her? Her desire for Diego?" he asked.

"Desire and love," I corrected.

"And Diego?" He had finally seen it and accepted it, as totally ludicrous as it had seemed just minutes before.

I opened the book of color plates from the art institute. There, on the thirty-first page, was a painting of Caitlin and Diego from the private study series of Alejandro Vargas. Caitlin and Diego…Grandma Kathleen and Del…me and Daniel. In a scathingly erotic pose!

Grandpa gasped. Daniel shuddered. Daniel looked up at me and muttered, "Then…!" but stopped, unwilling to put his thoughts into words.

"Diego is what Grandma, read Caitlin, saw in Del. Diego was a good person and they were deeply in love. But Del, the *real* Del, was not good. He was evil, truly evil, just like you said, Grandpa!" I explained, trying to make him understand that, while all of our physical appearances were identical and the attraction was irresistible, underneath it all we were all individuals, both good and bad.

"What happened to them after they reached shore?" Grandpa asked, still seeking logical consistency for this highly improbable tale.

"They were in heaven or at least Eden. They were so in love and free to love in this place. They avoided contact with colonists and natives, which wasn't that hard, since no one actually lived here back then. They lived off the land, constantly moving, loving and living as they were never allowed to before."

"But they didn't live happily ever after!" Grandpa concluded pessimistically.

"No," I confirmed. "Not unexpectedly, Caitlin became pregnant. Grandpa, she died in childbirth." This devastating shift in their fortunes did not sit well with Grandpa or Daniel.

"What became of him?" Grandpa asked, in shock, "and the baby? Did it survive?"

"I don't know," I said. "Her memories…my sense of her…end with her death."

We sat quietly, thoughtfully, considering the many questions that my revelations had raised but left unanswered.

The wine was starting to kick in and, as unsatisfying as the story was up to that point, even I was getting tired…and frustrated…and…

Daniel cleared his throat, screwed up his face as if performing complex mathematical calculations in his head, and pronounced out of the blue, "He left the island after she died. It wasn't Eden for him anymore,". As we looked on open-mouthed he continued, "He was mad with grief but he also knew the child would die without the breast of its dead mother, so he headed south into the Pine Barrens to a place called Scott's landing," he said. "Ever heard of it?"

I could now comprehend the amazement and disbelief that Grandpa had displayed in response to my story. When I had told Grandpa I knew almost everything, I was apparently mistaken.

"Sounds familiar," I responded noncommittally to his query.

"Diego placed the child anonymously on the doorstep of a local woman named Jane Leeds who already had 12 children. His hope was that she would take the baby in and feed him."

"Leeds?" Grandpa asked scratching his chin thoughtfully.

"Leeds," Daniel confirmed.

"When she spotted the bundle," Daniel continued, "she scanned the area for the source of the bequest. Unable to see Diego camouflaged in the forest, she picked up the baby. Her initial response was anticipation, as she apparently liked children. She must've to have had a dozen. But when she uncovered the face, she shrieked, threw the baby to the ground and rushed back into the house!"

"You see, it was a badly deformed child with the vestiges of a tail, some webbing on the hands and under the arms like wings. Physically healthy but, visually, it was a monstrosity! He looked like…"

"The Devil! The Jersey Devil!" exclaimed Grandpa. "That old wives tale."

"Legends sometimes have a basis in fact," I said, more inclined than Grandfather at this point to accept Daniel's metaphysical assertions.

"Diego, at his wits end, scooped up the child before the Leeds woman could return with witnesses. He tried once more with a woman named Mother Shourds with equally dire consequences. Eventually, he decided he would have to steal cow's or goat's milk. No woman would ever willingly suckle this abomination."

"You don't have a shred of evidence to support this, do you?" Grandpa interrupted.

"No, not one iota," Daniel admitted. "I did a little research, but no, no real evidence."

"If you just figured this all out today…now," to which Daniel nodded his head in agreement, "then when did you do research? And why?" challenged Grandpa, still understandably skeptical.

"They did an episode on the Jersey Devil on the *X-Files*. It upset me and I didn't understand why. I wasn't angry or horrified, like I became when you were describing Del's death. I was disturbed, weepy. I started crying during the show and kept it up, on and off, for nearly the whole next day. Not the usual effect the *X-Files* has on me. So I went to the Web and looked up some stuff," he explained.

We waited.

"Legend has it that, upon becoming impregnated with her 13th child, Jane Leeds became so frustrated at the prospect of yet another mouth to feed she said, 'I wish this child be born a devil!'" Daniel said. "With what I know now, I suspect that she did say something like that but perhaps had a miscarriage…or an abortion. If, soon after that, she encountered the deformed baby of Diego and Caitlin on her doorstep and interpreted it as her own dead fetus returned to haunt her for her devilish wish, it's not hard to imagine how the legend got started."

"After that, Diego just wanted the two of them to be left alone, but the Pine Barrens were more densely populated than Island Beach, to which he couldn't bear to return. And, on occasion, they were spotted," Daniel explained. "I'm beginning to understand," he said and stopped.

"What are you beginning to understand?" demanded Grandpa, embarrassed that he needed information from this interloper.

Still unfocused he said, "I got sick a moment ago because I remembered seeing Del being killed." Grandpa didn't react.

"By you!"

Unfazed by Grandpa's bullying, Daniel continued, "I also understand my irrational fear of you, Dr. Brace, and my irresistible attraction to Katy because of her resemblance to Caitlin and why my twin, my identical twin, doesn't even look related to me. That's what I'm beginning to understand!" he said, trying to come to grips with the ironies these revelations were unveiling.

"Katy, that's what I was doing while you were explaining things to your grandfather. First, I had to convince myself to even consider the possibility that what you were saying could be true. After that, with each new revelation, I tested it against what I was remembering," he continued.

"And?" I asked.

"And I started remembering things before you said them, and I know things that even you don't know," he said.

At this point, I wasn't sure if Grandpa was going to assault Daniel or just give up and, I don't know, die! He looked angry but despondent.

"Grandpa, it's time to go for a ride," I ordered, suddenly realizing what would be required to actually *convince* Grandpa, once and for all, of the impossible!

Chapter 36

Grandma Katy

Daniel drove, I sat in the middle and Grandpa rode shotgun in Daniel's old pickup. Talk about "Déjà vu all over again," we could have been Del, Grandma Katy and Grandpa headed out to the blowout on that first tense trip to recover the treasure. Granted, Grandpa was old now but, from his perspective, the two of us were recreating a scenario that had originally unfolded almost 40 years ago.

We went into the park and onto the beach at Gillikins. I ushered them to the blowout, where Grandpa had taken me that first week, where they found the treasure, where momentous events had transpired during the course of several lifetimes.

We walked up the hill and I stopped them. "This is it, isn't it?" The place where you found the empty trunk?" He nodded.

"Grandpa, Grandma Katy brought Del here to talk to him about the treasure. You know he was unhappy with *your* ideas about buying the park." I paused to let him absorb the implication.

"Are you trying to insinuate that it *wasn't* my idea to use the money to buy the park?" he asked.

"No, Grandpa," I corrected, "I'm not trying to insinuate anything. I'm telling you outright that Grandma Katy manipulated you into 'thinking up' that idea, the same way she made you believe it was you who figured out where to dig for the treasure along the trajectory from the ship to the chest," I proposed. He looked at me skeptically.

"She knew like I know" I explained, "from Caitlin."

"So she was…inhabited by Caitlin, too?" he asked, already knowing the answer.

"As were the others. She was even aware of Caitlin, I think, towards the end. She had to make it look like someone else found the treasure and figured what to do with it afterward. After all, she was a young girl in the '50s, with supernatural knowledge. It was simpler that way. It didn't pay for her to look too smart."

"But she didn't just know things," Grandpa protested. "She was smarter than any of us, even our parents and other adults," he said. "She outsmarted them all," he concluded.

"She not only had information but also access to the wisdom and maturity of several generations of very strong women," I said, knowing first hand that it was true.

"Like you do?" he asked.

There was no need to respond. He already knew the answer.

"How does she choose?" he asked finally, taking me off guard.

"I don't know," I admitted. "But it seems to me that it begins around puberty. I got my first period here, remember? That's when my looks started to change. We thought the drastic change in my appearance might be hormonal."

He remembered all too well. I was thirteen and Mother and Father deposited me with Grandpa for two weeks, visiting on weekends. The blessed event occurred on a Tuesday and resulted in Grandpa having to do some embarrassing shopping.

"Why weren't the others before her aware of the treasure?" Grandpa asked, seeking corroboration for my—well, now *our*—hypothesis.

"Because, at the time, finding it would only endanger the island and the person with the knowledge! Imagine the gold rush of treasure hunters tearing the dunes to pieces. It would have destroyed the place," I explained. I didn't need to mention that Caitlin would never have put the interests of mere humans ahead of her beloved island.

"So why, Katy?" he asked, needing to understand intimately the circumstances that had ruined his life.

"Developers were threatening the island, and the Federal Government's attempt to acquire and protect it had failed. Caitlin attracted Grandma and you here…and you attracted the others. The abuse caused the blowout which eventually led to the exposure of the treasure. With the proceeds of the secretly dispatched treasure you were killing two birds with one stone, protecting the island in two ways, from the *potential* devastation by treasure hunters and the *certain* destruction by developers!"

"So what were Katy and Del doing here?" he asked, but not really wanting to know.

"The first time they were here, when they originally found the treasure…" Daniel began but I interrupted, knowing it would sit better with Grandpa coming from me.

"Let me," I said before he could continue. "Grandpa, first you have to understand that, when I said I wasn't possessed by Caitlin, that wasn't completely true with regard to her passion for Diego and mine for Daniel…" I hesitated, "and Grandma's for Del."

"So she was here to be alone with him, to be intimate with him," Grandpa said, courageously confronting the worst fear of his life. But then denial kicked in and he stated, "No, *no*, it wasn't like that. She was drawn to him but she brought him here to tell him that it was over. She was a married woman now and in love with me. Then they stumbled on the treasure," he insisted, daring me to contradict his rationalization.

I just couldn't!

"No sir, I'm sorry to say that it wasn't like that," said Daniel. "Dr. Brace, they were intimate and it was consensual."

"No, you're wrong, or a liar—an evil fucking liar like your uncle!" Grandpa exclaimed. When Daniel didn't respond Grandpa slapped him on the side of his head with a brutal punch. Daniel went down without even attempting to dodge the blow, then got up and brushed himself off, wiping a tiny trickle of blood working its way down the side of his face. He faced Grandpa.

"Maybe you were entitled to that one for what my uncle did,

sir," said Daniel. "But don't ever lay a hand on me again," he warned. The intensity of his reaction was disquieting.

"Grandpa," I interjected, trying to redirect the focus of this rapidly escalating confrontation. "Daniel's telling the truth!"

He instantly raised his hand to strike me or, more likely, to strike Grandma Katy for what she'd done! But Daniel grabbed his arm and restrained him without apparent effort. Grandpa, even considering his age, was a large and very strong man, outweighing Daniel by a good 80 pounds. But there was no question of Grandpa striking me or doing anything. He simply could not move.

I don't believe he would have followed through, whether it was Grandma or me he was aiming for. But we'll never know.

Finally, all the energy, all the fight, all the denial of the hateful things he could no longer deny, left him. Whether he was ready to accept the truth or simply didn't give a damn, I don't know.

But then he sat, put his head in his hands and sobbed. Deeply but not for long.

"OK, I believe you. Now you tell me the rest," he began when he'd recovered. "No more illusions about my life, my wife, and how I thought things were. You've destroyed that. She destroyed that. So tell me everything. Don't hold back. Don't you dare try to spare me! Nothing can hurt me now," he challenged, looking up at us like a man with nothing left to lose.

"Grandpa, if you want the truth, then you must believe that what I'm about to tell you is the truth, even if it seems like I'm trying to spare your feelings," I said. Grandpa didn't respond.

"I doubt if I can make you understand this but the attraction between Grandma and Del, if it was anything like what Daniel and I are experiencing, was irresistible. Literally irresistible. If Grandma fell in love with you, married you, and had a child with you despite that overwhelming compulsion," I paused, hoping he could consider, objectively, what I was saying, "then you and Grandma must have had a deep and abiding love the likes of which few people will ever know."

No reaction.

"I know..." I started then stopped. "I know that Grandma couldn't comprehend why she was unable to control her attraction

My Island Beach

to Del. She knew it was wrong but, try as she may, and you know she was an incredibly strong person, she could not resist. And, Grandpa, if he hadn't killed her that night then her infidelity would have eventually destroyed her, one way or another."

"You might want to think that she was simply being unfaithful to you but, Grandpa, there's nothing further from the truth."

"Go on," he said finally. But I couldn't. I just didn't have the heart to hurt him anymore. "Go on," he repeated.

"She brought him up here the last time to offer to leave you and run off with him if he would forget about the treasure and Island Beach," said Daniel. There was no way to sugarcoat it so he didn't try.

"Grandma Katy was incredibly strong-willed in one sense and incredibly accommodating in another. The essence of Caitlin can be a moral compass to guide your heart in the right direction, or a selfish and overwhelming passion to surrender to. Or, in Grandma Katy's case, to open your heart to. Grandma Katy was a free spirit with a heart of gold and I believe Caitlin, for all her good intentions, took advantage of that. I, on the other hand, am now fully aware of Caitlin's predilections for Diego," I explained. "Daniel, however, is nothing like Del," I relented, recalling our "meteoric" tryst at the geotube when neither Caitlin nor Diego seemed in residence.

"Be that as it may, Grandma Katy, under Caitlin's influence, would have done anything to protect the island," I continued.

Grandpa absorbed what I was saying but remained unresponsive.

"But she overestimated her worth in Del's eyes. With that kind of money involved, Del could have any and all the women he wanted. He laughed in her face," Daniel explained, recalling more and more.

"I refuse to believe your grandmother was controlled by some sort of ghost!" Grandpa said, making one last attempt to refute the illogic of the story. "And I don't believe she would have run off with that reprobate!"

"Grandpa, did you know that you can ride horses in Island

Beach in the spring and fall?" I said, apparently sidestepping his objection. He looked at me, wondering where I was going with this now.

"They rarely ride horses here," he replied.

"Why?" I asked.

"Because there aren't any stables near here," he said.

"So why that silly rule?" I asked. "No stables, no one really takes advantage of it. Why a rule like that when no one's interested?"

"I suspect you already know the answer. It was your grandmother who insisted, anonymously, on the horses when the agreement was made to purchase the property for the state," he admitted.

"People must have been riding horses on the beach a lot back then, like the beach-buggy lobby?" I offered.

"Not really," he replied, defeated.

"But then, Grandma herself must have been an accomplished equestrian and wanted it for selfish reasons?" I asked.

"She never straddled a saddle, as far as I know," he answered, tired of waiting for the explanation.

"Then why, Grandpa?" I asked. He knew the answer, I was sure, but wouldn't admit it. "It was Caitlin, Grandpa, the little girl who lived to ride on her beautiful little pony. She wanted people to be able to use the island…to enjoy it as she would have," I concluded. "*She* insisted."

"So she was possessed. Call it what you like," Grandpa rushed to amend when it appeared that I would protest his semantics when, in fact, I was about to agree with him. "And it was Caitlin's desire for Diego that was behind Katy's attraction for Del?"

"Grandpa, near the end, Grandma Katy understood the nature of her attraction for Del. She knew it was not between her and Del, but between the parts of them that were Caitlin and Diego. She was willing to sacrifice her own happiness with you, I'm afraid, to save this place." There was no way to spare him this truth.

"And when the fool spurned her?" he asked warily.

"She tried to kill him with a knife she'd concealed here earlier, in anticipation of his refusal," I explained clinically.

"She was going to murder him? No, not Kate! I don't believe it!" he said, refusing to be persuaded by my explanation.

"Grandpa, Grandma was a good person and I know you loved her dearly but she was flawed. She was decisive, but impetuous. She was compassionate to a fault but intolerant of weakness in others. She wanted to right wrongs and was willing to do the hard things, to get her hands dirty, to make sacrifices and take responsibility. Whatever it took. She was the definition of 'zealot' for the things she believed in." I paused, not knowing whether to expect raging denial or grim acceptance of my evaluation of the love of his life, but no response was offered.

"Unfortunately, Grandfather, her fanatical approach to issues regarding the park would not allow her to dilute her vision of the right thing to do, either through consultation or compromise. Nor could she share the accountability for her sacrifices. She accepted sole responsibility for the consequences of her actions but she did so selfishly and arrogantly," I finished, without recrimination. I was starting to raise my voice.

"She put her righteousness, her passion for the fate of this Island Beach, ahead of her responsibility to you and her child! And, as just as that cause was—is—she *should* have somehow found another way!" I asserted vigorously, becoming increasingly animated as I continued. "Don't condemn her for her infidelity! That was positively inconsequential compared to the irresponsible way she sacrificed her family, you and Father…and me, without our consent or even awareness!"

"Enough!" he shouted, finally reacting to my railing against his widow.

"Let me finish!" I shouted back. He folded his arms and fell silent. I gathered all my poise and character, took a deep, cleansing breath and proceeded.

"If she had succeeded in killing Del, the outcome would have been the same. She would have had the arrogance to take responsibility for her actions, rather than the courage to try to get away with it and live an un-heroic lie with her family!" I concluded. "The outcome would have been the same. You would have been deprived of your wife, my father deprived of his mother and I deprived of my grandmother. That is the arrogance of martyrdom!"

"Are you through?" he asked.

"I'm through," I said.

He paused, gathered himself, and got a grip!

"I know you're right. I knew it even before today's revelations. But love is love; there's really not much you can do about it. And my motives in this little morality play would not stand up to close scrutiny, either," he confessed.

"A few years back, I realized that the depth and passion of the bond between Katy and me would never be repeated with another woman. I also came to understand that its all-encompassing nature prevented the type of, I don't know, the type of cultivated relationship that might otherwise be possible. The type that requires effort to maintain and conflict to evolve. That's when I started thinking about what might still be possible between Evelyn and me," he revealed, astonishing me yet again with his confession.

"Now finish your story," he requested, calmer now.

I continued. "But Grandma only wounded him. You saw the cut, I imagine, and some blood?"

"That's true," he confirmed. "I think that's when I knew he murdered her. In fact, the reason I managed to kill him was probably because that wound had weakened him. Your grandmother, for all her flaws, ended up saving me and the island. Arrogant or not, she was a hero."

"She was, Grandpa," I agreed sincerely.

"It wasn't self-defense, was it?" he said, finally prepared to confront the whole truth. "Del, I mean," he clarified.

"No, Grandpa. Initially it was. She'd attacked him first and, if it hadn't been for the influence of Caitlin and her reticence to harm Diego, I believe Grandma would have succeeded in killing him. But he survived the initial attack with only the one wound and subdued her completely, before he decided to kill her. He didn't need to kill her, except that she was coming between him and the treasure," I finished dispassionately.

"How can you be so all fired certain of what happened?"

My Island Beach

Grandpa asked finally.

"Because she knows—*we* know where to find her. Because we know he buried her here, where it happened!" said Daniel, whom we'd overlooked during our latest heated exchange.

"You found her remains here?" he asked Daniel nervously.

"No, Grandpa. But we know that this is where she is," I confirmed, "and when we find her, you'll have to accept that the other things that we know are true."

With that, I produced two shovels we'd brought to the site. Both the hurricane fences and time had started to reverse the deterioration of the blowout; it had had been gradually filling in since Grandfather's day. But we were on a pinnacle that had, if anything, ebbed and flowed over time.

We located the skeleton in short order.

I encountered the torso first, and then we carefully exposed the skull, arms and legs. The crest of the skull had been caved in by a brutal blow. I looked for a band on her ring finger and found it, as I had expected.

Grandpa gazed up at me with tears in his eyes. "After all this time! Is she—is your grandmother in you?" he asked querulously.

"No, Grandpa," I answered truthfully, "just Caitlin. And memories of what happened to Grandma and the others, as if Caitlin were a witness."

"And Diego," Daniel added, responding to Grandpa's questioning stare.

"I gave her a diamond engagement ring. A small diamond was all I could afford." I looked but didn't see it. "Oh, honey, don't bother. He had it on him when I killed him. Probably thought it would let the police identify her so he removed it. Or was so greedy, he was going to sell it."

The wedding ring was a simple affair, a plain gold band in the style of the times. "He must've thought it wasn't worth the bother," Grandpa said as he reverently removed it from the bone that was all that remained of her ring finger.

He examined it, caught his breath, and handed it to me.

I contemplated the delicate inscription on the interior of the band. 'True love is timeless. Philip.' And I started to weep.

As I ponder the irony of the situation, Grandpa, with considerable effort, removed the wedding band from his own fattened finger. He handed it to me and I read out loud, "Yours for all time. Katy."
We sobbed some more.

"Grandpa, there's something else I want to tell you, this time from me and no one 'inside' of me," I said faltering but determined. He acknowledged the implication of what I said. "We should rebury her right here, right now. Leave her to rest on the island that she loved so dearly."
"Of course," he agreed, enveloping me in his arms and holding on to me for dear life. Then, abruptly, he took me by the shoulders, held me at arm's length and said, "But only on one condition. When I go, I have to be buried here too."
I nodded in agreement.
"Katy, not so fast!" he interjected. "I'm putting the burden for this on you. I want your word that, no matter the circumstances or consequences, you'll see to the internment of my remains here. Right here, beside her."
"Do you believe in cremation?" I asked, considering the practical aspects of the commitment I was making.
"No!" he replied emphatically.
"They won't allow it," Daniel warned. "This is a State Park, not a cemetery. You're asking a lot, Dr. Brace."
"I'm asking for the world, darling," he said, ignoring Daniel and turning to me. "I'm asking for all eternity. I'm asking for more than I've asked of anyone ever before," he assured me. "Will you do it?"
I thought for several moments.
"Does it have to be done soon after you die?" I asked, again considering the pragmatic aspects.
He realized that I was committing to grave desecration and illegal transportation of a corpse. "Anytime before you die," he said. "No hurry but you have to promise or I won't leave her here."
"I promise," I said, giving up on being practical because I knew it was the right thing to do for her…and for him.

Chapter 37

The Whole Truth and Nothing But…

Grandpa and I had finally accepted the unbelievable explanation of the circumstances of Grandma's murder. After we buried her I was suddenly overcome with a feeling, a sense that I couldn't define but I couldn't deny either. "Wait!" I found myself commanding without explanation. They continued walking. "Wait!" I insisted. They looked at me as if I'd finally gone over the edge.

I felt like I had. Wait for what? I wasn't sure.

"For what, honey?" asked Grandpa, tolerant but impatient to go after re-interring his dead wife.

"I don't know…just another minute," I requested. "Wait!" I commanded once again when Grandpa started walking after the minute had passed.

He looked up at me impatiently. Daniel looked at me expectantly.

"Wait," I begged, feeling a compulsion but not knowing where to direct it.

They sat and waited silently, finally giving me time to concentrate.

I focused…then I knew.

"Dig!" I ordered, indicating a section a few feet to the north of Grandma's skeleton.

Our flashlights were beginning to lose power. Daniel had to shake one of them to keep it going. We dug.

Nothing at first. We shifted toward the west a bit, then toward the east, but always north of Grandma's internment. At one point I saw Grandpa giving Daniel a questioning look, as if to say, "Does this seem stupid to you too?" Daniel shrugged but, to his credit, remained neutral in this latest, incomprehensible quest.

I was afraid a mutiny was afoot when, at last, Grandpa's shovel finally scraped against something. Driftwood or a rock, perhaps? But his skepticism was transformed into advocacy as he fell to his knees to expose the source of the friction.

Soon the silhouette of a leg bone appeared, then another. Grandpa began searching for the torso but with no luck. It was as if a pair of legs had been cut off and placed here *sans* abdomen. Then Daniel, attacking from a totally different angle uncovered another pair of legs!

"Its' her!" I exclaimed, because I now knew what we had found. Two pair of parallel legs running east to west. To the north of that I dug again. It was almost impossible to see by now. Nothing! Shit!

"Over here!" I screamed, moving to the southern end of the two pairs of legs. Grandpa and Daniel joined me this time and we dug together.

Suddenly it was there…the skull. Bigger than a human, elongated, but smaller than a cow…like a giant Great Dane!

Suddenly I was overcome.

"*Silly Lilly, pony mine,*
Silly Lilly, tiny equine,
Silly Lilly, thee and me,
Play beneath the Banyan tree."

I recited this little ditty from memory only it wasn't *my* memory and it wasn't *me* talking. Then we wept, Caitlin and I, for that beautiful little pony of hers.

Suddenly Daniel was there too, pulling *us* up by the shoulders. Looking into *our* eyes.

Then they kissed us! Daniel and Diego!

We held that kiss for an eternity. How can I describe it? That kiss? I can't...I won't even try. On and on...until oblivion.

Then, as if coming out of a coma, we were back. Daniel and I...and Grandpa. What must he have thought? Grandpa was watching us, weeping and watching. No one said a word. There was nothing to say.

We buried Grandma without her wedding band. Grandpa placed it on his little finger. "Make sure I have both bands when I'm buried," he said. I nodded.

Afterwards we sat watching the moon, finally providing visibility to our eerie experience as it came up over the bay. As if we were coming out of a haze, each of us meditating on the tragically short life of Grandma Katy, and the devotion of a little girl and her pony to each other.

It was a brilliant moonrise with stripes of clouds across the pale sphere, reminding us of the insignificance of our affairs in the overall scheme of the universe.

"Katy," Grandpa began, "Do you believe that your grandmother and I did the right thing?"

"You mean attempted murder, in her case, and manslaughter in yours, not to mention grand larceny and fraud; all to protect the island from people in general and Del in particular?" I asked cynically.

I think I startled him with my uncensored assessment of the situation. "I suppose it was manslaughter," he said finally, unoffended.

"Accidental manslaughter!" I relented. Daniel, wisely, remained silent.

"Grandpa, in your position I don't know what I'd have done. Because when you really get down to it, the world needs to be protected from people—both evil people like Del and good people that happen to be businessmen or developers. Maybe what you and

Grandma did was against human law, but was the right thing for this place," I reasoned.

"Katy," said Grandpa, addressing me, but speaking to both of us. "Do you remember what I said about calling this place 'My Island Beach'?"

"I do. You called it a 'small vanity'," I said, recalling precisely what he had said.

"It was…it is. But don't misunderstand," he cautioned, "It's not meant to imply ownership. What it implies is responsibility."

"I know," I said.

"And I wish more people would refer to this place as 'My Island Beach' and take responsibility."

"Like Francis Freeman and Pete McLain?" I asked.

"Yes," he said.

"But Grandpa, you've dedicated your life to this place. It's different for you. You live here," I pointed out.

"Doesn't matter," he replied. "People may only vacation here or visit even once. But as long as they recognize and acknowledge that they have a responsibility to the island and to all the other special places on this planet, then those places will be 'theirs' too."

I thought about what Grandpa said and, even though I had to leave soon…even if I never returned, I had to agree this place had become 'My Island Beach'.

"Katy," said Grandpa interrupting my musings, always having to get in the last word, "Don't worry, you'll be back, to meet your obligation to me and for many, many other reasons!"

Chapter 38

Parting

"We haven't talked about so many things," Daniel offered during an uncomfortable silence at our last meeting before I left for the summer. He'd wanted to take me to the airport, but I told him that Grandpa had insisted and seemed to have some ulterior motive for the drama of my last moments on the island.

"There's nothing we need to talk about," I said sagely. I think the wisdom-of-the-ages thing was getting on his nerves.

"You understand why I gave you such a hard time the day after we were together the first time?" he asked.

"You were being a *prick*?" I responded, understanding exactly why he'd been that way but also understanding that he needed to explain his behavior for his own good as well as mine.

"No!" he exclaimed. "And you know why!" I keep forgetting that he has access to several generations of experience too.

Even if he knew and I knew, he still needed to verbalize it.

"I didn't understand why we were so compelled to be together. It was so wonderful…but so irrational. I didn't understand what was going on with my twin," he faltered. "I just needed to know that there wasn't some underlying scenario I didn't understand."

"Which there was," I pointed out. "But I didn't understand it either!"

I was tired of his unrelenting analysis of our situation. He wasn't.

"Look," I said finally, "we both know what was going on…the only question is what are we going to do about it?" I said.

"We should see other people," we said together, neither of us wanting it but both of us knowing it was necessary. Both of us were thinking about the second time we were together…when neither Caitlin nor Diego were present. The time that was clumsy, awkward and extremely…satisfying. I was unsure of Daniel's take on that experience and I was savvy enough to know that *he* was unsure of *mine*. Was there something there for him, because there certainly was for me!

"Katy," he asked, "when you did your research on the other couples like us, how many of them got married?"

"All of them," I responded. "Except Grandma Katy and Del. They were the exception."

"Were they all happy?" he asked.

"That's harder to say," I said considering his question. "Of the three I really know anything about; they married, had kids and stayed married. Based on the little information I could lay my hands on they seemed happy," I finally concluded.

"Did they know?" he asked.

"Maybe," I said, "but maybe they just thought they got lucky and that they'd found their one true love."

"But that's not always true," Daniel said, "Not for Katy and Del."

"No," I agreed.

"Which is why we need to see other people," I thought and I'll bet he did too.

Then I kissed him. I was really beginning to wonder if his endless analysis was a ploy to get me to be more sexually aggressive just to shut him up. I *hoped* so.

We spent the rest of the night, our last night of the summer together, trying to convince each other that it was true love.

I was convinced several times.

Oh—and by the way—it was clumsy and wonderful!

Epilogue

The Teller and the Story

Sitting in the waiting area for my flight, I thought back to another airport in another city when I had been waiting to journey here at the beginning of the summer. I remembered leaving the house in a mad rush after a fight with my father. I managed to move my flight up two days and was early for the modified itinerary, at that. In my haste to put distance between myself and my parent, not only had I packed poorly, I also had failed to procure any reading material.

Stranded as I was, with several hours to kill, I investigated the airport bookstore for something suitable to my mood—for the airport, my flight, and my sabbatical at the shore. Mystery? Maybe, but no, not really. Romance? Yuck! And I couldn't stomach another legal or medical thriller with their formulaic plots and contrived twists, where the reluctant heroine prevails against inconceivable odds! I was looking for something quirky, with well-developed characters in an intricate, if believable, intrigue. In short, a "Summer Read".

At that time, at the airport, I failed to discover anything that suited my needs.

That summer I frequented the local library, a branch at the

shore. The hours were limited and the staff was eccentric but affable. They had ecological and scholarly presentations by local luminaries and were not averse to offering a spontaneous cup of coffee and baked goods on a quiet night. Not the stern, whispering matriarchs (and spinsters) of yesteryear. I felt welcome there.

I sampled fare as diverse as the *Fig Eaters* by Jody Shield, a turn-of-the century mystical murder mystery set in Vienna, and *Switcheroo* by Olivia Goldsmith, an unlikely, yet entertaining romantic musical comedy farce, sans music. Not to mention the arduous, but worthwhile, *The Ground Beneath Her* by Salman Rushdi.

In *Anil's Ghost* by Michael Ondaatje, I confronted the contradiction of the Sri Lankans I knew, with lyrical names like Kithseri and Hiranthi that exactly matched their sunny personalities, yet contrasted with the fanaticism and cruelty of the politics of that island nation. The most consequential book I read that summer was *The Human Stain* by Philip Roth. As a privileged young white girl, I enjoyed the role of the perfectly objective observer of the courage or cowardice (take your pick) of an older black man who chose to pass for white and the irony of having his academic career destroyed by charges of racial prejudice.

Being an uninvolved observer was a role I relished.

From Grandfather's library, I read, or reread *The Seawolf*, *Robinson Crusoe*, and *Moby Dick* in their original and unmodernized forms and remained amazed and appalled by the dourness and fundamentalism of these classics…and, at the same time, struck by their genius. What would possess anyone to write a story about the conflict between a whale and a psychopathic misanthrope?

I found and read an old and short history of Island Beach by Patricia Miller. It told of Francis Freeman, the Phipps Family, and Operation Bumblebee, which I'd come to know independently during my summer furlough. Snippets of the history of the area were distilled from a treatise on Seaside Park, including old pictures of the Seaside Yacht Club, originally built on stilts in the bay before they added fill around it to make room for parking. Not to mention a 1931 photo of the depression-era Standard gas station,

My Island Beach

which is now a Mobil and, to this day, is the only gas station on this end of the island. It sports a black and white 1956 Corvette Stingray out front, hearkening back, perhaps, to the days when the auto was king of America. The B & B (Boekholt and Boekholt) and White Oak Market (in spite of the fact that white oaks have never grown on the Island) are other traditional Seaside concerns that have their roots in the 1930's.

In this surprisingly comprehensive branch library I stumbled upon a copy of the Army Corps of Engineers' original proposal to build the geotube that was eventually installed and became Daniel's launching pad for summer meteor showers in the Barnegat Inlet. It was as if the volume had been left out, specifically, so I would encounter it. My bent was strictly for fiction and I would never have pulled down such a dry and uninteresting tome for perusal. However, upon spotting it, I felt compelled to open it and consequently became engrossed in its maps and surveys, weighing the pros and cons of building a dike between the sedge and the inlet. I suppose they never considered doing nothing.

Which brought to mind the reference Grandpa had made in his beach story to the closing of New Inlet (since then referred to as 'Old Inlet' to the confusion of intermittent historians like myself) and the opening of Cranberry Inlet in that fateful storm in 1720. The Cranberry Inlet that resulted was a boon to the area, because it provided deepwater access to Toms River, immediately behind it. When another storm closed Cranberry Inlet in 1812, as attested to by David Mapes, the "colored" Quaker man Grandpa hijacked for his 1720 story, it was a major setback for shipping to the area. So much so that they tried to reopen it several times to no avail. The sea would not suffer interference from lowly humans, at least at that time.

I've heard the opinion expressed that, if it had survived, the area may have become a major commercial port, the likes of New York or Boston. This was yet another bullet that Island Beach dodged. Try to imagine it as a mini-Manhattan with accompanying bridges, tunnels and subways. Could Caitlin have had a hand in the manipulation of natural forces as well as the psyches of people?

No. Even I can't accept that.

But yet, after all my literary researches, perusals, investigations, and entertainments, I remained unfulfilled by the lack of a defining fiction to embody my summer. No *Lost Colony*, *Catch 22* or *Stranger in a Strange Land* would be equated with this particular summer. No *Lord of the Rings*, *Skystone* or *Dune* series would return my memories to this particular summer upon rereading.

That's when it occurred to me that the events and revelations of the past season possessed all the elements of the elusive narrative I was seeking. Romantic ambiguity, events of historical relevance, complex characterizations that require insight and analysis rather than simple acceptance, and motivations that were neither obvious nor uncomplicated.

And yet it was uncomfortable—disconcerting! *No*, it was *unbearable* to be the protagonist in this twisted tale of misdirected loyalty and idiosyncratic banality rather than the aloof muse. I craved detachment and objectivity but, instead, had experience and advocacy thrust upon me.

That's when I realized, in that discerning moment, that the "Summer Read" that I had been seeking was right there in front of my face. It was, in fact, *my* life—*that* summer—there on *My Island Beach*!

Author's note:

Much of what was described in this book is historically accurate. Francis Freeman was, in fact, the caretaker of the Phipp's estate, and one of the first individuals to recognize the fragility of this ecosystem. The Phipps family did originally intend to develop the island into a seaside resort, but were thwarted by the advent of The Great Depression. The park was purchased by the State of New Jersey from the Phipp's estate for $2.7 million, after the federal government, with the help of former President Harry Truman, failed to acquire it as a National Seashore, in 1953. The park opened in 1959.

Katherine Gray, the Garden Club president from Lavallette lobbied, successfully, to remove the Navy from Island Beach, after the success of Project Bumblebee, the first launch of a rocket ship in the United States. Her resemblance to the fictional Katy was, of course, strictly a product of my imagination.

Pete McClain is the individual who reestablished ospreys and peregrines to Island Beach and, in general, took up the cause from Francis Freeman in acting as a guardian and protector of Island Beach State Park. The reestablishment of the ospreys remains one of the most successful endeavors of its type on the eastern seaboard of the United States. Pete was also instrumental in organizing the initiative which resulted in the acquisition of the sedge for the state. And lastly, the initiation of pump-out boats at Tice's Shoal, which was attributed to Billy in the book, was yet another initiative of Pete McClain the indefatigable advocate of the island.

Jane Leeds and Mother Shourds were based on real characters in the town of Scott's Landing and implicated in the legend of The Jersey Devil. Their true involvement with the legend will likely never be known, but I can assure you that the explanation put forth in this manuscript is more fanciful than factual.

The foxes were a charming part of the park until a few years ago when the mange, sadly, wiped out most, but not all, of them. They are experiencing a resurgence.

The geotube is a controversial reality. The fisherman are

against it, as its absence allows for the influx of game fish to the sedge; clammers are for it, as it filters out the sand that inhibits the reestablishment and continued existence of the muddy clam beds. Advocates on both sides support their cases with politics, science, philosophy and emotion. The sponsorship of the geotube by the Army Corps of Engineers, on the other hand, seems to attract the ire of all parties, regardless of point of view.

The Old/New inlet that originally defined Island Beach did close in 1720, as described in the manuscript. And Cranberry Inlet opened at the same time Old Inlet closed and then closed itself nearly 100 years later in 1812 as described by an African-American gentleman named David Mapes.

The reality and details of the destruction of the Hindenburg are, of course, well-known and well-documented in American history.

Any historical inaccuracies are likely to be due to taking creative liberties or simply from ignoring facts that would interfere with the development of my tale to the desired conclusion; I don't apologize, but I thought that I should at least explain.

Robert E. Schwartz

schwartr@optonline.net

http://www.myislandbeach.net/

CPSIA information can be obtained at www.ICGtesting.com
Printed in the USA
BVOW070930250512

291106BV00002B/4/P